Maggie in Jamaica

Sequel to
The Mugs & Saucers Café

W K WAITE-GRACIE

To all my amazing friends and family who continue to support this inspirational adventure I'm on.

To the continued love and cheer leading from my two awesome kiddos.

To my sister from another mister, you were a major part in the writing of this sequel and I'm forever grateful for more time with Maggie and Billy.

Once again, my heart is full, and my passion grows.

Love and Light
Come One Sweaty Pie

INTRODUCTION

It's been two years since Maggie and Billy reunited and things are still just as sweet and sexy as ever. They've settled into living together and although they skipped over the getting to know each other beyond physical attraction, after their twenty-five years apart, they seem to be getting along swimmingly.

Billy's getting lots of work contracting and working at the garage and Maggie has added teaching belly dancing classes along with running her bookshop, as well as helping around Carla and Stu's farm regularly. All is right with the world.

But just when things seem picture perfect, an ex comes back into their lives and shakes things up in paradise. With old flames spending time together, reminiscing and catching up, Puts Out Pauline stirring things up again and Maggie and Billy spending less time together and not enjoying their usual intimacy, things start going wrong and the two lovers find themselves caught up in a lot of new and unknown dilemmas and issues they aren't sure how to work out.

A planned romantic trip to Jamaica changes course and Maggie finds herself alone and heartbroken oceans apart with Billy. Falling into sadness and not knowing what she'll do without him, Maggie crawls into her shell. Luckily, with her best friend Carla by her side and her youngest brother's surprise arrival, they manage to help Maggie out of her funk, but is it too late for the once insatiable lovers to make things right?

Will Maggie and Billy's love survive? Will they reunite yet again, and will their love stand the test of uncertainty and distance?

Fall back into the steamy depths of this lover's tale and join these beloved characters in the beautiful Caribbean waters of Jamaica. Who knows what adventures and surprises await and what new encounters might arise?

Table of Contents

Maggie in Jamaica PLAYLIST

Heavy Fuel - Dire Straits

Hotel California - The Eagles

Born To Be Wild - Steppenwolf

Harvest Moon - Neil Young

No Sugar Tonight/New Mother Nature - The Guess Who

What Is Love - Haddaway

A Little Respect – Erasure

Billie Jean – Michael Jackson

Tainted Love – Soft Cell

Wild Thing – The Troggs

Rhythm Of The Night – Corona

Dancing With Myself – Billy Idol

Little Jeannie – Elton John

I Guess That's Why They Call It The Blues – Elton John

Sad Songs Say So Much – Elton John

Blue Eye's – Elton John

Eye Of The Tiger – Survivor

Rock Me Gently – Andy Kim

Hungry Like The Wolf – Duran Duran

I Touch Myself – Divinyls

Trust Yourself – Blue Rodeo

Two Tongues – Blue Rodeo

Time – Blue Rodeo

After The Rain – Blue Rodeo

Who'll Stop The Rain – Creedence Clearwater Revival
Someday Never Comes – Creedence Clearwater Revival
Midnight Special – Creedence Clearwater Revival
Head Over Heels – Blue Rodeo
All You Need Is Love – The Beatles
Superstition – Stevie Wonder
Mrs. Robinson – Simon and Garfunkel
Witchy Woman – The Eagles
Legs – ZZ Top
Looking Out My Back Door – Creedence Clearwater Revival
Ain't Goin' Down Til The Sun Comes Up – Garth Brooks
Black Magic Woman – Santana
Livin' On Love – Alan Jackson
Daisy A Day – Jud Strunk
She Sells Sanctuary – The Cult
Dancing In The Dark – Bruce Springsteen
By Your Side – INXS
Cedar Lane – First Aid Kit
Everybody Hurts – REM
Power Of Love – Celine Dion
What Is This Love – Blue Rodeo
Long As I Can See The Light – Creedence Clearwater Revival
Listen To Your Heart – Roxette
No Woman, No Cry – Bob Marley and the Wailers
One Love – Bob Marley
Somethin' Bout A Boat – Jimmy Buffett
All I Have To Do Is Dream – The Everly Brothers
Ain't No Sunshine – Bill Withers
Always Remember Us This Way – Luke Evans

Just Like Heaven – The Cure
Like A Virgin – Madonna
Wake Me Up Before You Go Go – Wham!
Take A Chance On Me – ABBA
Come On Eileen – Dexys Midnight Runners
The First Time Ever I Saw Your Face – Luke Evans
You Never Can Tell – Chuck Berry
At Last – Etta James
Keep On Loving You – REO Speedwagon

CHAPTER 1

Billy sat back in his chair, closing his eyes as he rested, lifting his face towards the sun. He and Maggie had been working together all morning, in the backyard, building a shed for his motorcycle, and as the sun reached its highest point in the sky, the two of them decided it was time for a break. Coming out the back door and handing him a cold beer, Maggie sat down in the chair on the other side of the little table, taking a drink of her bubbly water. She smiled her big Maggie smile at him. Billy grinned and winked at her, opened his beer, and took a swig, before saying,

"We got a lot done today, Babe." She nodded happily, then grinned with lust in her heart as she watched Billy set his drink down and pull his shirt up and over his head.

"Ya looks pretty good too!" she said back to him, smiling as her eyes scanned over his chest and shoulders. She rested her head back against her chair and closed her eyes, grabbing her shirt, and giving it a shake in an attempt to cool herself down a little. It had been one of the hottest summers she could remember in Tamarack, and it was not fun working in it.

"I know we were hoping to get this done this afternoon, but what do you say we call it a day?" Maggie opened her eyes again and looked at Billy, his body glistening with sweat. Her mind wandered at the thought of running her own sweat-soaked body all over his.

"Sounds like a good plan to me," she agreed and took another big gulp of soda, then she held the cool can to her chest.

"Feel like hopping on the beast and going for a dip in the lake?" Billy asked, his eyes cheeky and hopeful. She didn't answer for a moment, not really feeling like moving, but then the thought of cooling off in the lake with Billy trumped her feelings of lethargy, and she stood up, walked over and stood in front of him, reaching out her hands as she spoke,

"With you, Lover of mine, I'd go anywhere." He chuckled and sat up, pulling her close to him. Then still holding her hands, he pulled her forward and stretched up to meet her lips, kissing her with a smile on his face.

"Excellent!" he answered.

"You're looking pretty sexy sitting there glistening in the sun Billy," she said, giving him another kiss, a little longer and harder than the last. She felt his hands sliding down and running across her back, and then down, giving her butt a squeeze.

"Mmmm, I was thinking the very same thing about you, Mag." After one more kiss, the two headed into the house.

They grabbed some towels, packed a small cooler with a few water bottles and ice, and were ready to go. As they were nearing the front door, they heard a "meow" and looked over to see Old Bill sleepily looking up at them from his favourite spot in the front bay window.

"You hold down the fort while we're gone Mr. Bill," said Billy with a grin, and Maggie stopped and gave her feline friend a scratch behind the ears, and a gentle pat on the head, then she followed Billy out the door.

She loved climbing on the back of Billy's bike, wrapping her arms around his strong body, hearing the roar from the engine, and feeling the wind in her hair. It was one of the many things Billy had introduced her to that pulled her a little further out of her shell, and one of the countless things she loved about him. It only took about ten minutes to get to the lake on the bike, and soon they pulled onto the dirt path that had been well worn from her and Carla's weekly fishing trips. Maggie climbed off and waited for Billy to do the same before putting her helmet down on the bike. Billy turned and smiled at her, the two embracing, looking at each other like a couple of love struck teenagers. The two years they'd spent back together had been filled with such love and laughter, and it was what they'd both waited for their whole lives. After twenty-five years apart, they really felt like they couldn't get enough of each other. Actually, to be fair, that had always been the case when they were together. From the first moment they laid eyes on one another, they were instantly connected. That connection and desire was still there after all these years.

"Still just as beautiful as the day we met Mag! Well, no, actually, more beautiful," he told her, and she squeezed him tight.

"Still so charming Billy," she teased. "You ready for this swim?" she asked, pulling away and starting to strip down to her birthday suit and making a run for the dock.

"Ohhh, Mag! Didn't know we were skinny dipping! I'm definitely ready!" He laughed and started peeling off his clothes, slowly making his way down to her, taking his time and enjoying watching her run off the end of the dock and jump in. She turned to grin up at him as he stood on the end of the dock looking at her with a smile.

"Why Mr. Stanton, how very nice to see you," she said looking him up and down, her eyes lingering between his legs. With a twinkle in his eye, he jumped off the end of the dock, splashing down nearby, and making his way over to where she was treading water. They smiled broadly at each other, giving each other a flirty look and a few kisses before Maggie started to swim away. The summer before, Billy, Maggie, and their friends Carla, and Stu had built a floating dock about forty feet out, in the center of the lake, and Maggie was making her way to it now.

"Catch me if you can, Sweet Cheeks!" she chimed at him teasingly.

"What do I win if I catch you?" She laughed to herself and kept swimming. It only took her a few minutes to get there, and grabbing onto the side of the dock, she turned to check Billy's progress, but was surprised when she didn't see him. She waited a moment, thinking maybe he was swimming under the water and would resurface any second. Still no Billy.

"Billy!" she called, feeling a bit worried, then hearing a splash, she heard him pop up behind her and felt his hands suddenly grabbing her and pulling her under with him, the two coming back up spitting and laughing, kissing in the water and holding their naked bodies close together.

"So, what do I win Mag?" he asked her again with a hopeful look on his face.

"Hmmmm, I don't know, maybe I could make you some cookies when we get home?" He shook his head smiling.

"Nah, don't feel like cookies, try again Mag." She kissed him again, then said,

"Okay, maybe some rice krispy squares?" His head fell back with a big chuckle and tickling her under the water he shook his head again. "Well, I don't know Billy, I just can't think of anything good." Maggie gave him a saucy smile, her green eyes flashing with mischief. He pulled her body even closer, kissing her hard and said,

"I think I could come *up* with *something!*" They were both giggling then kissing each other more passionately. "Hey Mag, what do you say we christen the floating dock?" Maggie looked at him, a little unsure and skeptical.

"Really, out in the open?" He grinned and nodded enthusiastically.

"We're pretty far from land Mag." He was now pulling himself up onto the dock and looking back down at her bobbing in the water. "Nobody out here except us and nature." She grabbed on with both hands and pulled herself up onto the dock beside him. He reached out, helping her up and pulled her close. The two of them standing in the middle of the lake, naked as jaybirds, with a rebellious, youthful fire growing in their hearts. She slid her hands from his stomach around to his back, he traced his fingers up into her hair, held her face and pulled her slowly towards him. They smiled softly at each other before their lips met, gently pressing into one another. Then, as their kisses became deeper, they started massaging each other's wet bodies and pressing up against each other tightly with a desire that needed seeing to. Holding her head in his hands again, Billy looked down at Maggie as her eyes slowly opened, rubbing their noses together softly, he kissed the end of her nose, and she grinned at him.

"Love you with a never-ending fire," he said in his sexiest raspy whisper, and her legs felt like jelly.

"Billy, you still make me weak in the knees," she told him, stretching up to kiss him again, their hands gently running along each other's bodies, hugging and kissing as the water rocked them back and forth on the dock. Bending down and sitting together, facing one another, Billy pulled Maggie's legs over his, so she could sit closer, while still sitting on the dock. This way they were able to embrace as close as they liked and could enjoy watching one another. They were once again running their hands along the curves of each other's bodies. Billy's strong hands rubbing up and down Maggie's back, lifting her long, wet curls and tracing his hands up to her neck, pulling her into a deeper kiss. Maggie's fingers trailed up his back, squeezing his shoulders, then up into his dark soft hair, kissing him passionately. Watching one another as their hands ran along their arms, across each other's shoulders, they became more aroused with each other's enjoyment and tender touch. Now kissing necks, cheeks, ears, and hands, then back to staring at one another. Maggie ran her tongue along Billy's lips, Billy's mouth opening slightly, then as his tongue found hers, their kisses became much more heated, their tongues tangled together, deep wide-open kisses. Their hands pulling into each other, grabbing, and squeezing. They had danced this dance so many times, and even after a whole lifetime, the passion and desire was as intense and delicious, maybe even more, than it had been when they were teens.

"If I get any splinters in my butt, you owe me Billy!" Maggie said, breaking their locked lips and grinning cheekily. He laughed, his eyes crinkled in amusement, then pulled her back to kiss her hard, holding the back of her head, trailing his other hand down her spine, sending shivers throughout her whole body. Feeling her quiver, Billy bent his face down to her shoulder, his lips ever so softly brushing across her skin. Then, still so softly, kissing his way from the top of her arm, over her shoulder, his hand brushing her hair away, he continued softly kissing his way up her neck. His lips, so warm and tender, pressing into her skin. Maggie was running her hands up, across and over his chest, down his shoulders, back up, and moving up either side of his neck. She gave his earlobes a little pinch, then traced her fingers back down and over his chest again, feeling his heart beating quickly under her hands. Billy's hands had dropped down to hold her breasts, Maggie's head falling back slightly with pleasure as Billy squeezed and caressed her, every so often pinching and pulling slightly as his fingers lingered on her nipples. Maggie reached down between his legs and grasped him gently in her hand. She felt him harden as she started to stroke him with long, even glides. He was back to kissing her neck, sucking, and licking, as their pulses quickened.

"You smell delicious Mag," he said quietly in her ear, and with another zap of shivered electricity through her body, she quickened her strokes and gripped a little more firmly.

"Billy, you make me crazy," she responded and now their lips were locked again, and they were back to holding each other's heads and pressing their faces together tightly. Billy laid Maggie down flat on the dock, still kissing her, Maggie's hands in his hair, sliding her tongue into his mouth. She reached down and grabbed his ass, squeezing tight as Billy pulled his face back and looked into her eyes. The look on his face made every part of Maggie stand at attention. She'd seen his desperate, insatiable desire before, but the hunger and deep need playing behind his eyes in that moment was beyond intense.

"I want to make you squirm Mag." She felt herself shudder and inhaled deeply as he started to make his way down her body with his mouth, so slowly, and taking time to look back up into her eyes every so often. Hardly touching her, just enough to make her want more, he kissed her neck, then her chest, grinning at her as he watched her body rise and her eyes close. Down between her breasts, right down to her navel and down to the soft hair above her center, then across from one hip to the other. Billy looked up towards her face as he kissed his way back up her warm wet body, and Maggie turned her head to the side, gazing back into his beautiful blue eyes, feeling like a wild animal might be waiting to pounce from within them. As he kissed his way back up, all the way to her mouth, he licked gently across her lips as she tried to kiss him, but he was already trailing his tongue back down her throat, sucking her neck for a moment, continuing his slow purposeful descent down her body. Her hips and chest rose, waiting for more. Taking both her breasts in his hands and squeezing them, almost in time with her heartbeat, then opening his mouth and bending down to suck on one of them, his tongue licking long and slow, he found his way to the other and began doing the same. Then he looked back into her eyes, and she saw a slight smirk as he grabbed her hands and held them down on the dock, moving his face back to her neck, her favourite side, and continued sucking and kissing her, feeling her body squirming now, as she ached for more.

"Gawd Billy," she moaned. He held on and kept sucking her neck. Feeling her legs moving, her desire tangible, he released her hands, running his fingers down her arms, over her breasts, down to her hips, and moving his face down her body, he kissed the tops of her legs softly. Then his tongue was between her legs, his hands stretched up holding her arms at her sides again, as he ran his tongue along her center, with pressure, flicking it against her clit.

She was trying to move her hands to pull him up, but he held them firm, licking with a constant rhythm, circling around every so often, then back to the rhythm she was excited by. He was enjoying her pleasure.

"Ohhh!" she cried, and he kept licking, a little faster now, still holding her hands as his tongue movement became more vigorous. She could hardly keep from screaming, feeling herself close to cumming. "Billy!!" she cried out again, her body moving involuntarily with delight as Billy continued the rhythm. Maggie was so close to bursting and then, reaching orgasm, her eyes rolling back, Billy kept licking. Maggie moaned and laughed with beautiful release. He let go of her hands and was kissing his way back up her body, still feeling her wriggling with pleasure. She looked up at him, their gaze intense, and she felt him push inside of her, his head falling back as a long, low growl escaped his lips.

"Ahhh." He was incredibly turned on after seeing her enjoyment. He slid in and out groaning with pleasure. The act itself, always delicious. The intensity and passion between them, always beyond ecstasy, and with that energy he was already so close to finishing. Billy's movements became faster, and looking right at each other, she soon felt him cum. His whole body shuddered as he stared into her emerald eyes intensely. She grabbed onto him tightly, as he laid himself down flat on top of her and both of them, still feeling a quiver in each other's bodies every few seconds, kissed deeply, wrapped tightly together, now noticing the rocking of the dock again.

"Wow!" she said, smiling at him. "You are one fine man Billy Stanton!" He smiled at her, that animalistic glint still in his eyes.

"Mag, you bring out such a hunger inside me," he said back to her. "I've never wanted or enjoyed doing the things I do to you, with anyone else," he added, kissing her softly, and holding his lips to hers for a moment.

"I think I know what your prize will be," she said, grinning sensually. His eyebrows raising and a smirk playing across his face, he asked,

"Oh really, and what might that be?" She gave him a kiss and grinned.

"You'll know when you get it." He laughed his sexy Billy chuckle.

"I thought this *was* the prize Mag," he added, then giving her one more kiss, rolled off her and laid beside her. They stayed like that, eyes closed, hands held between their bodies until the sun was just too hot. Billy sat up, then Maggie sat up next to him. Sitting quietly and looking around them at the woods and water for a few minutes, they decided to swim back and head home. Once they reached the land dock, they picked up their clothes and Billy asked,

"Wanna grab something to eat Mag?" She grinned cheekily at him. He kissed her, grinning back. "At the b and b?" he added. She pulled her shirt back over her head, and answered,

"Sure thing. Not really feeling like cooking." They walked back up the dock towards the bike, arms around each other, Maggie snuggled up close, Billy's head resting on hers. Then he pulled his helmet on and sat on the bike, and started up the engine, Maggie climbing on behind him. Billy turned on the radio. "Heavy Fuel" came on and he turned it right up, as they skidded slightly, driving back up the dirt driveway and out onto the road. Both feeling refreshed and glowing with satisfaction. "Hotel California" was blasting as they pulled into town, and Billy turned off the engine.

Mr. and Mrs. Slade were just coming out of the post office. Mr. Slade a few feet behind, shuffling along in his slippers as usual and Mrs. Slade casting evil, disgruntled looks in Maggie and Billy's direction. Billy laughed and Maggie grinned and waved, as they headed for the b and b. As Billy opened the door for Maggie to go ahead, they heard Mrs. Slade yelling something at her husband. Maggie and Billy just looked at each other and grinned again.

The usual old couple that frequently occupied the back corner of the restaurant were in their seats and there were a few others scattered around. Maggie and Billy walked over to an empty table and sat down. When Pat saw them, she smiled happily and made her way over.

"Well, hello you two, haven't seen you for a bit." Maggie smiled at her.

"Hi Pat, how are you?" she asked, trying not to sound too down.

"Oh, you know Maggie, I'm doing pretty well, thank you dear. I've got Beatrice and now her younger sister Jane helping me, and that nice young man, Jeremy, does all kinds of odd jobs for me. He's still young and has lots to learn, but he'll give anything a go, and often finds a way to make it work." Pat looked towards the young man gathering up dishes and taking them into the kitchen. Maggie stretched up her hand and gave Pat's arm a little rub.

"That's good Pat, glad you are managing." Pat smiled back at Maggie.

"And how are you Mr. Stanton? Still miss having you here." Billy smiled at her.

"I'm well Pat, thank you. You know you can always call us, for anything." She patted him on the shoulder.

"You are such a nice couple." She looked at Maggie and smiled.

"Found yourself a wonderful match Maggie. Now what can I get you tonight?" They weren't sure what they wanted yet, so they ordered coffees and had a look at the menu. Both had long since memorized their choices, but looking at it in black and white, somehow made it easier to choose. When Pat came back with their drinks she took their orders and headed to the cook at the back. They enjoyed their coffee as they waited for their food, playing footsies under the table and making eyes at each other. After they filled up on fries and wraps, they paid and said goodbye to Pat.

"So sad she lost Stan," Billy said, stopping and standing by his motorcycle.

"I know, they were such a lovely pair. Must be hard to be without him after so long." Maggie replied as Billy took her hand in his and pulled her close enough to give her a big kiss.

"Sure lucky aren't we Mag?" he said, smiling at her and giving her another kiss before they hopped on the bike and made their way home.

Bill was happy to see them when they walked through the door together, hopping down from the window to meet them and then running ahead, leading them to the kitchen where he was eagerly waiting for his dinner, then weaving in and out of Maggie's legs, meowing at her.

"Ok, ok Old Bill, here you go," she said to him, placing his food down on the floor.

"Hey Mag, are you going into the shop tomorrow?" she heard Billy ask from the front hall.

"I was thinking I might, for a few hours, why Babe?" she answered, as Billy came around the corner and sat at the island.

"Just have some errands to do, and thought I'd do them when

you weren't home, so I didn't miss time with you." She grinned at him and walked over to wrap her arms around his shoulders, sitting on his lap and kissing his face all over.

"Oh Billy, you are a softy aren't you!" she teased, and he gave her a big squeeze around the middle.

"Hey, when's your girl's night with Carla?" As Maggie got up Billy slapped her butt. She grinned at him, then went over to the fridge, grabbed a club soda, and turned to look at him. Without asking, he nodded, and she grabbed him a ginger ale.

"Um, I think she wants to do it Friday. And she's decided we're going to take her camper to the lake." Maggie laughed a little at the thought. "So, no hydro!"

"Oh, well that should be interesting Mag. What will you girls do?" Billy took his drink from her, opened it and had a mouthful.

"Not sure, but knowing Carla, it will involve alcohol." Maggie grinned.

"So drunk Carla, sober Maggie and no hydro?" He got up and headed to the living room, Maggie followed. "You know Mag, if you want, I could spend a night in the camper and you two could have your night here." She sat next to him on the couch, Old Bill jumped up beside her, turned around in circles a couple times, then laid down to have his after-dinner bath.

"Really? Thanks, I'll run it past her tomorrow when she drops off the mail." Maggie leaned over and kissed his cheek, and he winked at her, flashing his cute Billy grin.

"What time is it, Babe?" She looked at the clock over on the kitchen wall, just out of view from his spot on the couch.

"7:30" she answered. He put his hand on her leg and smiled at her.

"TV? Board Game? Sex?" he asked her, his cheeky smile growing. She put her hand on his thigh, sliding it up a little and giving his leg a squeeze as she leaned over to give him a long loving kiss, then grinned at him. With her sexiest whisper, right in his ear, she answered,

"TV." He laughed, pulled her close and the two of them snuggled up together. Billy grabbed the remote hoping to find something for them to watch. There wasn't much on. News, hockey, infomercials, and an old spy movie that they settled on. It ended up being pretty good, a bit cheesy but Maggie loved those old black and white movies, *especially* the cheesy ones. Billy had fallen asleep before the end of it, and it was still only 9:00, so Maggie thought she might give him his prize she'd promised from earlier. She managed to slide out from under his arm without waking him and let his body slide down gently, so he was almost flat on the couch. Then she unzipped his pants and with some effort and patience not to wake him up, pulled them and his underwear down enough to return the *favour*. She lifted his shirt a bit, then, starting by letting her hair drop over his skin, she swept her caramel locks over his lower stomach and down and over the tops of his legs. He moved a little but didn't wake. Then kissing all around his pelvis and into the hair around his unaware but hopefully soon to be happy dick, Maggie continued to kiss around the tops of his legs. She slid her hands under his shirt, softly pinching his nipples, noticing things starting to stiffen up slightly. She ran her tongue from the base to the very tip and he made a quiet moaning sound as she took him into her mouth. Moving him in and out, feeling him harden and making sounds of pleasure. She held him and licked over and around the end of his now very hard dick, running her hand up and down every so often licking long wet strokes with her tongue. Then after licking the base, and licking back up to the tip, she slid her mouth down and took him in again deeply and sucked gently before sliding back to the tip.

"Maag," he suddenly growled her name and groaned with enjoyment. She reached her hands up and over his hips and around to his back, sliding her head up and down, making very wet, consistent slides from base to tip, his hips rising and his breathing heavy. She looked up at him with a sultry stare as she licked the end of him teasingly, then going all the way down on him again, she felt his hands in her hair, and he was groaning louder.

"Oh God, Mag!" She held him at the base again, licking the end a few more times, sucking and moving sensually, knowing he was close to cumming. She finished him off with a hand job, kissing all around his hips and as his body shuddered, he groaned out her name as his hips pressed forward and his pleasure was unleashed with complete enjoyment. Maggie's hand was still holding him as he came, his body shuddering again. She looked up at him and saw his head lying back down on the couch, his chest rising and falling, as she kissed her way up to him, smiling as he looked at her.

"Better than cookies Billy?" she asked, and lifting his head, breathing heavily, he chuckled, then dropped it again, and still grinning, answered,

"Well, maybe not oatmeal raisin!" laughing a little, Maggie playfully slapped him as he pulled her down on top of him, hugging her and kissing her.

"Real funny Billy!" she said to him. He held her in his arms for a few minutes, as she kissed his neck and lips softly, sleepily running his hand over her back.

"Ready for bed, Beautiful?" he asked her, she nodded and got up, handing Billy the box of Kleenex with a smile. She walked over and turned off the TV and the lights, making her way down the hall. Billy was soon right behind her and rubbing her ass all the way up the stairs. They got ready for bed and climbed in, snuggled tightly.

"Love you my Maggie," he said as she turned off the lamp and laid down again in his arms.

"Love you my Billy," she said back, and they soon fell asleep, both with big grins on their faces.

CHAPTER 2

Maggie got up early the next morning and had a shower before Billy woke up. She was already downstairs, enjoying her second cup of coffee when he came down, just in his boxers, looking very handsome and edible.

"Good morning, handsome lover of mine," she said as he walked towards her. He grinned broadly at her and wrapped his arms around her.

"Good morning, Beautiful," he responded and the two of them kissed a long kiss, pulling each other's bodies tight. Still holding tight, he looked down at her and smiled.

"So, what time will you be home from running errands?" she asked him. He kissed her forehead and walked over to the cupboard to grab a coffee mug and poured himself some coffee as he answered,

"Not sure exactly Mag, hopefully by five." She finished her coffee and sat the mug in the sink, walking over to give him a kiss goodbye.

"Okay, I'll see you later then, Billy." He nodded and took another sip of his coffee.

"Yep, see you later Babe." Maggie grabbed her lunch and keys and headed out the door.

The sun was bright, and the morning was already quite hot as Maggie walked to her bookshop. She was glad to go inside where it still felt a little cool. She was only open two days and one evening a week and the crochet and knitting group had put their weekly meetings on hold, as one of the regulars had broken a hip and was in the hospital, and another was staying with a sister for the summer.

Maggie opened up the blinds and unlocked the door, flipped the sign in her door window to "open" then started up the computer and put away a few books she still had on the counter from the week before. She came back to the counter and sat on the stool. It was Billy's 46th birthday in November, and she hadn't planned anything yet, but wanted to do something special. She hopped on the computer and started searching for ideas. Seeing lots of things that just didn't feel Billy-ish enough to her, and thinking she'd worry about it later, she heard the door open and looked up to see Carla walking in.

"Hey Mags!" Carla said with a big smile. "How's things?" She closed the door behind her and walked over to the counter with Maggie's mail in her hand.

"Hi Carla, things are great, thanks, how about you?" Carla slid the mail towards Maggie, shrugged her shoulders and answered,

"Aw, you know, same as always." Maggie nodded at her. "Ready for our night away Mags?" she asked her hopefully.

"You bet. Hey, Billy said he'd go stay in the camper for the night if we wanted to stay at our place. What do you think?" Carla's smile grew.

"Oh, that'd be good eh Mags! Ya, I'll take'm up on that offer! Good ol' Sweet Cheeks." And she was already headed for the door. "Sorry I gotta run Mags, lots of errands today!" She waved at Maggie with a smile and was gone. Maggie picked up her mail. Electric bill, magazine subscription, an upcoming fall fair harvest party notice for the county south of Tamarack and a couple things for Billy. She sat the envelopes back down on the counter then turned back to the computer. *Wait a second* she thought to herself, *that's it! Billy and I could have a double party during Tamarack's fall gathering, and have people dress up. A fancy Halloween dress party, with a theme.* She was quite pleased at the idea, and soon decided on the theme being "dress as your favourite film character" and as their birthdays were only a few weeks apart, it would be fun to celebrate together. Satisfied with her idea, she decided to talk to Carla about that in a few days when they had their girl's night and work out the details for making it happen.

Just before lunch a half dozen people came in and spent about an hour looking around, sitting, and reading some books, thanking her and then going about their day. No one else showed up by three, so she decided to close up and head home.

Billy wasn't back yet, and Old Bill was eager for some snuggles, so she sat in the front window with him for a bit, enjoying the calming effects of his happy purr. He voiced his complaints at being moved when Maggie got up and she gave him a soft pat on the head before walking away. She ran up and grabbed her yoga mat, rolled it out near the bay window where Bill was still curled up and did a fifteen-minute practice. She was just finishing up when the phone rang.

"Hello," she said into the receiver, but it was quiet. "Hello!" she said again, then heard the line go dead. "Hmm, weird," she said to herself, then went around the island into the kitchen to figure out what to do for supper. She went to the fridge to survey what she had to work with. There was some left-over chicken from the other night, still lots of lettuce and she noticed a lemon in the crisper, so she decided on a chicken Caesar. She pulled out the mayo, parmesan cheese and the lemon, and got to work making her dressing, then washed and ripped up the lettuce. She planned on throwing the chicken back on the barbecue closer to dinner, so she shredded it up, tossed it with some of the dressing, another squeeze of lemon and a dash of Worcestershire sauce and wrapped it in tinfoil, then stuck it back in the fridge, grabbed some bubbly water and went out back to sit in the evening sun. The ivy was doing well and growing in a thick canopy on the pergola, and she sat looking at it with a smile. Maggie had always loved ivy and her memory was cast back suddenly to her younger days on the farm, when she'd go out after dinner, take Benny, her horse, for a ride and then they'd find themselves in Maggie's favourite spot in the woods, under her willow tree, daydreaming and happily absorbing the beauty of the vines, and moss and ivy growing on the tree trunks while the barn cats and her dog would come and sit with her. She missed having a dog. She'd thought about getting one as company and protection when she first moved into her house, but the thought had escaped her after she and Billy reconnected. Now she thought she would really love to have one again and maybe that could be her gift for Billy. She was still lost in thought when she heard Billy's deep voice calling.

"Mag?" she heard from inside.

"Out back," she called, and he came out and bent down to give her a kiss.

"Hey," he said, smiling at her. "How was your day?" He walked around the small round table and sat in the chair next to it.

"Pretty good, how about yours? Get everything done?" He nodded,

"Just about, yep." She looked over at him and asked,

"You hungry?" Maggie stood up and headed over to the barbecue.

"Yes, I didn't get a chance to grab any lunch today." She started it up and opened the lid to scrape down the grill.

"Ok, I just need to warm up the chicken," she told him with her back towards him. She felt his hands on her shoulders, then sliding down her back, and wrapping around her waist as Billy snuggled his face next to hers.

"Mmm, you smell good Mag," he said in her ear. She grinned and her shoulder came up instinctually as his words tickled, and she turned her head to give him a kiss.

"You always think I smell good," she replied. He kissed her softly and made a little growling sound.

"That's because you always *do* smell good. Good enough to eat!" Maggie giggled as he kissed and nibbled her neck.

She slid her hand into one of his and they walked inside, into the kitchen. Maggie stopped and put her arms around his shoulders, and Billy wrapped his around her waist, pulling her against him.

"Missed you today Beautiful," he said looking deeply into her eyes and giving her a little kiss on the end of her nose. She grinned and stretched up, pulled him down a little, rubbed her nose softly on his, grinned and tenderly kissed his lips, the two of them hugging each other close, rocking slightly, then smiling again and breaking apart. Billy walked over to the cupboards and got them their plates as Maggie grabbed the left-over chicken and took it out to the barbecue. She came back to him, setting the table, both smiling lovingly.

They enjoyed dinner together, happily chatting. Maggie told him about Carla thinking his plan sounded great, Billy said he'd be going into work the next two days, to finish up a repair on a car he started working on the week before. He was still doing his odd jobs contracting but was now working part time, as needed out of the gas station, repairing cars and trucks. After they ate, the two of them did the dishes together, listening to the radio as Billy washed and Maggie dried. It was still set on a classic rock station that Billy liked, and they sang along to "Born To Be Wild", "Harvest Moon", and danced around with each other to "No Sugar Tonight/New Mother Nature" before finishing up the dishes.

Maggie fed Old Bill, then told Billy she was going up to take a bath.

"Sounds like a good plan, Mag." He winked at her, and she nodded at him knowingly. They often enjoyed long baths together. They had some of their best talks in the tub, and sometimes even enjoyed dessert.

"I'll go run the tub, meet you up there," Maggie said, smiling and heading upstairs. She filled the tub and stripped down, climbing in and resting her head back. She loved a good bath and was glad she'd treated herself to a big soaker tub when she was still in the beginning stages of renovating and fixing up the house. There was a little knock on the door, then it opened, and Billy walked in with a cheeky look on his face. She smiled up at him, ready to enjoy his naked body and was pleasantly surprised and giggled a little as he gave her a little strip tease before climbing in and sitting across from her. He slid his legs along the outside of hers and lifted her feet and rested them back down on his thighs.

"Awww, what could be better Mag?" he asked with a smile,

closing his eyes and resting his head back. She looked at him lovingly, thinking about how handsome he was, and how strong his shoulders and arms were, how safe he made her feel, how he always made her smile, and how she never wanted to be without him. Then she closed her eyes and rested her head back again, smiling to herself. They stayed that way for a few minutes before she felt him move and opened her eyes to see him watching her, his blue eyes dark and alluring. She grinned at him, feeling slightly self-conscious and embarrassed at the hungry stare he was giving her.

"What?" she finally asked, and he grinned, a twinkle in his eye as he answered her.

"Just thinking about how I woke up last night Mag and couldn't help but feel like jumping you." she giggled and felt her cheeks redden.

"How is it that after all we've done together and at our age, you still make me blush Billy?" He grinned more broadly, and she felt his hands running up her legs.

"Guess I'm just that good," was his reply. She laughed and nodded.

"Well, you are good Billy, but I wouldn't want it to go to your head." He gave her legs a little pull and she grabbed the sides of the tub with a little squeal, the two of them laughing as they leaned in closer, tracing their fingers into one another's hair and holding each other's heads as they looked into one another's eyes. Then as their lips met, they started kissing slowly and deeply, stopping, and gazing at each other again. They sat there for quite some time, Maggie adding some hot water at one point, as they chatted and kissed, loving on each other as they usually did. Billy watched Maggie climb out with a happy look on his face.

"Never get tired of seeing your wet naked body!" Maggie turned in time to see him grinning.

"Hope you still say that when I'm 64 Billy!" He chuckled.

"I hope *you* do too Mag." She flashed her big Maggie smile at him, her green eyes twinkling.

They dried off, and Maggie threw on a short, light summer nighty, Billy just in his boxers and an old T-shirt and they went back downstairs and outside to sit on the patio together. They watched the sun set, enjoying the cooler air, until the mosquitos got too bad, and then they went back in.

"What time do you have to get up?" Maggie asked Billy as he slid the back door closed.

"Probably around six, Mag." She was bent down giving Old Bill some scratches and rubs, and Billy ran his hand across her shoulder as he passed her. She grabbed it and he pulled her up smiling affectionately at her.

"Dance with me," she said to him, and jokingly, he let go of her hand and started doing the chicken dance, with a goofy look on his face. Maggie shook her head, then she laughed as she watched him chicken dance his way over to the radio in the kitchen.

"You got it Babe!" he said, shaking his hips as he turned on the music. He played with the dial for a moment, and she smiled to herself, knowing he was listening for something she liked. "What Is Love" was playing, so he turned it up and spun on the spot looking at her with a big grin. 80s music held a soft spot for them, and he knew she'd be loving his choice of the station. He danced towards her, not being goofy anymore. His eyes locked on Maggie's, making sensual controlled movements to the beat, as he moved closer to her. She couldn't help but grin, watching him dancing in his boxers, feeling her heart light and full, as *he* enjoyed the dance but knowing how much he enjoyed making her feel happy too. She was dancing on the spot now, rocking to the music, the two of them dancing separately for most of the song, then Billy reached out and took her hands, pulled her in and they danced together. The song was over, and "A Little Respect" started. Billy spun them around and dipped her, pulling her back up quickly, kissing her, then continuing to move back and forth with her to the beat, Maggie grinning away, Billy singing as he moved her out of the kitchen, and around the dining room and living room. Maggie broke away and danced on her own and gave him some intense eyes, as she danced her way back to him. Billy chuckled with delight. They reached out for each other again and hugged while they danced. Then, still swaying together, his hands moving up her body into her curls and holding her head, he leaned down and kissed her, long and hard and she reached up and held his wrists, kissing him back with a love so big, it couldn't even come close to being explained with mere words.

"How about we continue this dance upstairs?" Billy suggested, in his sultry raspy whisper, and winked at her, still holding her face. Maggie grinned at him.

"Whatever you say Lover Boy," she replied, and she saw his eyes laughing before he turned, holding her hand and led them upstairs. As they stepped onto the landing Maggie pushed him back against the opposite wall and let her hands fall to grab his ass. Billy smiled and kissed her; she kissed back a little harder and his hands found their way down to squeeze her ass too. Then he spun them and pushed *her* against the wall, still squeezing her ass and now pressing himself up against her and kissing her hard. He let her go, holding her hand again and started to lead them down the hallway towards their room, but before they got past the banister, Maggie pushed him against the hallway wall and stretching up to kiss him, she slipped her tongue in and reached her hand down the front of his boxers to grab him gently. She felt him rise a little and she grinned. Then Billy's hands were holding her head and lifting her chin so he could suck on her neck. She felt her legs go weak. He turned her around and moved them to the banister, where she grabbed onto the railing and felt Billy's hands slip under her nighty and then quickly pull her underwear down to the floor. Running his hands all the way up her legs on his way back up, back under her nighty to grasp her already freely hanging breasts, he gently squeezed them, as he pressed himself against her and she felt his growing excitement. She stood up straight and he kissed the side of her neck, then she felt him pulling his boxers off before bending her over the banister and sliding himself between her legs. Back to fondling her breasts, massaging them, and squeezing them as he slid back and forth, making her as wet as he could before...

"Oh! Billy," she cried as he held her hips and slid inside, so slowly, moving his hips around while inside her, then gliding back out and in again, still slowly, as she bent forward a little more.

"Mag, you feel so good," he breathed, and she felt him glide a little faster. She couldn't touch him, she couldn't reach him, he held all the control, and it was making her crazy, with arousal.

"Billy, you're so hard," she whispered, and both of them started to breathe heavier, Maggie getting wetter, Billy gliding faster. He was still holding her hips, banging against her body harder.

"I want to feel you cum." Maggie's whole body tingled as she felt herself starting to let go. "Tell me how much you like it, Mag."

he said to her, and Maggie was almost exploding.

"God Billy, you make me so hot." Both of them, moaning with pleasure now. "Don't stop Billy. Oh God Billy, don't stop." And they were cumming, bodies vibrating, Billy making shorter movements deep inside her, Maggie crying out in delight, Billy calling out "Maggie" as he slowed to a stop and draped his body gently over hers for a moment to hold her. They stood up and Maggie turned to face him, Billy backing them to the wall behind him, both breathing heavily and kissing passionately.

"Well, that was new and kicked ass Lover of mine!" Maggie said to him. Billy laughed and kissed her again.

"Yes, we'll definitely be trying that again, you sexy woman!" he replied. They walked to the bedroom and landed on the bed, still trying to catch their breath.

"Don't ever hesitate to bend me over the banister Billy!" Maggie said, turning to look at him with a grin.

"You got it Babe," he replied with a chuckle, and they fell into a lip lock, hugging each other close, legs wrapped around each other and loving one another deliciously.

CHAPTER 3

Maggie didn't remember anything after that, and she woke up to a beautifully sunny morning with a smile on her face. She turned to see that Billy was gone, and closed her eyes again, resting her hands over her heart, smiling and thinking, *I may have waited most of my life for such happiness, but damn, it was sure worth the wait.* She felt Old Bill jump up on the bed and lie down against her leg. She knew Billy must have fed him as he wasn't squawking at her to get up, so she enjoyed laying there, relaxing, still basking in the previous night's deliciousness and having a nice snuggle with Old Bill. When she finally rolled out of bed, Bill followed her down the stairs. She walked into the kitchen and saw a note by the coffee pot, picked it up and read 'Thanks for the banister banging sexy woman'. Maggie giggled, feeling her toes curl slightly and a shiver run up her spine, and thinking about when she'd kiss Billy again.

It was a Wednesday, so as usual she wasn't going into the bookshop, but she'd be going on Thursday. She and Carla had started a belly dancing class in place of the usual knit/crochet meetings. Tomorrow afternoon was the first class. The subject came up one day between the two friends, of wanting to learn and wishing there was somewhere to take classes. After talking about it, they got to thinking, *why don't we teach the classes ourselves,* so they started a short practical program to learn how to teach, spending lots of time practicing their moves at home, and they were really looking forward to the new endeavor.

Maggie spent the morning singing along to the radio and cleaning up a bit, trying out some of the moves she'd learned. She left it on the station she and Billy had danced to the night before and was happily working and dancing to "Billie Jean", "Tainted Love", "Wild Thing", "Rhythm Of The Night", and "Dancing With Myself". She managed to get quite a bit done, dancing and singing her way around the house. She made Billy one of his favourite dinners, a big green salad, baked potatoes with sour cream, and steak with fried mushrooms and onions, which she had ready to go onto the barbecue when the time was right. She stopped to have a little snack around mid-day, then got some laundry done to some of her favourite Elton John tunes, "Little Jeanie", "I Guess That's Why They Call It The Blues", and "Sad Songs Say So Much". She had the potatoes cooking about half an hour before Billy got home. While singing her heart out to "Blue Eyes", the volume turned right up, working away in the kitchen, Maggie turned around and saw Billy smiling at her from the other side of the island. She grinned at him, and kept singing, looking into his deep blue eyes, and walked to the island where she leaned over and met him halfway for a kiss. She turned around, walked to the radio and turned it down a bit, then turned back around to look at him.

"Hello Sweet Cheeks!" she said with a smile.

"Hello Beautiful," he said back.

"How was your day?" Maggie asked.

"Hot and greasy," he replied, looking down at himself. "I'm gonna jump in the shower before dinner Mag." She gave him a hungry look and, noticing the sparkle in her eyes, he added, "Care to join me?"

"Not sure we should try that, Lover. We're not teenagers anymore." They both grinned broadly, remembering one very hot, slippery, passionate shower together, many moons ago.

"Ok Babe." Grinning, he turned around and left the room, Maggie stood there for a moment with a reminiscent grin on her face as she enjoyed watching him walk away.

By the time Billy came back down, Maggie had set the table and had the steaks and veggies on the grill. Billy came over to her and hugged her, Maggie wrapped her arms around him and gave him a big hug back. Still embraced they smiled at each other, exchanging a few short, sweet kisses.

"Been thinking about coming home to you all day," he told her, and she gave him another kiss.

"I was dancing with you today, Lover," she said back to him. "I loved my note this morning." He grinned at her, gave her a few more kisses, than Maggie put her hands on his chest, and suddenly said,

"Oops, the grill!" She hurried out the back and opened the barbecue. Everything was fine, but it was time to take things off. "Dinner's ready!" she called in to him and Billy came to the door to take the tray from her.

"Mmm, looks good!" he said, setting the food on the table and waiting for her to sit before sitting down across from her.

"So, hard day Babe?" she asked him, adding a big scoop of sour cream to her baked potato.

"Oh, just finicky work Mag. I was trying to put new brakes on an older car, and I had to pretty much take the car apart to get to where I needed. Glad to be home," he said, hungrily eating his dinner. "The place looks great, Mag. Looks like you were busy today too." She nodded.

"Ya, thanks. I did manage to get a lot done today. Are you working the same hours tomorrow?" Billy nodded, having just had a mouthful of potato and mushrooms. "Should we plan to eat out then?" He grinned cheekily at her, as he finished his mouthful.

"Sure Mag, wanna just meet at the b and b at 5:30?" he asked. Maggie was taking a drink from her water glass, and as she sat it down she replied,

"Sounds good." As usual, after they ate, they cleaned up the dishes together, then before Billy landed on the couch, Maggie grabbed his hand, and he stopped and looked at her.

"What's up Mag?" he asked her. Maggie didn't say anything. She slid her arms around his waist and hugged him, he wrapped his around her and gladly hugged her back.

"How about a back rub Lover?" she said to him.

"Mmmm, that sounds great." Maggie looked up at him with a smile. Again, before he could head to the couch, she held his hand and led him upstairs. "Oh, the full package. Nice!" he said grinning as she pulled him towards the bed. He pulled off his shirt and laid down face first on the covers at the foot of the bed. Maggie grabbed the coconut and lavender oils and climbed on top of Billy. Before doing anything else, she laid down over his back and hugged him, then kissed his shoulders softly and sat back up. She added a few drops of the lavender to her hands and after getting a small scoop of coconut oil she ran her hands all over his back. She started to rub gently, making sure to spread the oils around. As she began to knead and rub harder, Billy let out a low, happy moan.

"You're growling, Lover," she teased.

"You always get my motor going Mag." She smiled as she kept

massaging. After about ten minutes, she felt his muscles go from stiff and tense to supple and relaxed. She was working on his upper arms, and making her way back over his shoulder blades, when he turned over, holding Maggie in place so she was now straddling him at the top of his legs, and he pulled her forward so he could kiss her.

"Thanks Babe, that felt great." Maggie looked at him with a sexy grin and he held her face smiling at her, that Billy twinkle in his eyes. "Think I'd like the other part of the package now Beautiful," he added and pulled her face close again, still looking at each other, as he ever so gently kissed her mouth, her chin, her nose, then her mouth again. Maggie's eyes closed as she smiled softly. Billy gently moved the curl hanging down off her face and tucked it behind her ear. Maggie sat back up, her hands on Billy's chest, and she trailed her fingers across and over his shoulders, her fingers still oily. Continuing to run her hands up his neck and to the base of his head into his hair, she pressed her body against his. Then running her hands back down to his shoulders and onto his chest as she sat up again. Billy was now reaching down to pull her shirt off, Maggie lifted her hands up and pulled it off the rest of the way. She leaned forward again and pressed her lips to his, warmly, with a long kiss, Billy's hands running up her back and into her hair, then tracing all around her back and down to squeeze her butt. Maggie sat up and smiled as she looked at him for a moment, then leaned forward. Her hands in his hair, she kissed his forehead, down his cheek and to his ear where she took his earlobe in her mouth and sucked it gently. She felt Billy shiver as she gave his ear a little lick and nibble before moving a little further down, then slowly and opened mouthed, kissed his neck and down to his shoulder, her hands still running through his hair, his hands caressing her back softly, as she kissed down and all over his chest.

"Mmm Mag, how'd I ever get so lucky?" he asked, holding her face again and bringing her close. Slowly, their lips slightly parted, his warm lips touched hers, and he softly, so she could *just* feel him, kissed her, Maggie not kissing back yet. With more pressure they kissed deeply, moving sensually, tongues sliding, hands caressing each other lovingly. Maggie felt Billy grab her firmly, then flipped them so he was on top of her, still kissing each other fiercely. As her hands ran over his body, she was thinking about how beautiful and strong he was, opening her eyes to look at him and drinking him in. Now Billy was kissing down her neck, lingering there for a moment before traveling down to her chest and the tops of her breasts. His lips were hot on her skin, making her body tingle. Billy pulled Maggie up to sit, undid her bra and slid it off her, laying her back down. Then he reached for the coconut oil, and put some in his hands, rubbing them together for a few seconds. Letting it melt slightly, he ran his hands across her breasts and gave them a squeeze, grasping them gently and with slow deep squeezes, massaged them, leaning forward to kiss her rising mouth, running his oily hands all over the front of her, over the front of her shoulders and down her arms, kissing each arm from her shoulders to her wrists and back up to her mouth. Maggie wrapped her arms around him and kissed him deeply. He stopped kissing her and was staring at her, his eyes deep in thought as he ran his hand over her hair, holding her curls and looking at them, his fingers playing in them, kissing her softly and looking into her eyes again. Maggie's hands tenderly traced up and down his spine, gazing lovingly at him. He held her face in his hands again and kissed her like it was their first. She felt electric shivers through her body, starting from her toes, moving right to the top of her head and pulling him closer, she kissed him with such desire and adoration. She squeezed his ass, slow and hard, pulling his hips tighter against hers. Then Billy sat up and reached down to pull her long skirt off, his fingers teasingly trailing as they moved, and Maggie lifted herself slightly to help him slide it off. Billy bent forward again to kiss her, kissing straight down to her chest and between her breasts as he grasped them in his strong hands. As he moved back up to look at her, Maggie reached down and undid his pants, sliding her hands down the back to hold him tight again. Billy leaned back and pulled them off the rest of the way and slid his body up hers to lay on her. She wrapped one leg around him, and he pressed himself against her, his hand holding her leg and squeezing her thigh, pulling her in tighter, the two of them still softly kissing every inch of each other they could get to. Maggie felt for the coconut oil and picked it up. Billy sat up a little and watched her run her fingers through it and reach down to slide her oily hand over his already very firm cock. His head fell back slightly, and he inhaled suddenly, his eyes closed for a moment, looking down at her with hot desire. He stuck his fingers into the oil now too and sitting up a little more, reached down between her legs and ran his fingers across her center. Maggie inhaled sharply and reached up to pull him down to her, grabbing his ass firmly and pulling him inside her. They could feel the coconut oil dripping down, and with his oily fingers he played with her nipples as he slid in and out slowly, teasingly stopping and pulling out of her and leaning down to suck on her breasts, then pushing himself back in, Maggie fondling his balls gently each time he came closer to her.

They played with each other like this, teasing and creating such anticipation for so long, then, not able to take one more second, Maggie pulled him in hard and they were back to kissing deeply, Billy sliding in and out, faster and faster, until he was moaning with an explosive force, Maggie so close as she felt him cum. He pressed his lips to her neck kissing and sucking, reaching down and rubbing her until she gave a cry of pleasure, and he felt her cum too. Kissing each other deeply and holding each other's heads in their hands.

"God Mag, I love you!" he breathed happily. Kissing and holding each other close, until he laid down beside her and she put her head down on his chest and snuggled up to him.

"I love you Billy," she said to him, her hand playing with the hair on his chest, as he ran his hand up and down her arm.

After they laid together for some time, they got up and grabbed their underwear and summer housecoats, went down to get drinks, and took them out back to watch the last of the sunset. Smiling at each other, hand in hand across the little table, then heading to bed early together, they snuggled close, until they fell asleep.

***

"Morning Mag," she heard Billy say and felt him kiss her as she opened her eyes smiling up at him.

"Morning Billy," she replied.

"Have a good day Beautiful." He gave her another kiss and turned to go. She closed her eyes again and laid there feeling like a queen. She had her Billy, Old Bill, a beautiful home, good friends, her health, and not to mention a hotter sex life than she'd had with anyone else. She enjoyed a few minutes of nothingness, happy in thought, then coaxed herself out of bed and into the shower. Old Bill was up on the counter washing his face and paws when she walked into the kitchen.

"Aw, Daddy fed you eh Buddy," she said, giving him a rub and he pressed his head up into her hand with happy blinky kitty eyes. After a coffee and some toast, Maggie grabbed her things and headed out the door. She was thinking about her night with Carla now and decided she'd head over to the grocery store on her lunch break to grab some snacks for them.

Pat and Beatrice were out front of the b and b, and as she passed, Maggie stopped to say good morning. After a short chat she carried on a few more doors down to her bookshop, unlocked it and went in. She loved walking into her shop, with the smell of all the books surrounding her. Books had always helped her get away from things when she was growing up. She loved that you could travel anywhere, anytime inside a book and smiled remembering all the people, places, space, and time she'd visited over the years through the many pages she'd turned.

Soon after opening the shop, Maggie had a run of customers. A few people from out of town stopped by and they chatted happily with her. They were a group of young people traveling in a van together, and they asked her all about Tamarack, about how far it was to the next town or city and told her about some of their adventures so far. They bought a number of books between them, and Maggie enjoyed watching them and being pulled back to old memories of her time at the cabin. Remembering the people she spent the week with and wondering how their lives had turned out. Smiling at the thought of the beginning of her love with Billy, and then the heartbreak of losing him for twenty-five years. Then, remembering even more fondly, the day he walked back into her life, when he stepped through the doors to her bookshop, and how the two of them picked up right where they had left off. They were still like teenagers together, so in love and full of energy, and all over each other, just like their week at the cabin. Maggie's thoughts faded as she heard the group in the store talking about their plan for hitting the road again. They thanked her and said their goodbyes, Maggie smiling broadly at their young, eager thirst for adventure. It was a lovely start to the day, that made Maggie's morning go by quicker than usual.

At 12:30, she turned the sign to "closed", locked the door, and headed to the grocery store. There were a few oldies meandering up and down the aisles, surveying products like it was their daily duty. She grinned to herself, picturing her and Billy slowly moving along the aisles, talking about what kind of soups were the best, how soup had changed over the years and those darn prices. She only hoped they'd be so lucky. She grabbed some more bubbly water, a couple bags of chips, popcorn and pretzels, a cheesecake and the fixings for chicken fajitas before piling everything onto the counter.

"Heya Maggie," said Debbie, the woman who ran the store with her sister Denise.

"Hi Debbie, how are you?" Debbie nodded slowly, she was always kind of Eeyore-like, but very friendly.

"Ah, you know Maggie, same as always." Maggie smiled at her and nodded back.

"I hear ya Debbie. Say can I take a couple of those scratch tickets too please?" Maggie pointed to the $2 tickets under the cover on the counter. Debbie slid the tray out and let Maggie pick her own. She paid and thanked Debbie, smiling as she left the store and headed back to the shop.

The beginning of the afternoon dragged on a bit, only a couple of people came in. Maggie sat and scratched her two tickets, not winning anything but was able to pass some time. After that, she started getting things ready for the belly dancing class, and time passed quickly. She moved the chairs and tables against the walls, put out a number of yoga mats and popped a home burned CD into the player. Then she changed into some comfier clothes. She was all set when Carla came in, in a Willie Nelson T-shirt and pink jogging pants, and carrying a big bottle of water.

"Hey Mags, ready to shake your money maker?" she asked, laughing.

"Hi Carla, yes, it should be fun. I think we have eight people signed up," she told her friend, walking over to grab her water bottle. Just then the door opened, and some of the ladies started coming in. They chatted happily while they waited for the others to arrive, then Carla locked the door and stood beside Maggie at the front of the group.

"Hello ladies," Maggie said grinning. "We are really looking forward to learning this with all of you. Now, first things first," she said more seriously. "If anyone here has any issues with their hips, this might not be the class for you." She saw the women looking around at each other and whispering, but everyone stayed put. Maggie and Carla had put up their posters for the class a month in advance. The posters said all women, of any age, are welcome to join, and they ended up with quite a mix. Young teenage Beatrice and a friend of hers named Kate, Lu from Mugs & Saucers and her sister Helen who were both in their late 50s, Mrs. Barret and two of her friends, Martha and Tilly, who were in their 60s, and Denise, Debbie's sister from the grocery store, about the same age as Maggie.

"Ok, ladies we're going to start with some very basic moves today, it's not rocket science, but finding the movement and rhythm can be a little tricky at first." Carla clapped her hands once, and said,

"Ready ladies?" and Maggie laughed, before continuing talking, thinking her friend would have made a great cheerleader.

"We'll start with hip lifts, shimmies, belly rolls and figure eights. Okay, feet flat, about hip width apart, good," she told them, smiling as she looked around. "Now, pelvis in, shoulders back and bend your knees. The more they're bent the easier it will be to practice the hip lifts. Excellent. Okay, now starting with your right leg, straighten it, while keeping the left leg bent, now right knee bends and straighten the left."

She walked around everyone, checking as she encouraged them to continue this movement over and over. "Notice when you straighten your leg, your hip lifts, this is how you will find the correct movement for later." Carla was still up front, arms out working on her lifts. "Okay ladies, I'm going to turn the music on and we'll try it with the beat." Maggie walked over and pressed play. She had made a mix CD of Middle Eastern music, and it started playing as she took her place again. "Ok, now, right...left...keeping your feet flat, yes, that's it...right...left... that's it Mrs. Barret," she encouraged, grinning, "Nice Beatrice, alright, now a little faster girls." And they tried to keep time. Some became very uncoordinated, some laughed but they kept trying their best. They went back to the original tempo.

After half an hour they took a bathroom and water break. "Ok Ladies, let's come back and finish our next 20 with some shimmies." Everyone came back to their spots, smiling and ready. "Now, remember, our posture is very important, feet flat, feet hip width apart, soft knees, remembering not to lock them on the lifts, good. Pelvis in, shoulders back. Hands out at your side, almost like you're spinning your hula hoop. Now, right... left... straighten... left...good...left... keep the rest of your body still ladies, good, now let's go a little faster, remember your posture." And off they went, Carla walked around the room checking people's posture, Maggie carried on at the front.

"Okay ladies, that was great!" she said, smiling at them all as they finished up. "Next week, let's all bring some belts, scarves, tutus if you have them, and we'll really be able to see our hips shaking. Oh, also, your homework, keep practicing your shimmy, fast or slow. While you cook, brush your teeth, standing at a counter, whenever you can, shake those hips girls!" Everyone laughed, said thanks and goodbye and left the shop happy.

"Mags, that wasn't half bad! Yer a good teacher!" Carla declared as they left the bookshop together.

"Ya, it was fun, wasn't it?" she grinned. Maggie laughed as Carla started trying to shimmy to the truck. "Loving the shimmy Carla!" Maggie said as her friend waved and shimmied on.

"See ya tomorrow, Mags." Maggie walked to the b and b still grinning. She was feeling quite hungry, having skipped lunch to go to the store, and only snacking on a few dry crackers before belly dancing. It was about quarter after five when she walked into the restaurant. The regulars were already eating their dinner, looking up to see who had come in, Maggie waved and smiled at them, a few waving and smiling back. Pat came over with a big smile on her face.

"Maggie, twice in one week. Well, isn't this nice." Maggie smiled back at her.

"Hi Pat, good to see you."

"Good to see you too dear." Pat looked behind Maggie.

"Now where's that handsome fella of yours?" she asked. Maggie laughed and spoke,

"Hopefully on his way soon, Pat." She started towards a table, Pat following her.

"Oh, that's good. Did you want a coffee while you wait dear?" Maggie nodded at her.

"Thanks Pat."

She finished her coffee by the time Billy arrived, turning to look at him after hearing him say hello to Pat when he came in. She noticed he wasn't in his work clothes, and his hair was still wet from showering. He bent down and gave Maggie a kiss.

"Hello, Beautiful," he said, sitting next to her. "Sorry if you had to wait long, I was covered in dirt and grease and had to shower first." She smiled at him.

"Worth the wait, and you smell delicious." He grinned at her, and they leaned in for another quick kiss. Pat came over and took their orders then Maggie and Billy started chatting.

"How did it go today, Billy? Did you get that car finished?" He nodded, as he answered.

"Yes, thankfully! What a bugger that was! But I don't have to go in again till next week, Wednesday and Thursday. Oh, I've got the roof repair at the post office on Monday too." She smiled at him again and he looked at her cheekily. "What is it, Mag?" She grinned at him a little longer before answering,

"Just thinking about how handsome you are. And, maybe a

little about you fixing a roof." Billy grinned back, eyes twinkling.

"Mmm, yes, roof fixing..." he said with a quiet growl at her, then leaned close and held her cheek, moving in for a tender kiss. They both drifted back to their first time for a moment before Billy spoke again. "Oh, hey, how did your class go, Mag?" he asked, smiling at her.

"Really well Babe, and we had a lot of fun!" His eyes smiling at her, he added,

"Do I get a private show?" Maggie laughed.

"Maybe, later, Lover." They leaned towards each other for another kiss. "You sure you don't mind staying in the camper tomorrow?" she asked him as Beatrice brought their food over.

"Course not Babe!" he replied, getting started on his dinner. Maggie smiled at him lovingly, finding it hard not to be aroused by his appetite.

They sat and enjoyed a coffee after dinner, then Maggie remembered her groceries at the shop, and Billy waited for her at the b and b while she grabbed the two bags. Each with a bag in their hands, and holding each other's free hand, they walked home together, enjoying the saskatoon-berry trees just starting to bud as they reached White Tree Lane. Old Bill was sitting up in the bay window watching them walking towards the house. He had heard the front gate open and was eager to say hello to his favourite people. They walked into the sound of his persistent meows. Billy took the bags and Maggie scooped Old Bill up and gave him a hug all the way to the kitchen, where she got him his dinner, Maggie laughing at his hungry, bossy eagerness. The three of them watched some TV for a little while, then headed to bed early, Old Bill following happily up the stairs.

CHAPTER 4

They awoke to another beautiful sunny summery day and enjoyed their coffees out back together.

"Guess we can finish up the shed on Sunday, eh Mag?" Billy suggested, getting up to grab another coffee. He reached out for Maggie's cup too as he was passing her.

"Another coffee?" he asked.

"Yes, to both questions," she said with a smile, turning to watch him walk inside. "Some sweet cheeks you got there, Lover." Billy gave his hips a little shake. Maggie laughed.

"I'll miss you tonight Billy!" He was pouring the coffee at the counter now but turned to smile at her as he came back out and set the coffee down. He bent down and held her head, gave her a kiss and winked at her.

"Well then we'll just have to make up for it the night after, won't we Beautiful?"

Billy left shortly after to go pick up the camper and get it ready for the night. He decided to just park it in one of Carla and Stu's back fields, instead of going all the way to the lake. After he headed out Maggie got a few things ready for the "sleepover". She inflated the double air mattress, found as many pillows as possible and brought them all into the living room, put all the snacks on the table, made sure there was beer and club soda in the fridge and got things ready for their fajita dinner. When Billy got back, she was blasting "Eye Of The Tiger" dancing around the house. He, of course, grabbed her and danced with her for a minute, then carried on with getting his stuff packed up. Maggie had made him some dinner and snacks too, and as Billy packed up the small cooler adding a few cans of beer, Maggie cut him a piece of cheesecake, popped it into a container and slipped it into the cooler.

"Thanks Babe," he said, stopping to grab her and hug her, the two holding on and kissing like they didn't want the other one to forget just how much they loved each other. "Have fun Mag," he said, kissing her again. She grabbed his butt and squeezed.

"K, probably not as much as I will tomorrow night!" She kissed him, giving him another squeeze. He flashed his cheeky grin at her.

"KNOCK KNOCK" came the sound at the door, then they heard,

"Hey you two sweet lovers, put some clothes on quick, it's me!" from Carla as she came into the house. Maggie and Billy laughed and started smooching again. "Ha! Just what I thought!" Carla said and they broke apart and smiled at her.

"Hi Carla," said Billy.

"Hey there Sweet Cheeks, how's it hang'n! Say, don't you two ever get enough?! Gawd!" She screwed up her face for a second then laughed and said "Only tease'n! Hey Mags, how's it going?" she asked as she came over to her and they gave each other a hug.

"Great Carla! I've got one sweet hunk of man..." grinning at Billy who winked at her, "and I'm about to have a kick ass slumber party with my bestie!" Carla fist pumped the air and said,

"Hells ya Mags." Billy chuckled and shook his head, gave Maggie another hug and kiss, then with their noses almost touching he said,

"Love you, Beautiful." She kissed him again and said,

"Love you, Handsome." He turned to grab his bags, and his guitar, smiling at Maggie.

"You girls have fun," he told them, and as he passed Old Bill near the bay window in the front hall, they heard him say,

"You make sure those two don't get too wild Mr. Bill." Then hearing the front door open he yelled,

"Bye ladies."

Carla was over at the stove checking things out,

"Smells good Mags, oh ya," and she turned to grab a six pack off the counter and slid it into the fridge. "I brought a couple movies Mags. Good ones!" she laughed. "Not those chick flicks you love!" And she handed them to Maggie. Maggie sorted through them, feeling her stomach flipping just reading the titles, "The Exorcist", "Psycho", "Friday The 13th", and "The Shining".

"No way am I watching all of these Carla!" she said putting them back down on the island.

"Oh come on Mags, they're just movies." Maggie shook her head.

"Nope, Nope, Nope!" Carla gave her a pleading look. "Okay, I'll watch *one* of those, but that's it." Carla nodded happily. "How can you even enjoy those movies, Carla?" Maggie asked her with a look of fear on her face. Carla laughed.

"Oh come on Mags, don't you like get'n your heart race'n and that feeling like something might jump out and get ya?" As she spoke she jumped at Maggie, Maggie started a little and gave her friend a smack on the arm.

"Now don't start that or I won't even watch *one* of them with you." The two of them laughed together.

"Hey Mags, I managed to get my hands on something I've

always wanted to try with you." Carla told her, looking around like she expected there to be people listening in on them. Maggie looked at her funny.

"Oh ya, and what's that Carla?" Carla looked around again, Maggie thought maybe she was losing it, and Carla motioned for her to come closer.

"Weed Mags," she said quietly. "You know, whacky tabacky." Maggie burst out laughing.

"Ya right Carla!" Carla looked at her, almost hurt, and didn't say anything, which worried Maggie even more. "Carla, you're serious, aren't you?" Carla nodded.

"Ya Mags, Stu's brother and nephew were over last weekend and the four of us rolled one up and smoked the thing. Shit Mags, never laughed so hard in my life!" Maggie could hardly believe what she was hearing. "So I got Leroy, that's Stu's brother, t'roll one up for me," and as she said it she walked over to her bag and pulled it out. She handed it to Maggie with a grin. Maggie took it and looked at it like she couldn't even imagine what you'd do with it and Carla laughed. "So, what'a ya say Mags?" Maggie gave her a goofy look.

"I don't know Carla." Carla was rummaging in her bag for some matches.

"Ever done it before Mags?" she asked, looking up at her friend and already heading towards the back door. Maggie shook her head, then had a vague memory of the cabin.

"Oh, wait, had some magic brownies once." Carla looked at her with surprise.

"Way to go Mags!" Maggie giggled.

"Remember the skinny-dipping story with Billy? That was

courtesy of the brownies." She was walking to the back door with Carla now, still unsure but thought she'd probably never do this with anyone else, and why not. The two stepped outside, Maggie closed the door and they sat at the patio table. Carla looked ridiculous as she stuck it in her mouth and tried a couple matches before getting it lit, then coughing and hacking as she hauled on it.

"Mmm, looks like fun," Maggie said sarcastically, as Carla passed it to her. Maggie gave it a couple hauls and started coughing too, but Carla was still hacking, so she just held it for a moment, then took another drag once she had stopped coughing. Carla was back up and breathing so Maggie handed it back to her. She had a few more puffs, then they put it out and left it on the patio table for later.

"Feel anything yet Mags?" Carla asked her from across the table. Maggie was staring out at the back yard watching the trees with deep interest. "Mags!" Carla called again. Maggie looked over at her with a blank stare. She felt fuzzy, kind of like she was in slow motion and could feel herself smiling like she'd just got laid.

"Well, I'm not, not feeling something," she answered, and Carla burst out laughing.

"What?" Carla asked, laughing harder still. Then both of them were in hysterics for ten minutes before they could calm down.

"I'm starving!" Maggie suddenly declared and stood up and walked back into the house, on a mission. She walked straight to the fridge and pulled out a soda, cracked it open and chugged it. Carla slinking in, and making her way over to Maggie, pointed at her and through another fit of laughter said,

"That's not food Mags!" Maggie laughed and spit her mouthful out, then the two laughed even harder, and were practically rolling around on the floor. Crawling back to the island and pulling themselves up, they grabbed plates and piled on all the food for the fajitas. Carla grabbed a beer, Maggie grabbed another club soda, and they took their food over to the living room and sat on the couch. They didn't talk for the longest time, just stuffing their faces and smiling through bursting mouthfuls as they attempted to tame their appetites a little. "Hey Mags, where's the weirdest place you ever had sex?" Carla asked from out of the blue. Maggie giggled.

"Just one Carla?" and laughed as Carla's eyes bugged out of her head.

"Not Maggie Two Shoes?" she said to her with such a serious look, Maggie burst into fits of laughter again.

"Recently? Or over the years Carla?" she asked, quite enjoying her friend's surprise. Carla shrugged, having just stuffed her face again with another mouthful of fajita. Maggie thought about the floating dock, but then thought maybe she better not mention that, as they all used that dock. "Hmm, okay... a balcony," she answered. Carla nodded.

"Cool Mags, sounds fun." Maggie envisioned the experience with fondness.

"Very cool actually." And she started giggling again.

"How about you Carla?" Carla was back to stuffing her face, now into the popcorn, and looked up at Maggie suddenly, confused, like she'd thought she was alone.

"Me what Mags?" Maggie was killing herself laughing again. Carla looked at her for a minute, then started eating more popcorn. "Hey, Mags, put a movie in would ya," she said between mouthfuls. "One of mine Mags!" Maggie stayed put, wondering if there was any way she could *will* the movie to jump off the island and into her outstretched hand, but to no avail. She got up and grabbed one at random and popped it in the player. "What did you put in Mags?" Carla asked, now sitting on the floor in front of the bag of popcorn like she was protecting it and would take out anyone who tried to steal it from her.

"Don't know Carla." But as the opening music started to play and Maggie saw the name Alfred Hitchcock, Carla sat up straight and said,

"Ooooh, I loooove this one." Maggie felt a brief moment of fear but then found the big-eyed serious look on Carla's face hysterical and burst into laughter, bringing Carla along with her. Then the two of them grew serious, as the music and the opening credits continued. Maggie was starting to feel a little creeped out again, then was happily surprised when she saw it was two secret lovers together and found herself watching eagerly.

"Carla, this is a love story!" she said grinning. Carla laughed.

"You just wait Mags, you just wait." Maggie slid down to the floor and started to make a dent in the chips, eyes glued to the screen. So far, she was loving it. It was an old black and white. Just two people in love, wanting to be together. How bad could it be, she thought? Carla got up and grabbed another beer and Maggie a soda, Maggie taking it quickly, still feeling very thirsty.

"Oh shit!" Carla said, startled at what just happened in the scene, then laughed at herself as she remembered she'd seen this movie hundreds of times.

"What Carla?" Maggie asked, not taking her eyes from the screen. "Hey Carla, her boss just saw her." Carla laughed again.

"I know Mags, that's what I was shit'n about." Carla was

giggling away again, then turned back to watch the movie. One thing after another, of the woman getting noticed as she traveled to her destination, Maggie thinking, ohh, she's gonna get busted for sure. Then she pulls into a motel, the young man working seems to be very lovely, even kinda cute. "Aw, sicko!" Carla yelled at the TV as the 'nice young man' stood peeping at the woman. Maggie didn't notice Carla get up and leave the room as she moved herself closer and closer to the TV, watching intently. Then just as the woman was enjoying her shower...

"REET REET REET" Carla jumped up behind Maggie. Maggie jumped right up to standing and screamed, Carla killing herself laughing and reenacting Maggie's reaction.

"Oh Mags, 'Ahhhh!'" she mimicked, and laughed. Maggie was whacking her with a pillow now, then the two of them were back on the floor, sitting on the air mattress laughing until they couldn't breathe. They paused the movie and took pee breaks. Then Maggie grabbed some bowls and spoons so they could eat cheesecake while they watched the rest of the movie. Right before they sat down, the phone rang.

"Hey Carla, you're closer, grab that would you please?" Maggie asked and Carla turned on the spot and went to the island wall to pick up the phone.

"Mags's phone," she answered. Nothing. "Hullo!? Hullo!" Carla said. "Hanging up now arsehole!" she added, Maggie laughing from the living room. Then Carla heard the other end disconnect, shrugged, and came to join Maggie back on the mattress. "Nobody there, Mags," she told her, taking her piece of cheesecake. Carla only managed to scare Maggie once more near the end of the movie.

"Hey Carla, speaking of scary," Maggie said as the credits were ending. "I want to have a surprise Halloween birthday party for Billy, well, a double party for both of us, and we all dress up like film characters for the Autumn Festival." Carla nodded happily.

"Ya, that sounds effn' great Mags!" Maggie was stuffing cheesecake in, chewing quickly, then added,

"Ya I know right! So can you get the committee to plan it for the Saturday night dance?" Carla nodded again.

"Ya ya Mags! Noooo problem." She shoveled in a huge mouthful of cheesecake, her cheeks bulging, Maggie giggling at her.

"You won't forget, will you Carla?" Maggie asked worriedly.

"Course not!" she answered, having another big mouthful, then added "Best tell me again tomorrow though Mags!" and they were back to laughing.

They were both too full and too stoned to do much and ended up watching one of Maggie's favourite "chick flicks" and falling asleep. Maggie had some weird dreams about Paul from Breakfast at Tiffany's, but of course they called him Fred, and there was a big orange cat named Holly who smoked and liked cheesecake. When Maggie woke up the next morning all she could think about was how full she still felt and wondering where the big cat went. Carla was still zonked out on the floor, so Maggie got up and got the coffee going then headed up to the washroom to take a shower. Carla was still sleeping when she came down, so Maggie poured a coffee and sat on the couch with Old Bill.

"Put it down Stu!!" Carla suddenly yelled sitting up straight, and looking at Maggie.

"Carla?" Maggie said to her. Carla silently stared at her for a few seconds then laid back down. Maggie shook her head and laughed to herself, then went back to petting Old Bill and sipping her coffee. It was almost 10:00 by the time Carla got up, which Maggie knew was much later than her usual rise and shine. She was usually up before sparrow fart, as Carla liked to say, and out before the sun came up, running the farm and doing all her other jobs too. She brought her friend over a coffee and Carla sleepily took it upstairs with her.

Maggie had started to gather up their mess when she heard the front door open, and Old Bill went running.

"Hiya Babe," came Billy's deep voice. She was in the kitchen tossing the garbage when he came down the hall.

"Hey Handsome," she replied with a smile, and they walked towards each other, happy to hug and give each other a big, long kiss.

"Missed sleeping next to you, Beautiful," he told her, giving her another kiss, holding her tight, and moving in a gentle rocking motion.

"Me too, Sweet Cheeks," she replied, and they stood there grinning at one another.

"Where's Carla, Mag?" he asked, looking around.

"Upstairs trying to wake up." Billy looked up at the clock automatically.

"Wow, really? She must have had more to drink than usual!" He gave Maggie another hug then let go to grab a coffee for himself.

"Ya, something like that," Maggie said with a little grin before Billy had turned back to her.

Carla came down a few minutes later, looking a little refreshed, and smiling away at the two of them.

"Hey Sweet Cheeks!" she said, giving him a pinch as she walked past to top up her cup. Billy chuckled.

"Hi Carla."

"Good night in the camper?" she asked, turning around. He nodded and took another sip of his coffee, making his way over to the couch with Maggie, the two of them sitting side by side, Carla followed and landed in her favourite chair.

"Think I'll head out after I finish this Mags!" she announced, holding her coffee up. "God knows what state Stu's in. He had pool last night, so..." and she trailed off, Billy and Maggie quickly flashed each other a grin.

"Okay Carla. Thanks for a fun night. Don't forget your movies." Carla waved goodbye and was soon out the door. Billy sat his coffee down and grabbed Maggie's and did the same. He pulled her closer and snuggled her, Maggie wrapped her arms around him tight.

"*Really* missed you last night. Not sure I can wait till later Mag," he told her, and she looked up at him and saw the tell-tale twinkle glinting in his eyes.

"Ohh?" she said flirtatiously. Billy leaned in for a kiss, then continued talking.

"Spent most of the night thinking about you Babe and how hot you are." Maggie grinned at him.

"Oh, you did, did you?" Billy nodded, his eyes becoming more twinkly, his hunger starting to grow.

"Mmhmm, yes, then while I was thinking about how hot you are, my mind wandered to what I might do to cool you off." Maggie raised her eyebrows questioningly.

"And what did you come up with, Lover?" She was starting to feel intrigued and slightly aroused now. His cheeky grin turned to a mischievous smirk, and he stood up, pulling her up with him.

"Care to find out?" he asked her, pulling her up close and kissing her hard. She reached up and held his face in her hands and looked at him.

"I think so," she answered, and he chuckled a little.

"Hey Mag, remember that time on the balcony?" He was grinning broadly now, and a smile spread across her face quickly.

"Oh, quite vividly!" she answered, thinking she felt like she had just thought about that very experience recently, but things were a bit fuzzy. "What about it, Billy?" He was walking them out of the living room smiling at her.

"Well, if my memory is correct, it was quite cold and judging by your body's response to the temperature, that seemed to, well, work for you." Maggie felt her cheeks go a little red. Laughing with a little embarrassment as she answered,

"Well yes it did." Billy moved her ahead of him, gave her ass a slap and said,

"I'll meet you upstairs in a minute, Mag." He winked at her. She looked at him questioningly. He was still standing waiting for her to go. "Say Mag, how about you get ready by waiting for me in your birthday suit." She couldn't believe how big his smile was.

"But Lover, it's not my birthday yet." He motioned for her to go and gave her another wink.

"Go on Mag, it'll be like a preview of your birthday." She grinned, turned, and walked down the hall to the staircase, then made her way up to their bedroom, and waited for... something unknown.

She left the curtains closed, and there was just enough light in the room to see one another in the day's growing sunshine. She stripped down to nothing, climbed into bed and pulled the sheet over top of herself to wait. Billy came into the room with a bowl and a grin.

"What are you up to Billy?" she asked, hating, and loving not knowing. He sat the bowl down on his end table so she couldn't see what he had, then pulled off his shirt and dropped it on the floor, still looking at her with mischief. *Gawd he's hot* she was thinking as she watched him undoing and pulling down his jeans and letting them land on the floor, then he started crawling towards her on the bed.

"Close your eyes Mag," he said to her.

"Billy, what are you up to?" she insisted.

"Trust me Mag. Close your eyes." She looked into his blue eyes as he smiled, with the look he gave her when he was ready to take her. She closed her eyes slowly, opened them again and he laughed.

"Come on Mag!" She grinned.

"Okay, okay." She closed them again. She felt his hand on hers, taking it, then kissing it and then he kissed his way up her arm, kissing her neck and then feeling the warmth of his breath near her face and his lips gently kissing hers.

"Keep them closed Mag," he whispered. She was already so aroused. He reached over her body and grabbed her other hand and kissed it too, then put both her hands above her head and she felt him wrapping something soft around them to keep them together. She opened her eyes and his hand reached down and gently covered them.

"Closed," he whispered again. She felt him moving on the bed and it was a few seconds before he touched her again. He placed something over her eyes and lifted her head gently to wrap it around to the back.

"Billy?" she said to him, and he kissed her lips ever so softly.

"Relax, Beautiful," he assured her in his deep sexy voice. She felt him lowering the sheet, down to her waist, and Maggie moved her body with unknown anticipation. She realized her hands weren't just tied together, but to the headboard too. Then something cold dripped onto her chest, and she wanted to open her eyes but even if she did, she couldn't see anyway. He kissed her lips gently again, and she felt something very cold... wet... what was it? Ice, slipping over her breasts, and Billy trailing it along her hot body, over her neck, down to her shoulders, Maggie's body rising and exploding with this strange, new, delicious feeling. He ran a piece across her mouth and as it melted a little, her lips became wet and Billy licked them, then kissed her, their mouths opening wider and kissing deep slow kisses. Billy was running the ice around and over her nipples and Maggie's pulse was racing.

"Oh my God Billy," she said softly. He kissed her harder. He moved the ice all over her arms and neck, sliding it slowly, over her chest and around her stomach, then she felt him pulling down the sheet, and throwing it off of her. Billy ran the ice up one leg, almost to her center, then the same up the other leg, this time into her center, where it melted almost instantly. Unable to participate, Maggie's body was at his mercy, and he grabbed more ice and made his way all over her body, now licking and kissing along the wet trails the ice left behind. He was circling a piece around her clit as he licked her nipples, her body was squirming with explosive pleasure, the ice melting faster with every second and she became more aroused.

"Billy," she called out to him, wanting him so bad. He was busy, licking around her center now.

"Maggie," he breathed her name back and she felt his hands run over her breasts, her nipples so hard, his body pressed to hers as he lifted the scarf on her eyes and slid his tongue into her mouth, his hands in her hair holding her face and kissing her passionately. Then he was sucking and kissing her neck, his mouth open and wet on her skin.

"Billy," she whispered. He looked at her with a sultry, powerful gaze, his hand sliding down as he stared into her eyes intensely and she felt a finger slide inside of her, moving himself down her body again and sucking on one of her breasts. She couldn't stay still; she wanted him inside her. She wanted to hold him.

"Mag, you're so hot when you want it this bad!" he said, licking his way back up to her ear and sucking her earlobe. Her hips were moving, squeezing her thighs together, her feet and legs sliding up and down together. He grabbed another piece of ice and she watched him pop it into his mouth, then he leaned forward and placed his mouth over one of her breasts, circling his tongue and the ice around her nipple as she moved more, her body rising to feel him against her. Then finally, with a grin, looking right into her eyes he pushed himself, thick and hard and very erect, into her hungrily aching body. The water dripping down over her body, her hands above her head, the taunting foreplay he'd provided, it was all so erotic and arousing. She was cumming instantly, and did, multiple times as he slid inside of her, then out to kiss her body again. Then taking her legs and bending them to slide in right against her body and letting them down again to slowly penetrate, he was now groaning with his own pleasure.

"Mag, you turn me on like no other," he said as he was about to cum.

"You feel so good," she breathed, and his body rocked harder against hers.

"Mag, Mag!" he yelled, and she felt him explode.

"God Billy, untie me!" she said to him, and with his hips still moving against her, he reached up and undid her restraints, she grabbed his ass and squeezed, running her hands up and down his back and scratching and grabbing him, kissing like they were going to eat each other's faces. She wanted him again. She was on fire and needed him to put out the flames. Her face rubbing softly down to his neck, kissing him and licking him, biting his ears and reaching up into his hair and holding on as she pressed her hips into his, her legs wrapping around him. His hands now underneath her, holding her tight as she moved them to flip him.

"Mag!" he said, sounding a little surprised at her ravenous energy. Flipping over together, so she was now on top, she kissed from one ear, sucking and licking, down his neck and to the other ear, breathing heavily and whispering,

"Billy, I want more." Kissing back down to his chest, her hands in his hair again as she moved her center over his, grinding circles on top of him. His hands holding and squeezing her ass, then she reached down and held him, feeling him getting hard again. She reached a little further and teasingly fondled his balls, gently squeezing and then running her fingers up the base of his increasingly hardening dick. She grasped him and rubbed her wet body up and down a couple times before sitting up and riding him like she'd never done before. Head back and arms in her own hair, she rose and fell in long rhythmic glides, crying out with absolute enjoyment.

"Oh my God, oh God!" she was yelling, riding up and down,

Billy's hands beside his body, bracing himself, his head back calling out her name over and over.

"Mag, oh Mag!" Until she was making shorter, faster glides and leaning forward, Billy holding her breasts.

"Ohhhh," she cried.

"Gaaawd, Maggie!" he yelled.

"Billy! Ohh... Ohh... I'm so close," she said, gliding faster still.

"I'm gonna cum Maggie!" She felt his pelvis lift as he yelled "Awww! God!" Maggie laughed with delight as she came, her body still squeezing him inside of her as she fell forward, and they kissed so passionately again. Both of them panting and laughing and kissing, until she fell right next to him, both huffing and puffing with satisfaction.

"Billy," she said. "What the hell?" He laughed his Billy chuckle.

"Just something I thought might be fun to try Mag." She rolled to face him and looked up at him.

"Well, just when I think you couldn't be more delicious you best yourself again lover of mine. God, you really got my motor going this time." Maggie laughed pantingly, and gave him a hard kiss.

"Damn Mag, that was amazing," he said with a smirk, kissing her back. "I could hardly stand watching you squirm like that, and I certainly wasn't expecting to do it again." The two of them laughed and lay in each other's arms trying to catch their breath.

"Well, next time I'm tying *you* up Billy!" she told him with another kiss. "It's not easy not being able to hold you while you're making me so hot." He grinned at her, and rolled over on top of her.

"Okay Mag, you're on." And they were back in a lip lock, eyes dreamy and deeply watching one another. "Hey Mag, I'm going to grab a shower," he said after a bit.

"Okay Lover, I think I'll hang out here and wait for you, then hop back in myself." He sat up, then looked at her and leaned down for another kiss before leaving her. She was almost sleeping when he came back and kissed her.

"All yours Beautiful." She grinned and made her way to the washroom. After she finished her quick shower and threw some clothes on, she went down to find Billy sitting out back. He was playing his guitar and singing "Ain't No Sunshine".

"Hey Babe," he said, smiling.

"Hello Handsome Lover," she replied. "My legs are still shaking Billy!" she said with a laugh. He chuckled.

"Ya, that was crazy Mag!" He continued playing and singing, Maggie went and sat in her chair, and leaned her head back against the wall with her eyes closed, listening to him and loving it as always. After he finished the song it was quiet for a minute, then,

"Hey Mag, what's this?" he asked grinning at her, and Maggie looked up to see him holding the stub of the joint.

"Oh, Carla brought that last night." He raised an eyebrow.

"Oh, so that's why she slept so late. Well, you two really did have a good time then?" He laughed, seeing her anxious face.

"Ya, I think so. Don't remember much," she answered. He laughed again and sat it on the table.

"Trip down memory lane Mag?" he asked her, and she laughed.

"Ya, no brownies this time though." He didn't say anything else for a minute then asked,

"Any cheesecake left?" They both burst out laughing when she answered with a sheepish look on her face,

"Nope!"

The rest of the day was spent lazing about. There were still some fajita leftovers, so they finished that off for dinner, then went back to lounging about. Old Bill happily lounging with them. They were both pretty worn out and called it a night fairly early, lying in bed talking for a little while and chatting about their plans on finishing up the shed the next day. Billy said he was planning on adding a pull up bar, hoping to get back into his old work-out routine. Maggie snuggled up to him, smiling as she pictured his beautiful body.

"Mmm, you're already perfect!" she told him happily.

"Thanks Babe," he replied and kissed the top of her head. "I'd like to stay that way for a while longer yet." She looked up at him and they smiled flirtatiously.

CHAPTER 5

They were up early the next morning, had coffee, and breakfast and were outside working by 10:30. They managed to finish the shed by 4:00, and were feeling quite proud of their work.

"Looks great Mag," Billy said as they packed up their tools, and had a shed to store them in.

"Ya Babe, we did good," she replied and smiled at him.

"We make a great team Beautiful." Billy hugged her and gave her a big kiss. The plan was to make it big enough for tools, and yard equipment, that sort of thing, but also a place to park his beast. They had built a nice wide double door and added built-in shelves all along the back wall and along one side a long work counter. Billy's pull up bar was up in the front corner.

"Say Mag, let's see if we can manage what I have planned for us." Maggie looked at him apprehensively. Billy walked over to the bar, rubbed his hands together and reached up. Not as quickly as he would have liked, but succeeding just the same, he pulled himself into a chin up. Maggie walked towards him grinning.

"Very nice Mr. Stanton," she purred at him and ran her fingers down his chest and stomach. Billy gave her a kiss, breathing a little heavy from the pull up.

"Okay Beautiful, your turn." Maggie gaped at him and laughed. "What Mag, I bet you're better at it than you think," he told her smiling. "You're a farm girl Mag!" She grinned at him and gave him a quick peck.

"Okay, I always say I'll do whatever you like, Lover." Billy growled at her sexily and grinned. Maggie had to jump up to reach the pole. It took her a second to find the right muscles, then she slowly pulled herself up, her head level with the bar. Then she stretched out and dropped down again. "Holy crap Billy! That's hard!" Billy chuckled as he pulled her close and hugged her.

"Ya but, you got yourself up there!" She giggled through heavy breaths. "So, there's more to this Babe. Remember when we first met, I may have been showing off for you when I got you to grab on while I did pull ups?" Maggie grinned reminiscently at him, her eyes twinkling. "Well, we're going to do them together." Maggie gaped at him again. Billy laughed. "Come," he said, grabbing her hand. "Okay, Mag, you're going to wrap yourself around like I'm wearing you," he started, winking cheekily at her, then continued. "And we're both going to hold the bar and pull ourselves up together."

"Mmm, very motivating work out Lover! You've got yourself a deal," she said with a giggle. Standing under the bar, Maggie jumped on, Billy grabbing her as she wrapped her legs around Billy's middle and reached for the bar. Billy grabbed the bar on the outside of her hands. He looked at her and they were grinning at one another.

"Ready Mag?" he asked, and she nodded. They both started pulling, slowly at first, they could feel the raw, straining power in each other's bodies as they pulled themselves up and looked over the bar at one another. Then stretching down, Billy landed gently on the floor and held Maggie for a kiss.

"Let's do that every day Lover," Maggie suggested with a big smile. Billy's head fell back with a chuckle. Maggie slid down his body to the floor and they took each other's hand as they headed into the house to clean up and figure out what to do for dinner.

While they were eating their grilled cheese, fries and a hardy pile of raw veggies from their little garden, Maggie's thoughts fell on Billy's early comment about them making a good team. She looked up at him, then back down at her plate, second guessing herself for a moment. Then, looking back up again she said,

"Billy, do you ever think about the two of us getting married?" He looked up quickly, his eyes twinkled, and a little smirk was playing around the corner of his mouth. Looking at her thoughtfully before answering, he replied,

"Oh, we don't need a piece of paper, do we Babe? We're doing fine just the way we are, aren't we?" He leaned over to give her a quick kiss. Maggie smiled and gave a little nod.

"Ya we're great," she answered, and he went back to eating. "Would be nice to make it official though, don't you think?" Billy gave her a little smile and shrugged.

"I know I want to spend my life with you Mag. Why do we need a piece of paper to say that?" Maggie was going to say something else when the phone rang. She got up and answered it. It was Carla.

"Hey Carla, how's things?" Maggie asked cheerily.

"All good Mags. Say, is Billy around?" Maggie smiled at him and answered "Yep, just a sec, for you Babe," she told him, and he got up to take the phone from her. Maggie sat down again, ate a couple more french fries, and the last of her carrot sticks, then took her dishes to the kitchen.

"Hey," Billy said into the phone. "Oh right, almost forgot...

Yep okay, lunch? Right... Yep... Bye." and hung up. Maggie heard him sit down again.

"Everything okay?" she asked from the sink.

"Yes, all good Babe. Stu just needs some help with his truck." Maggie finished filling the sink halfway with warm soapy water and Billy joined her, sliding his dishes in on top of hers and started to wash them, passing them to Maggie to dry.

***

"Love ya Babe," Billy said, giving her a quick kiss the next morning and heading out the door.

"Bye Lover, see you later," she said, watching him leave. Carla had canceled fishing, because she had some extra errands to run, so Maggie decided to start on getting things organized in the shed. She couldn't help but think about Billy's answer about marriage. He was right, they *were* great, but she was actually surprised he didn't want to marry her. He was such a romantic, she thought he'd think it was a great idea. She put it out of her mind, finishing up in the shed, then working on plans for their party.

The summer was quickly fading and by the end of August Maggie and Carla had organized all the details with the committee for the party. They were having it the second night of the gathering. Carla had invited everyone when she delivered the mail, stressing the secret and surprise part as much as possible. People were excited about dressing up and celebrating with Maggie and Billy.

Maggie was now looking for someone with puppies so she could give Billy one as his present. Carla and Stu had settled on Fred and Wilma for their costumes, and Maggie had bought her and Billy Zorro and Elena costumes and was really looking forward to wearing them at the party. She'd asked Pat to make the cake, and she accepted gladly, with grand plans of making it fit the party theme. People were told gifts weren't necessary but asked to bring a dish, for a potluck dinner and any alcohol they might want to add to the table.

Billy was busier than usual with work. He was at the car shop three times a week and still running all over the place doing odd jobs and contracting work almost every other day. They weren't getting to see much of each other, and he was understandably beat most of the time, and headed to bed early every night. They weren't talking much and their lack of communication with each other, which was new for them, was causing slight friction between them. They hardly saw one another and hadn't made love for more days than they'd ever gone, which was an important part in Maggie and Billy's "communication" with each other. It was making both of them feel a bit unwanted, and paranoid, as well as frustrated. They were just *off*. They'd never not been there for each other, attentively before. Except of course when they lived in different worlds for twenty-five years. Maggie felt sad and missed time with him.

With the distance between them, Maggie started wondering what was up after a few separate occasions when she came home to Billy on the phone and he'd suddenly finish the call, when she'd walk in. If she asked him about it, he'd just say, "Oh, just some contracting clients." But Maggie's gut was telling her something wasn't right. She had thought about those calls too, where the person calling didn't say anything, then would hang up after a few seconds. And that had happened a number of times.

"Carla, you don't think Billy's messing around on me, do you?" she asked Carla one day when they were setting up for their belly dancing class. Carla looked at her with wide eyes.

"Are you crazy Mags? Billy's only got eyes for you and in case you haven't noticed, you turn him on big time Mags!" Maggie shrugged as she rolled out the yoga mats. "Mags, you're not seriously worried, are you?" Carla asked.

"Well, I don't know Carla, things just don't feel right. Maybe I'm just being paranoid, you know with all the cheating Pete was doing while we were together. But I feel like Billy's keeping something from me. You know I even brought up marriage and he shot it down." Carla looked away, then busied herself with the box of hip scarves.

"Nah, I doubt it, Billy would never cheat. I'd be one of the first to know around here. Plus, think he's quite content bumping uglies with ya Mags, and it's not like he doesn't get it often enough!" Maggie laughed a little. She could always count on Carla to cheer her up or shake her up. She knew Carla was probably right, and took a deep breath, trying to push the thought from her mind.

"Say, you coming by for a ride this week Mags?" Carla asked after a bit of silence.

"Oh, ya, I think I will, maybe Wednesday." Maggie's cup filling back up a little at the thought of riding Black Beauty.

"Oh, and by the way, I was delivering some eggs to the Crofters farm yesterday and their golden retriever just had puppies Mags!" Maggie looked at her friend excitedly.

"Oh, that's awesome, I can't wait to see Billy's face when I give him a pup." Carla grinned.

"Ya, think that's a great gift Mags." Maggie nodded, smiling.

"You know, he had a dog growing up. He mentioned him while we were at the cabin. He was worried about how sad the dog would be when he went away to military school. I don't think he's had one since, Carla." Maggie was feeling much better now, and, as always, felt better spending time with her friend and chatting with her. Belly dancing with their group of ladies seemed to release her worries too.

When Maggie got home, she headed straight upstairs to shower. They'd stayed a little later than usual, some of the ladies hanging around to chat a bit. Neither Maggie or Carla had anything to hurry home to that night. She climbed out of the shower and dried off, then threw on her summer nighty, rolled on her vanilla oil and went downstairs. She wasn't sure when Billy would be home, so she had no plans for dinner. She was feeling a bit lost with Billy gone so much. *What did I do with myself before he came back into my life,* she wondered. She walked over to the radio and flipped it on. Old Bill hopped up onto the island and gave her a meow.

"Hello old buddy," she said, as she smiled at him and gave him a good rub. He always loved it when there was music, and Maggie turned it up a bit when she heard "Rock Me Gently" playing. She started dancing around the kitchen and around Old Bill, singing and being silly. She turned it up a little louder and danced away. She danced around to "Hungry Like The Wolf" and then "When I Think About You I Touch Myself." She had her back to the island at that point, dancing around the kitchen again as she grabbed a drink and something to snack on, then heard,

"Hey Babe." And turned to see Billy grinning at her. She danced over to the radio and turned it down. Smiling at him.

"Hi Sweet Cheeks," she said back to him, "feel like dancing?" He smiled but said,

"No, I'm going to jump in the shower, then I have to head out again." He smiled at her then headed back down the hallway.

Ok, what the hell, she thought to herself. *No kiss, no hug, no dance, leaving again.* Maggie turned the radio off and went and sat out back. She was feeling very frustrated by the time he came back down and stepped out on the patio. He leaned down and kissed the top of her head. She didn't look up.

"I'll see you later Mag," he said, putting his hand on her shoulder. She didn't respond. "Mag?" he said again. Then he was standing in front of her, bending down to face her. "Mag? What is it?" he asked her. "I'll try to get back as soon as I can. I gotta go Babe!" he added and kissed her lips.

"See you later," she responded, coolly. He looked at her with some frustration, hesitating for a moment, then walked towards the back gate and left. She was pissed. She was sure there was something going on. Looking down, she saw the end of Carla's joint still on the table. She grabbed the barbecue lighter and lit it up, taking the last few tokes off of it, then put it out on the patio stones. It was enough to feel a little buzzed and she felt her shoulders relax a bit. She sat there for ages, feeling old wounds reopen. Anxious feelings she'd felt throughout her marriage with Pete, but never before with Billy. The ugly self-doubt and negative self-talk started up in her mind, that she hadn't heard for years now.

Maggie went back inside and made herself a cup of tea. She grabbed her CD player and headphones and brought them with her as she went upstairs and filled the bath, adding some oils and salts, hoping to soak away all the negative vibes. As the tub filled up, she did some yoga stretches, trying to wring out the tension in her body, ending with child's pose, then climbing into the warm water. Old Bill pressed his face into the crack between the door and the frame, pushing the door open, and sauntering in to sit on her clothes on the floor next to her. She turned on her music and closed her eyes and lost herself in song. Singing along with Blue Rodeo always soothed her heart. She finished her bath, and taking the CD player with her, grabbed her thin summer housecoat and went downstairs, Old Bill following along behind her. She put the player on the table and unplugged her headphones so she could take it out back and listen at the patio table. It had started to rain softly while she sat there, and it was getting quite dark. She turned to check the clock. It was already 8:40, and still no Billy. She walked back in and grabbed the phone, dialing Carla's number. It rang and rang, then finally,

"Yah?!" came Stu's scruffy voice, sounding quite annoyed at being disturbed.

"Hey Stu, it's Maggie." She heard him grunt. "Can I talk to Carla please?" Maggie continued.

"Huh? S'not here is she. She's out with your Billy. Should be eff'n home by now too," he said, sounding grumpier.

"What, Carla's with Billy?" Maggie asked.

"That's what I just said to ya! Saw him pick'er up with my own two eyes!" he snapped.

"Okay, thanks Stu." Maggie hung up. What in the actual hell was going on? Why were Billy and Carla together, without Maggie knowing about it? She went back out and sat down again, the rain had started to fall a little harder now. "Trust Yourself" just finished, then "Two Tongues" started to play, and Maggie heard the front door open. She got up and walked in just as she saw Billy coming into the kitchen.

"Hey Mag," he said smiling. She walked right up to him, almost hopping.

"Where have you been?" she asked angrily.

"Whoa Mag, why are you so worked up?" he asked, backing up slightly.

"What's going on between you and Carla, Billy?" she pressed. Billy looked surprised. "Are you cheating on me Billy Stanton?" she asked, standing almost right against him, looking up into his shocked face.

"Mag, what are you talking about?" he asked, trying to hold her. She pushed his hands away and backed up.

"Billy, I want to know if you're cheating on me!" He shook his head in disbelief.

"How could you even think that, Mag?" She stared at him, not saying a thing. "Mag, I can't tell you where I've been, but I'm not eff'n cheating on you." He was starting to sound angry too. She could hear "Time" blasting out back now and the rain coming down harder. "I can't even believe you'd think that, Maggie." She was standing with her hands clenched looking at him.

"Well, what am I supposed to think Billy, when I keep getting hang ups, you're gone all the time, not telling me what you're up to, we haven't even had sex for over a week." She was starting to cry, which made her angry at herself and she turned and walked back out to the patio. This was new territory for Maggie and Billy and the lack of experience navigating through uncertainty and jealousy was making their thoughts cloudy. Billy stood there for a moment in shock. He walked to the back door and saw Maggie standing in the middle of the yard in the rain. There was just enough moonlight shining through the clouds to see her, casting a blue-ish light over her silhouette.

"Mag!" he called but she didn't budge. He hesitated for a moment, staying under the small patio awning, looking up at the falling rain, before he headed straight for her. Grabbing onto her arms and looking at her, the rain dripping down their faces, their hair already soaked, her housecoat clinging to her body. "Mag," he said again, more softly. She didn't look up. "Please, look at me Mag." She finally looked up at him, her eyes wet with tears and rain drops. "Dammit Maggie, I'm not cheating on you! I hardly went near another woman in the twenty-five years we were apart because you were the only woman I ever loved. Why would I lay with another, now that I have you?" She felt herself soften seeing the look in his eyes, she knew he meant it. "I can't tell you what I've been up to because I've been planning shit for your birthday." She reached up and held his wrists as he slid his hands up to hold her face. "You really are the only one for me," he said and leaned down and kissed her slowly and softly. Then looked back into her eyes. "*You* are the reason it never worked out with anyone else Maggie." She felt herself melting a little more than usual.

"After The Rain" was playing when Billy tried to coax Maggie back to the house; she stopped him and pulled him back. He looked at her questioningly, and she looked into his eyes, pulling him into her deep emerald trance, and he knew she needed him to mend this sting with more than just words. Sliding his hands around her waist, holding her in his arms, he lifted her up. Maggie wrapped her arms around his shoulders and kissed him. As she slid back down to stand in the grass, he started to dance with her, she still had her arms around his shoulders, and he had his hands resting on the top of her hips, holding her tight. The rain washed over them as they moved to the music. Kissing each other's wet dripping faces lovingly. It was the last song on the album. Now all they could hear was the rain's pitter patter on the ground around them. They stood there hugging and caressing each other and pressing their lips together with such force, holding one another snuggly. He peeled her housecoat back and off her shoulders, letting it drop to the ground. She pulled his shirt from his jeans and lifted it up, he finished pulling it off and dropped that too. As he did, she was already undoing his pants, and he pulled them down, along with his boxers, and slid his hands back to grab her ass, lifting her right up off the ground again. With her legs wrapped around him, still kissing each other wildly, caressing, they started to kiss more deeply. Their bodies hot, even in the coolness of the night's rain, squeezing each other tight. The physical connection they'd both been missing was washing away with the rain pouring over them, somehow wiping the slate clean. Their hearts pressed together, the beat pulling them back into their deep love for each other. Maggie had felt so lost in their lack of time and intimacy with each other, but now, with their bodies pressed together she was filling up again and felt their lifelong magnet pull, locking back in place. Kissing lovingly, still holding on tight, Billy walked back towards the house and carried her right upstairs. Sitting her feet down on the bedroom floor, she sat down on the bed and pulled him forward towards her. She moved back further on the bed, their eyes softly locked. He followed, then laid down on top of her, their wet hair dripping, their bare bodies shivering slightly. They spoke not a word. Kissing each other gently, kissing along each other's necks as they moved together, Billy sliding himself in and out with long slow glides, holding on tightly and hugging each other as they made love, the rain pounded on the front porch roof outside the bedroom window as their bodies continued to move in rhythm with the rain drops. It was so tender and deep, Maggie almost cried, feeling such a release of worry and so enveloped by his true pure love for her and hers for him. When they finished, they still didn't speak. Maggie laid her face on his chest, Billy's arms around her. She ran her fingers over his chest, Billy played with her hair, and they laid there hugging each other tight.

CHAPTER 6

She didn't remember falling asleep, but when she woke up, Billy was gone, and there was a single daisy lying on his pillow next to her. He'd picked it from the garden out front and left it for her. Maggie picked it up smiling, bringing it to her nose and smelling it deeply. Her heart was full and more peaceful than it had been recently. She smiled softly thinking, on her way to work today, she'd stop by the garage to say hello before opening the shop.

"Oh, hiya Maggie," came the voice of the gas station owner, Eric, when she walked into the garage in search of Billy. She turned and smiled.

"Good morning, Eric," she replied.

"Billy's not here, if that's who you're looking for," he added, and she felt herself starting to fret again.

"Oh," was all she could say.

"Ya, he won't be in until tomorrow Maggie." He turned to walk back outside to serve a customer at the pump. Maggie walked back to the shop and went inside. *Birthday stuff?* she wondered. The phone rang and snapped her out of her deep thoughts.

"Ashberry Books," she answered with a smile. Again, no response. She'd never had these calls at the bookstore before. "Hello!" she said, getting angry. Then click, as the person hung up. She heard the door open and looked up to see Carla, smiling happily.

"Morn'n Mags!" she said walking towards her. "What's up with you?" she added looking at Maggie as she tilted her head slightly.

"Think I'm losing it Carla. I accused Billy of cheating last night. Actually, I asked him if something was going on with the two of you." Carla made a face at her.

"What the hell ya talk'n bout girl?" she said to Maggie "You think I'd do something with your man? Geeze Louise, Mags, you are losing it!" she said with an annoyed look on her face.

"Ya, I know, I'm sorry Carla, he's just been so secretive. Now I just got another one of those hang ups, here!" Carla pulled another face.

"That's weird Mags. Secret admirer maybe?" and she winked. "Listen Mags, I'm not supposed to say anything to ya, but Billy's not cheat'n, he's just working out a surprise for your birthday." And Carla beamed at her.

"Ya, that's what he said last night Carla. Thanks." Carla walked around the counter and gave Maggie a hug.

"Now you quit with this cheat'n stuff, eh Mags!" Maggie smiled and nodded.

"Ya, I will Carla, thanks. So what brings you in, this morning?" Carla grinned at her.

"Well, I'm supposed to invite you over one day, in a few weeks..." she started, winking goofily at her, then going on, "so you're out of the house for a few hours." She winked again. Maggie laughed.

"Okay. I won't let on," she said with a smirk. Carla touched the side of her nose and smiled.

"See ya tomorrow Mags," she told her happily and headed out

the door. Maggie chuckled to herself, feeling a bit stupid for worrying so much. She knew a lot of it had to do with all the years of Pete cheating on her, and that it was something she needed to work on. She still had a hard time feeling like she could trust a man.

Billy came by the bookstore just before closing.

"Hey Mag," he said, almost timidly, and Maggie giggled slightly at him. He was looking a little worried she might freak out again. "Heard you stopped by the garage looking for me. You're not going to throw anything at me are you?" he asked, a cheeky look now playing across his face.

"Ha ha," she said, and they walked towards each other and hugged. "What are you doing here?" she asked, smiling up at him. He leaned down and kissed her.

"Just wanted to see my sexy woman and walk her home," he replied with a wink. She gave his butt a squeeze and grinned at him.

"Nice. Feel like taking your sexy woman out for dinner too?" she asked him.

"You bet," he answered, giving her another kiss.

"K, I'll just shut down the computer and we'll go," she said with a smile and walked back to the counter. They left the shop hand in hand and walked to the b and b. After a filling dinner, they made their way home wrapped tightly as they walked, Billy leaning down and kissing Maggie every once in a while. The two of them talking and laughing like their usual selves again.

"We going apple picking this year Mag?" he asked as they approached the front gate.

"Sure. We'll need apples for our crisp, won't we!" she grinned at him as he unlocked the front door and let her walk in ahead of him. Bill was meowing at them eagerly. "Could you feed him

Babe? I just have to run to the washroom," Maggie asked, already heading up the stairs.

"Sure," he answered her, "Come on Mr. Bill," he said and off they went. Maggie heard the phone ringing just as she reached the top of the stairs. It rang about five times then stopped. She closed the bathroom door behind her.

Billy managed to put Bill's food down for him and answer the phone before it stopped ringing.

"Yep?" he said as he picked it up. Nothing. "Hello," he said. "Who is this?" he could hear the person breathe, then,

"Hi, is Maggie there?" came a man's voice.

"Yep, just a second." Billy sat the phone down, walked to the bottom of the staircase and called up to her. "You gonna be long Mag?" he asked.

"No," she yelled back. Billy walked back to the kitchen and picked the phone up.

"She'll just be a minute, can I tell her who's calling?" The man didn't say anything for a few seconds, then finally,

"Ah, ya, tell her it's Peter. Peter Baker," he said, just as Maggie walked in. Billy's face fell slightly as he covered the phone with his hand. Maggie was smiling at him and then saw his face.

"What Billy, is something wrong?" she asked, feeling worried.

"Um, no, well I don't think so Mag." She reached out her hand.

"Is it Carla, I was going to call her?" Billy held the phone and shook his head, Maggie's hand dropped down again. "Billy!" she said.

"Mag, it's Pete." Maggie felt like the wind had been knocked out of her. She opened her mouth, but nothing came out. "What do you want me to do?" he asked her, still covering the phone. She reached out her hand again, sitting down on one of the stools.

"I better take it Billy, might be about someone from home." Billy handed her the phone and stood there for a second watching Maggie. "Hello," she said, her voice sounding far away, even to herself.

"Hey Maggie? Is that you? It's Pete," he said, sounding quite happy.

"Ya, hi Pete, is everything okay?" she asked him, shrugging at Billy. Billy went over to the living room and sat on the couch.

"Oh well, ya, everything's okay Maggie. Wow, it's so great to hear your voice," he said, Maggie feeling more and more confused.

"How did you get this number Pete?" she asked him.

"Your number, oh, well I'm home again, and so I swung by your farm, hoping to see you. I was surprised to see you'd sold it. Luckily I ran into Mason in town, and he said you'd moved away, so he gave me this number." Maggie quickly made a mental note to call her brother and thank him for that.

"Oh, I see. Yes, I moved here about four years ago now, after mom and dad passed on. What are you doing back home?" She felt like she was in some kind of strange fever dream.

"Well, like I said, I came looking for you Maggie." Maggie didn't respond for a moment, thinking *what am I even supposed to say*, then asked,

"Didn't you and your wife move to Michigan, Pete?" and now Pete was quiet.

"Oh, well, yes, but Lucy's gone Maggie." Maggie had a brief second of thinking *oh, now you know what it's like to be left for another,* then Pete added. "She was sick for a while, and we lost her a couple of months ago." Maggie felt terrible, glad she hadn't voiced her previous thought.

"Oh my God Pete, I'm so sorry to hear that," she said to him.

"Ya, thanks," he responded.

"So, are you moving back home then?" she asked him, trying to move the conversation along.

"No, just home for a bit, then back to Michigan." Maggie looked over at Billy, he had the TV on but she saw it was on mute. "So, you're with someone then Maggie?" Maggie was feeling less and less comfortable with this conversation.

"Yes, that was Billy who answered." Pete didn't say anything for a second.

"Married?" he asked, and she felt a bit of a sting not being able to say yes as she answered.

"No, we're not married. Pete, was there a reason you called?"

"Like I said, just wanted to hear you, see how you were." Maggie was gobsmacked.

"Okay, well, here I am. I am just on my way out though Pete." She said to him, lying but wanting to finish the call.

"Oh, okay Maggie. Well maybe we can chat again some other time." And before he could say anything else she said,

"Ok Pete, I'm sorry to hear about Lucy. You take care now. Bye." She hung up before he said another word. She sat there on the stool, the moment feeling surreal. Billy was back, sitting down next to her.

"What was that about Mag?" She shook her head.

"Not really sure. Called to tell me his wife died, and that he just wanted to talk to me." Billy looked a bit grumpy.

"Oh, that's too bad to hear he lost his wife, but why did he call you?" Maggie looked up at him and shrugged.

"Weird," she said, and they grabbed drinks and went to the living room to watch TV. Neither one mentioned Pete again.

CHAPTER 7

Billy was gone again by the time Maggie got up. She was going over to the Myers farm for most of the day, taking Black Beauty out for a ride and then finishing up the details of the birthday party with Carla. Stu was headed out in his old truck when Maggie pulled in and beeped and waved at Maggie as they passed each other. She wandered around for a bit, hoping to find Carla. She finally found her, milking the cows, and when she said 'good morning' Carla looked up at her with a big smile.

"Hey Mags, you made it!" she said happily.

"How far have you gotten?" Maggie asked her.

"Oh, just got Freeda over there left to do." Pointing to the cow in the corner. Maggie grabbed a bucket and a stool and took them over to the cow. "Aw, thanks Mags," Carla said with relief in her voice. Maggie pet Freeda lovingly and placed her head against her as she sat down. Then, as she milked, she told Carla all about the call from Pete.

"What the eff Mags!?" she said, getting all worked up and causing the cow she was milking to moo loudly at her. "Sorry Bessie!" Carla said, patting the cow's side. "Think that's been the hang ups Mags?" she asked. Maggie hadn't even thought of that.

"Now that you mention it, ya, probably Carla." Maggie sat there thinking for a moment. "You know, I haven't heard from Pete since we went through our divorce Carla. Why is he calling me now?" she said, feeling super annoyed.

"Think he wants ya back Mags?" Maggie shook her head at the thought.

"No, he was done with me a long time ago."

"Ya, well, he's probably getting randy and remembering old times! What did Billy hafta say about it?" Carla asked after they sat in silence for a few minutes.

"Not much, confused too. We didn't really talk about it," she answered her friend with a shrug. Maggie finished milking Freeda, then left Carla to go to the stable. She happily walked over to the majestic creature and reached out her hand to rub his face. He whinnied happily as she said hello to him, opened the door, walked towards him, and gave him a hug. "Ready for a run, Beauty?" she asked him, his head gently butting against her, one of his front hooves happily scratching the dirt floor. She saddled him up and walked outside with him, then in one fluid motion, stuck her foot in the stirrup and was mounted on him and kicking him on. Instantly, everything and anything that brought any anxiety melted away with the sound of his hooves hitting the ground with a "clip clop clip clop" taking her away from all worry and thought. Her body became part of his as they rode towards the fields. She laughed, feeling his muscles contracting as he grew excited at the chance to run with her. As they approached the back field, Maggie slid off and opened the gate, he snorted his impatience and she laughed, rubbing his face, placing hers against his as she patted him. She walked him through and closed the gate behind them and was back on top of him and running wild in seconds. It was like she was flying, and Maggie loved the freedom she felt, mixed with the wild joy emanating from the horse. It was like heaven to her. They rode hard for a while, then she led him down one of their favourite trails, stopping by a little brook where he could have a drink before making their way back. As soon as they reached the back field he broke into a gallop again, Maggie laughing and loving it just as much as he did. It was close to 1:00 when she finally got him unsaddled, rubbed down and back in his stall where she gave him some snuggles.

"Thanks for the ride old friend," she said, stopping to visit Oatmeal for a bit. He soaked up her love, and enjoyed being brushed, but as usual was mostly happy about the hay she gave him. Leaving him happily munching, she left the stable and headed into the house to chat with Carla. She was busy working on some dinner prep when Maggie walked into the kitchen.

"Good ride Mags?" Carla asked her as she sat down at the table watching her friend chop veggies.

"Yes, lovely, thanks. You need any help with that Carla?" Maggie asked.

"No, all finished Mags, thanks though. Tea?" she asked her, and Maggie got up and grabbed the kettle, taking it to the sink and filling it before Carla could, sitting it down on its base and flipping the switch.

"You having one too?" Maggie asked and Carla nodded. Maggie grabbed them each a mug and put tea bags in, walked to the fridge and got the milk, adding some to each of their mugs. Then she went and sat back down at the table. Carla grabbed the cookie jar in the corner and brought it over to the table, then went back to pour the boiled water into their mugs, adding a couple spoonfuls of sugar to her own, then, sitting down across the table from Maggie, she sat their drinks down. The two friends chatted, enjoying their tea and a few cookies together. Plans for the party were finished and they were both looking forward to it. Carla told Maggie about how Stu was off his "want'n to do'er" again, so she was feeling a bit grumpy and randy lately. They talked more about Pete's unexpected call and Maggie even tried coaxing out Billy's birthday surprise, but Carla wouldn't budge. They cackled the afternoon away, until Carla had to get back to work.

"Gotta start on the feeding and milk'n again Mags," she said, pulling on her boots and they walked out through the kitchen door together.

"You know I'm always happy to help Carla," Maggie told her as Carla headed for the barn.

"I know Mags, thanks." And off she went with a wave. Maggie was thinking she'd make a habit of coming by a couple of times a week to do some of the chores with Carla. It took a couple hours to milk the cows, and even if that's all Maggie did, that was a couple hours extra for Carla to get other things done. She hopped into her car and headed home, stopping by the grocery store first to grab some ground beef, hamburger buns and a jar of pickles. She already had onions and knew there were a few big ripe tomatoes on their plants in the yard, so she didn't have to buy any. Of course, Bill was sitting up looking out the bay window as she walked towards the house, and she smiled happily at his face watching her open the door. As soon as she walked in, he jumped down to meet her. She bent down to love him up as usual then he followed along, weaving in and out of her legs meowing away. She sat the groceries down on the island and got him his food, then she washed her hands. She pulled out a couple eggs, and the onion, Worcestershire sauce, and garlic, and mixed it in with the ground beef, forming four nice sized patties. Maggie washed up, then went out to the yard and picked two tomatoes, washed them, sliced one for the burgers, and used the other to add to the salad she was now making. She had just gone out back to fire up the barbecue when she heard Billy's motorcycle revving out front. Thinking about how much she loved him, then hearing his sexy voice call out for her.

"I'm home Babe." She grinned to herself.

"Out back, Lover," she called back, and he came and stood at the back door. He was dirty and greasy again, so she blew him a kiss and he grinned.

"Time for a shower Mag?" he asked, and she nodded at him.

"Of course." She went back in and set the table before starting to cook the burgers, and as she sat a beer at his spot and a bubbly water at hers, he came back into the kitchen and walked straight for her with a hungry grin. He grabbed her and spun them, put her down and kissed her hard.

"Damn you look good today Mag!" he exclaimed, and she looked at him almost sheepishly. "How was your day?" he asked, kissing her again.

"Good, I helped Carla a bit this morning, then went riding for a couple hours." His grin broadened.

"Ahhh, that's why you look so good." Billy gave her a little wink. She tilted her head at him inquiringly and he chuckled. "You rode your stallion. That *always* makes you glow." Maggie laughed.

"Oh, yes, I guess it does. But Billy, I *haven't* ridden my stallion yet today." His head fell back with a laugh, and she squeezed him close. Billy held her face and gave her another kiss.

She let go of him and grabbed the tray of burgers off the island, took them to the grill and dropped them on gently. Then she went in and washed her hands and Billy grabbed his beer and took it out back to sit down with her while she tended to the grill.

"So, how was your day?" she asked as she flipped the burgers.

"Dirty Mag. And not the good kind." He took a swig of his beer. "Glad to be home Babe." Maggie turned and smiled at him.

"Glad you're home too," she replied. He pulled her closer to him, turning her and moving her backwards onto his lap, wrapping his arms around her front and snuggling up to her. His nose finding its way to her neck, then kissing her and making her giggle as his kisses sent shivers up her spine. She tried to stand up and he pulled her back, the two of them laughing. "Billy, the burgers!" she said, and he let go still grinning. The burgers were soon ready, and they took the food in and ate.

"Mmm, so good! Love when you make burgers Mag," he said, about to take another bite. She smiled at him, sliding her foot up the inside of his leg, and laughing as his eyes grew bigger and he sat up straighter. She laughed saucily at him and put her foot back down on the floor. His eyes twinkling and smiling watching Maggie.

While they cleaned up the dishes, they had the radio going, and they did their usual dancing, singing, and goofing around as they worked. Billy had another early start and long workday, so they went up to bed together early and Billy was soon sleeping. Maggie rolled out her mat and did her short nighttime stretches, then crawled into bed. She laid there reading for a while before turning off her light and falling asleep too.

***

"Time to get up Mag." She felt Billy close to her face and smiled.

"Okay, thanks Babe," she answered. He kissed her cheek.

"See you later Beautiful," he said, and she heard his footsteps going down the stairs. Getting up and stretching, she hopped into the shower and started her day clean, perky, and ready to face the world.

The day was pretty quiet at the bookstore. Maggie did her weekly dusting and vacuuming, and someone had dropped a box of books off that she went through happily before putting them out on the shelves. Carla came by with the mail and chatted for a bit, then headed out to do her many jobs. Maggie was happy to see a letter from her brother Frankie and opened it eagerly.

"Hey Sis, how are things? I'm back home for a while and finding it's not as much fun here without you." She smiled thinking about her little brother. It had been so long since they'd seen each other. "Ran into Pete, he's back Magster, and was asking about you. Told him you were with someone, and you were happy. You know Pete though. Apparently, his wife died. FYI, Mason gave him your information, so he might call you." Maggie laughed, *yeah, thanks bro,* she thought to herself. "I'm headed to Florida next month with a couple old friends. Leaving in a few days. We'll only be gone for three or four weeks, then I'm not sure what I'll get up to. Would love to see you, Magster." She held the letter to her heart thinking the same thing. "Hope that Billy guy is treating you right. Love you always, Frankie. Ps. Hope you're treating him right too sis." She slid the letter back into the envelope smiling. He was always such a light for her on the farm. It made her so happy that he was traveling and enjoying his life.

By 4:00, Maggie decided to close up and head home. She passed a few people along the main street and stopped to chat for a few minutes with each of them, then turned the corner and walked towards White Tree Lane, thinking about Frankie and all the fun they used to get up to. She had just reached the gate when she heard Billy coming down the street on his bike. He stopped but didn't turn the engine off. Maggie walked over to him, and he pulled off his helmet, running his fingers through his hair before giving Maggie a kiss.

"Hey Beautiful, wanna ride?" he asked grinning. Maggie laughed.

"Well thank you kind sir but I don't have a long walk home, so I think I'm fine." He smiled.

"Good one Mag. No, wanna go for a ride?" She looked at his clothes, noticing he was out of his work things already. "Already home and showered," he said, winking at her, then opened the back compartment and grabbed her helmet for her.

"I better just feed Old Bill," she said to him.

"Already done my Love," he informed her, handing her the helmet. She smiled her big Maggie smile at him and put the helmet on, climbing up behind him and hugging him tight.

"Where are we headed?" she asked, giving him another squeeze.

"Wherever Babe." He revved the engine, turned them around and headed up the street and onto the main road. They drove for about half an hour, then Billy pulled over and turned the bike off. Maggie looked around, not seeing any reason to stop.

"Everything okay?" she asked as he climbed off the bike, took off his helmet and reached out his hand for hers. She took it, and swinging her leg over, slid to the ground. She pulled her helmet off and looked at him expectantly. He sat the helmets next to the bike and took her hand, leading her into the woods. Maggie had no idea what he was up to.

"Billy, what are we doing?" she asked, and he held his finger to his mouth. They came to a hidden driveway and at the end was an old rotting cottage. The roof was almost completely caved in. Maggie went to speak again, and Billy bent down, and pointed to a spot at one end of the building. The grass was very long, and nature had already started taking over, so Maggie didn't notice at first, but then she saw movement and a brown foal was grazing happily in the grass. Billy looked at Maggie and they smiled at each other. Whispering, she asked,

"Billy, how did you know?" He grinned.

"One of the old guys that comes for oil changes was up here earlier today, looking for any materials that might still be usable, and saw it." Maggie stared at the little horse, her eyes lighting up with love. "Stu and Carla are on their way too, Mag," he said looking at her with a smile, as she continued to watch the horse grazing.

"Well, where's its mother I wonder?" Maggie said without looking away.

"Ah Mag, that's the sad part. The old guy found the mother." Maggie looked up at him quickly, fear in her eyes.

"Ya, where is she, Billy?" she asked urgently. Billy shook his head slightly. "She died Mag." And he ran his hand across her back.

"Oh," was all she said. Both were quiet for a moment before Maggie spoke again. "So, are Carla and Stu taking the foal home?" she asked. Billy chuckled, watching the childlike wonder in Maggie's face, hugged her against him and kissed her forehead.

"Yes, they're taking it to the farm." They heard a beep, and Billy slowly stood up walking back to the road to meet them.

Maggie stood up too but was ever so slowly making her way closer to the little horse. She stopped and watched it again, scanning over its rump right to its beautiful nose, thinking it couldn't have been more than four months old. She crept a little closer still, the horse looked up at her, Maggie stopped, waiting, and grinned from ear to ear, as she watched it go back to grazing. She continued to creep towards it and was only about three feet away from it when it looked up again. Its body language showing signs of wanting to make a run for it. Maggie stopped walking and started talking to it.

"Hello, you pretty, pretty horse." It gave a little snort but stood watching her now too. "I'm sorry about your mother," she said, stretching her hand out towards it. The horse scuffed the ground with one hoof and bent its head back, making a little whinny sound. "You must be very sad and lonely." It scuffed the ground and bowed its head with a grunt of complaint. The horse looked up at Maggie and they watched one another for a moment. "You really are so beautiful," she whispered, taking another small step forward. "It's okay, it's okay," Maggie said to it as its head bent down and shook, scuffing the ground with its front hoof again. Maggie took another step, now only a couple feet away. She had both hands stretched out and she kept talking to it. Her voice was calm and loving. Carla, Stu, and Billy were standing back at the driveway watching quietly. Amazed as they watched and listened to Maggie, still talking to the horse, patiently waiting and moving ever so slightly closer to the young creature. All of a sudden it started to walk towards her. Snorting and scuffing as it inched towards Maggie's hands. "That's it, you're okay," she coaxed and finally its nose bunted up into Maggie's hands. She stayed still and let it feel her out, then inched a little closer, enough to pat its head softly, still chatting away to it, and Maggie ran her hand down its head and neck, patting it happily. The little horse was hugging against her as she giggled quietly and hugged it back. She now realized she hadn't thought about what she'd do next to keep it. So, gently lacing her fingers into the horse's mane, reaching down, and grabbing a nice big handful of grass, she held it out in front of the horse and led it closer to Carla, who was walking slowly towards them with a rope. The horse whinnied and pulled back a little when it noticed Carla. "It's okay," Maggie said again, patting it and holding her hand on the horse's side. The horse seemed to calm down. Talking like she was still speaking lovingly to the horse, Maggie said, "Carla, throw the rope as close to me as you can." She kept feeding it grass while walking it closer to the spot where the rope landed. She saw Carla motion something to Stu and Stu turned to say something to Billy. The three of them were spreading out slowly to surround the horse. Maggie was able to get to the rope and tied it into a slip knot around its middle.

"Nice Mag!" she heard Billy call. Still loving the horse up, walking it back to the others.

"Shit Mags, you are pure magic!" Carla said, her eyes big and shaking her head. They managed to get the horse into the trailer without too much trouble.

"What are you guys going to do with it?" Maggie asked them as they climbed into the truck.

"Burgers!" said Stu with a gruff laugh. Carla smacked him.

"Stu!!" she yelled, and Billy laughed along with Stu. "Hoping to raise it Mag. That's if you'll help us?" said Carla grinning at Maggie's big smile. Stu had already started up the truck and Carla pulled the door closed, rolling down the window, she stuck her arm out and waved as they made a U-turn and headed home. Billy wrapped his arm around Maggie as they watched them drive off.

"Mag, that was amazing!" he said, grinning at her.

"Oh Billy, that poor horse. I can't believe it survived without its mom," she sympathized.

"Carla didn't know how on earth they were going to catch it, Mag," he said, chuckling. "Should have known, you'd be able to do it." Still grinning, he bent down and gave her a long kiss. They headed back to the bike and rode home. Maggie was excited at the prospect of visiting it as much as possible.

"Hungry?" Billy asked as they approached the main street.

"Starving Lover," she replied.

"How about I run in and order dinner, drop you off at home, then come back and pick it up." She nodded and he pulled up in front of the b and b and went inside. He was only there for a couple of minutes, then hopped back on the bike and took Maggie home before driving off again. She had time to go in and wash up a bit. Bill was very happy to see her but a little put out at how late it was. She gave him some extra snuggles and soon heard Billy coming in. They ate their dinner quickly, both of them were very hungry, and it was already 8:00 when they finished.

"I'm going to head over to Carla's in the morning," Maggie informed Billy while they were finishing up. Billy's eyes crinkled up as he smirked at her.

"Mmm, didn't see that coming." She smiled at him. "Okay, Mag. I have some running around to do in the morning, but I'll be home around 2:00." Maggie nodded as she got up with her garbage and took it to the kitchen, Billy close behind her with his things. "Bed?" he asked her, stopping her and wrapping his arms around her shoulders and sliding his hand up into her hair.

"Mmm, yes," she answered, hugging him and looking up at him with a glint and a grin. She closed her eyes, as his face came closer and she felt his lips warm and soft against hers. They kissed each other tenderly. Then walking side by side with their arms still around each other, turning off the lights they headed to bed.

CHAPTER 8

Maggie and Billy had just finished some much needed showers after their morning work-out in the shed together. Playfully getting dressed, they flirted as usual and then enjoyed a coffee together before going their separate ways for the morning. Maggie was eager to head over to the Myers farm to check on the foal.

"Hey Mags!" came Carla's happy greeting as Maggie walked towards the stable.

"Hi Carla," she called back. "How'd things go last night?" Maggie asked Carla, walking to the stable together.

"Oh fine, gave the little filly some milk and got'er into her own stall." Carla was pointing over to the corner. Maggie eagerly went over and peaked over the door. "She and Oatmeal have taken a real shine to one another Mags. Awful cute when they graze together." Carla laughed. Maggie smiled and walked to the door.

"Hello friend," she said, and the horse looked up at her. Maggie opened the door and went in, reaching out a hand and talking to her. "Good morning, you pretty thing," she said, and it butted her hand and came over to give her a hug, Maggie filling with joy as she petted her. Carla was hanging over the door now, grinning.

"So, what'er ya gonna name'er Mags?" she asked, laughing when Maggie turned to her with a confused look on her face.

"Me?" she asked. Carla nodded, laughing again.

"Course Mags! You whispered'er, you name'er!" Maggie looked

back at the little brown face, she had a tiny white spot above her left eye, but the rest of her was completely brown, and her mane was like french vanilla ice cream, almost like coffee with cream.

"Hmmm," Maggie said, checking the horse out and running her hands all over her. Then she laughed to herself. "Well like you pointed out, she fancies grazing with Oatmeal, and we found you grazing too, so how about 'Grazer'?" The horse whinnied happily.

"Think she likes it, Mags," said Carla. Maggie grinned and patted her again.

"We'll call you Graze or Grace for short." The little horse pushed her muzzle into Maggie's hand.

"Say Mags, the vets coming over in about an hour to check her out. Stick around so you can hear what he has to say too would ya?" Maggie nodded and came out of the stall.

"Sure Carla. Hey, have you milked yet." Carla shook her head.

"Nope, on my way t'do that when you pulled up. Why?" Maggie caught up to her.

"Why don't I help with the milking while I'm here." The two friends walked off, arms linked, and headed into the cowshed. An hour later, they met the vet at the stable. Watching as he did his exam, said all was well, and told them he'd be back in a week to see her progress. Maggie stuck around a little longer, then headed home where she drew a nice warm bath and climbed in. She had the radio going and Old Bill was happily lying on her clothes on the floor. She hadn't been in the tub for long when she heard Billy come in.

"Mag?" he called out. "I'm home," he added. Then she heard him coming up the stairs and knocked as he opened the bathroom door. "My oh my, I do love it when you don't add bubbles Mag," he said grinning broadly and walking over to the tub. She smiled up at him as he leaned down and kissed her.

"Room for one more Lover," she told him. He was already peeling off his clothes and climbing in. The two leaned forward and met in the middle for a long, sweet kiss. Resting back again, massaging each other's feet as they talked. Maggie asked how his morning had been. Billy asked how things with the horse had gone. Bill even meowed a couple times adding his two cents to the conversation. They topped off the tub a couple times with some more hot water and were becoming prunes by the time they climbed out. Billy chased Maggie to the bedroom in just their towels, Maggie giggling as she ran, Billy tackling her on the bed and the two rolling about laughing with each other playfully. After a short make-out session, they put their pajamas on and headed down for dinner.

***

Maggie went back to the farm every morning for the next 2 weeks, even on the days she worked in the bookstore. Grazer was growing stronger and out frolicking with the other two horses quickly. On the days Maggie didn't work at the shop, she did the morning milking for Carla, and was really enjoying being a farm girl again. *Can't take the farmer out of this girl's heart,* she thought as she plugged along in her rubber boots, bringing the milk inside for Carla every morning.

"Thanks Mags!" Carla would call as Maggie headed home or to work.

One day when the two friends were out doing their Monday morning fishing, they were talking about the fall gathering.

"Did you pick your pup Mags?" Carla asked her.

"Yep, Mr. Crofter and I settled things last week Carla. Oh, I can't wait to see Billy's face!" Carla smiled.

"When do you get it?" she asked.

"Sunday afternoon, he's bringing him over around 4:00 I think." They packed up their catches for the day and headed back.

"Looking forward to the party Saturday," Maggie said as they approached town.

"Ya, everyone's real excited about the surprise dress up party Mags. Think there's gonna be a lot of Marshal Rooster Cogburn's and Annie Oakley's though. Probably a good amount of Daisy Dukes and Boss Hogs too," she said laughing. Maggie laughed along with her replying,

"That'll be an interesting sight, Carla." The two were still laughing as Carla dropped her off outside her house. "See you later," she called as Carla waved out the truck window and beeped.

The next day, Maggie had just come home from the farm and was doing her morning yoga before getting ready to go into the shop when Billy came downstairs. She was in a downward dog pose as he sat down behind her with his coffee.

"Hey Babe, nice view!" he said, grinning. Maggie smiled to herself. "Do you mind if I move a couple things around in here today?" he asked her nonchalantly. She looked through her legs watching Billy grinning and sipping his coffee.

"Sure, what things?" she asked him.

"Oh, maybe just that table and chair, I have a bookcase I'd like to put there." Maggie walked her feet forward to meet her hands, hanging like a rag doll for a few seconds before slowly standing up straight and reaching up above her head, as she answered,

"Ya of course." She stretched tall, bent down again, rolled up her mat, and walked over to grab her lunch, stopping to give him a kiss before leaving.

"Later Babe," he called as she headed for the front door.

"Have a good one, Lover," she called back.

As usual, the store was quiet, the occasional customer popping in. Most were coming in to talk about the party.

"So, we dress up on Saturday, right Maggie?" Maggie counted about nine people who asked that same question and each time she smiled and said,

"Yes, that's right, the night of the dance, you dress up as a film character." And off they'd go. Some coming back and asking which character they should be, and Maggie letting them know it could be anyone they wanted. She stopped by the b and b on her way home to make sure everything was good with the cake prep. Pat was already well prepared and excited to put it all together.

"Oh Maggie, it's so nice that you're surprising Billy. I am so glad you two have each other dear." Maggie gave her a hug, knowing she must be missing Stan terribly.

"Thank you so much for making the cake for us Pat," she said smiling and saying goodbye.

When she arrived home, Billy was in the kitchen, listening to the radio, singing and dancing to "Wooly Bully", wearing his apron. And nothing else.

"Oh my!" Maggie said laughing as she walked up to the island and put her things down. Billy, still singing away, turned and faced her, smiling and dancing. Maggie couldn't stop laughing. "Hello there, Sweet Cheeks," she said. He came over to her and grabbed her hands to dance her around. She couldn't stop grinning at him.

"Hey, Mag, welcome home," he said, giving her a big kiss, then turning and dancing away. Maggie staring at his fine bottom.

"What are you cooking Lover?" he turned back with a grin.

"Nothing yet Babe." She went over and stood in front of him, undid his apron, pulled it over his head and started running for the stairs with it.

"Hey!" he yelled, the two of them laughing, Maggie already halfway up the stairs and Billy close behind her. She grabbed the banister and used it to pull herself around and run down the hall to the bedroom, turning to laugh again as naked Billy came running at her. She braced herself as he ran at her and once again tackled her, both falling onto the bed laughing hysterically. He was kissing her face all over and she couldn't stop laughing.

"Billy, you're too much!" she told him, slowly stopping her laughter. They grinned at each other, pulses racing, then their expressions changed to desire. They suddenly grabbed each other's faces and kissed quickly and passionately, as if they had to hurry to make love before someone stopped them. Billy frantically pulled Maggie's clothes off, Maggie helping him, still kissing hurried and intense kisses. Pushing her further up the bed and sliding his hands under her body, up her back and lifting her up, sitting himself on the edge of the bed, Maggie straddled over him. They stopped their frantic kisses for a moment, Maggie holding his face in her hands, looking down at him with a grin, placing her feet down on the floor to lift herself up, then with an intense gaze, staring into Billy's eyes, she slid down onto his very eager cock. The hurried frantic attack started again. They were almost clawing at each other, tongues sliding all over each other, hands grabbing and pulling into one another hurriedly, Maggie lifting and lowering herself quickly, sliding him in and out of her warm, wet body. Billy was holding her hips and moving her up and down, faster and faster. Their heads falling back, both of them panting quickly and heavily.

"Billy, ohhh Billy," she cried with each lift and fall.

"Don't stop Mag, God don't stop!" he called out and she slid up and down faster still.

"Maaag!" he yelled, and pulled her closer, their bodies skin to skin, and she made shorter rises and falls, still moving quickly until they were both laughing and cumming, crying out with pleasure. Maggie slowed down and leaned into Billy, and they kissed intensely again, hands in each other's hair, sucking face and breathing heavy.

"God Mag!" Billy said as Maggie climbed off of him and they lay down beside each other grinning, their chests still rising and falling rapidly. Maggie inhaled deeply, then kinda laughed the words,

"That was delicious!" Billy chuckled.

"Thought we could have dessert first tonight, you glorious sex goddess!" Billy replied, with his cheeky smiling eyes. Maggie laughed and reached out to hold his hand, Billy's grasping instinctively.

"Mmm, that's my favourite way to dine with you, Lover." They wrapped around each other and kissed slowly. Lips softly pulling and smacking. Billy reached up and ran his hand across her cheek and combed back her hair with his fingers. She looked at him and smiled gently and adoringly. Billy pulled her face towards his and kissed her with slow, deep pressure. Pushing into her, and Maggie could feel her stomach full of wonderful butterflies. The tingling electricity between them sent warm, loving, awakening vibrations throughout her whole body. She held his face and pulled back to look at him.

"Billy, I'm so in love with you." He pulled her in for another kiss, rubbing noses as he pulled away, and grinning, he said,

"Always and forever my Love." He kissed her nose.

Snuggling for a little longer, Maggie said she actually really *was* hungry, so they dressed and went downstairs, still all over each other. Stopping along the way several times to make out, for brief moments.

"So, good look'n, what else ya got cook'n?" she asked, going up behind him and wrapping her arms around him tightly.

"Hmm, give me fifteen minutes and you'll find out," he answered, turning in her arms and grinning cheekily at her. And about fifteen minutes later she found out it was pizza. "Mmm, perfect post sex food," said Billy. Maggie laughed.

"Nah, deli sandwiches all the way Babe," she replied, giving him a little nudge and grinning. Billy shook his head at her, chuckling. "This *is* really good though Lover, thank you." She took a big cheesy bite. Maggie didn't want to admit it, but the pizza scored pretty close to the sandwiches.

As usual they tidied up together, chatting about their day. Maggie fed Old Bill while Billy washed another plate.

"What's up for tomorrow?" she asked him, taking the plate, drying it and putting it in the cupboard.

"Work 8-3," he answered, looking a bit bummed.

"How about you?" Maggie shrugged, she had some party stuff to do, but of course, couldn't tell him.

"Visiting Graze, milking cows, then I'm not sure," she

answered, smiling.

"Well, sounds like we can spend the afternoon together then," he added, smiling at her.

"Sounds good to me," she replied with a smile back.

"Say Mag, did you know we were supposed to dress up Saturday?" he asked, hanging the dish cloth over the tap and turning to face her.

"Oh, ya, don't worry, I got us costumes." Billy raised an eyebrow.

"Oh, and what did you get us Mag?" She grinned.

"You'll just have to wait until Saturday, Lover." He pulled her in and kissed her, then looked down at her.

"Batman and Robin?" he asked. Maggie laughed.

"No, Robin, of course not." Billy chuckled and gave Maggie another kiss. "Feel like playing me some tunes?" she asked as they walked to the living room.

"Well, maybe Mag. If you promise to sing with me." She tilted her head down to the side, giving him a sexy grin.

"Only for you." Billy grabbed his guitar from off the 'Carla chair' and sat down on the couch with Maggie.

"Actually, wanna sit out back Mag?" he asked, getting back up. Maggie nodded and followed him out back. They sat in their spots and Billy did a quick tuning, then as he started strumming, he looked at her and asked,

"So, what shall I play my love?" Smiling her Maggie smile as she answered,

"Hmm, how about some CCR." Billy nodded and started playing "Who'll Stop The Rain." Maggie was in heaven listening to him play his guitar and loving his voice, staring at him googly eyed. She joined in when Billy looked up at her, his eyes smiling as they sang together. They sang "Someday Never Comes", Maggie harmonizing with his deep voice. Then she sat and watched, listening with a smile on her face as he sang "Midnight Special". His voice cracking in all the right places. She sat and swayed as he sang his heart out, finally singing along by the end, not able to hold the music in. They sat singing, Billy strumming for a few more songs, then as the sun set, they made their way back inside. Billy wrapped one arm around Maggie and grinned at her.

"Ever miss having a piano Mag?" he asked, and she looked up at him.

"Almost every day, Billy!" He kissed the top of her head.

"Bed, Babe?" he asked her, and she nodded.

***

When Billy got up Maggie was downstairs getting ready to go.

"Morning, Beautiful," he said, coming over so they could hug and kiss.

"Morning, Gorgeous," she answered, giving his butt a squeeze and smiling up at him. "I made lunch for you," she told him, pointing to some things on the counter.

"Ah, thanks Babe." Billy gave her another kiss, then walked over and grabbed himself a coffee.

"You heading out already?" he asked her, coming back over and running his hand along her ass and kissing the top of her head.

"Ya, hoping to get the milking done early, so I can go for a ride," she replied, turning and stretching up to kiss him. "And get back home to be with you."

"Mmm," Billy growled with hunger, "I like when you've gone riding." With one more kiss, Maggie left with a feeling of delicious arousal and a smile on her face.

The day passed quickly. Maggie was busy at the farm for a few hours, then headed back to town, picking up some things she'd need for the new pup. Food, a bed she'd ordered through the vet, and some chew toys to have ready when she surprised Billy the following Sunday. Maggie kept everything in her car, so Billy didn't see any of it, and went inside. She'd been keeping their costumes at Carla and Stu's, and had brought them back with her today, so she headed straight upstairs to the spare room to hang them in the closet. Old Bill was squawking his complaints as Maggie passed him and continued up the stairs.

"Well, come on old boy!" she said to him, and he ran up beside her, meowing happily. It was going on 3:00, and she knew Billy would be home soon. Deciding to have a quick look before closing the closet door, she pulled her costume back out and unzipped the clothing bag it was in. She'd had a hard time deciding between the white undergarment costume and the red and black dress, but in the end decided it was probably better to wear more clothes at the gathering and went with the red dress. It was absolutely beautiful and looked just like the one from the movie. Gold lace around the neckline, frilly puffed sleeves, white lacy sheer's hanging from the ends of the sleeves, the long black velvet skirt with white frilled layers at the front. She even bought some black lace and put her silver locket onto it to wear as a choker. She wasn't sure what she'd wear on her feet yet but was thinking her bike boots would look good. For Billy, she chose the classic black Zorro outfit. Black, pants, shirt and gloves, wide black and silver belt, hat, cape, and mask. She bought a kid's sword to go with it and knew his motorcycle boots would work with the look. She had just stuck everything back into the closet when she heard the front door open.

"Hey Babe, I'm home," he called out. Maggie closed the closet door quietly and went downstairs. Billy looked up at her as she descended. "Hello Beautiful," he said with a big smile.

"Hi there, Handsome," she replied, smiling back, and giving him a kiss as she passed him. He was covered in dirt and grease, so it was a quick peck.

"I'll be back down in a bit Mag," he told her, heading upstairs for his shower. "Hey Mag," he called, and she stepped back to the bottom of the banister looking up at him.

"Hmm?" she answered with a smile. He grinned at her.

"How long have you been home?" he asked.

"Just got in before you Lover. Only had time to visit the washroom before you came in." He grinned impishly at her, and she turned her head slightly, looking at him questioningly.

"Why?" she asked.

"Oh, just curious." And he continued to the top landing. "Hey Babe, do me a favour? I forgot my things in the back of the bike. Would you grab them for me?" She heard the bathroom door close as she turned around and headed out the front door. Maggie walked down the path, enjoying the flowers in the front yard, noticing the bugs and butterflies landing and flying away. Breathing deeply and happily, grateful for her life. As she reached the gate, she opened it. Billy's bike was parked right out front, and she saw a bouquet of wildflowers sitting on the seat. She smiled and walked over to pick them up. There was a small card stuck in the flowers and she picked it up to read; 'Mag, if music be the food of love, play on. Happy early Birthday my Love'. She stood there for a moment, smiling broadly, sticking her nose into the flowers, and smelling deeply.

"Hmmm…" she said aloud to herself. *One of my favourite quotes, but what does he mean?* she wondered. She couldn't find anything he might have forgotten and smiled at his romantic ways and trickery into getting her out to the bike. Turning back towards the house with her flowers and walking back in grinning happily. She was still looking at the card, absentmindedly smelling the flowers again as she walked towards the kitchen, not even noticing anything different as she found a vase in the cupboard, filled it with water, then stuck the flowers in. Then her brain woke up and something said *wait, was that a big red bow?* And she turned around to face the spot Billy had wanted to clear. Sitting against the wall, between the sliding dining room doors and the big living room window was a piano, with the biggest red bow she'd ever seen right on the front of it. Maggie walked towards it, her heart soaring, tears coming down her face as she smiled from ear to ear. She sat down on the bench in front of it and lifted the fallboard. She placed her fingers down on the keys and played a couple chords. It sounded beautiful and her heart was bursting. She couldn't wait to thank Billy and ran upstairs. He was still in the shower. Maggie walked right in, pulled back the curtain and stepped into the shower with him, still in her T-shirt and long skirt, grinning from ear to ear. Billy smiled back broadly as Maggie threw her arms around him, water coming down over both of them as she kissed him over and over, saying

"Thank you, thank you, thank you!" in between kisses.

"So, you like the flowers, Mag?" he asked, laughing.

"Yes, they're lovely," she answered, grinning. She grabbed his face and kissed him, long and hard. Both smiling at each other, Maggie now soaked, as they hugged and kissed some more.

"Billy, thank you so much!" she said as they pulled apart. He kissed her softly and looked at her lovingly.

"I love seeing you happy Mag, and I know how much playing the piano fills you up. Plus, you look pretty damn hot tickling the ivories Babe." They laughed at Maggie standing there soaked in her clothes. Billy turned off the shower and climbed out, grabbing his towel and handing Maggie a towel too as she peeled off her wet clothes and left them in the shower and stepped onto the bath mat.

"You're the best Babe," she told him, snuggling up beside him as they held each other walking to the bedroom.

"Love ya," he said, smiling at her.

After they dried off and put clothes on, they headed down. Maggie went straight for the piano, and started playing all her old favourites. She was happy to find out her fingers hadn't forgotten the songs after a number of years of not playing. While she played, Billy sat smiling and listening, feeling Maggie's joy with each key she pressed. Then, "RING RING", came the sound of the phone and Billy got up and answered it.

"Hello?" she heard him say. "Who? "Oh, hello, ya, just a sec." She stopped playing and turned around. "Hey Mag, it's your brother Frankie!" He held the phone out to her, she hopped off the bench eagerly and took it.

"Frankie?" she said happily, surprised.

"Hey Magster, how are ya?" he answered back.

"Oh, my goodness, it's so great to hear from you!" she told him.

They talked for ages, and he told her he was staying in Florida for a bit longer than he had originally thought, but then had plans to come and visit her next month. She said that would be amazing and she'd get the spare room ready for him. They made plans to chat again before he headed her way. Maggie hung up the phone beaming. "Wow. This day just keeps getting better!" she said as she and Billy headed to the kitchen. They made some dinner and ate, and Maggie told Billy about the conversation and how excited she was about Frankie visiting. Billy's heart was full and so was Maggie's, and after dinner, they curled up on the couch together, snuggling, chatting for a while and loving on one another. They finished the evening watching one of their mutual favourite movies, "Smokey And The Bandit", wrapped up under a cozy blanket with Old Bill snuggled up in Maggie's lap.

CHAPTER 9

Maggie came down early and sat at her new piano. She played for about half an hour, then grabbed a coffee and went out back with it. Both her and Billy had to work, and he came down to join her on the patio for a coffee before they did their workout together, then parted for the day.

She was feeling too excited about everything to focus on work. She now had a beautiful piano waiting for her at home, she would be bringing a puppy into their home soon, and the fall festival started tomorrow. The surprise party was the following night, and then she was surprising Billy with his gift on Sunday. How could she possibly dust and sort books? Maggie was happy to see Carla around 4:00, when she came to get ready for belly dancing, and could tell by her friend's face that she had known about the piano all along.

"Hey Mags! How's things?" she asked with a big grin. Maggie smiled at her friend.

"How long have you known?" Carla shrugged.

"Known what, Mags?" but she couldn't keep from bursting. "Soooo, pretty eff'n awesome huh, Mags?" she asked, almost hopping on the spot. Maggie laughed.

"Ya Carla, totally awesome! So that's what you two have been up to. Oh man, what an idiot I am," she said.

"Ah, Mags, no worries. Got ya though. Were you surprised?" Maggie was laughing, Carla's eyes were huge.

"Yes, very! I just want to close up and go home and play it!" she replied, beaming. "I'll be shaking up a storm tonight." Maggie answered, laughing.

"Better wear the belt with bells Mags, so we can all keep up with your jingling." The two laughed and finished getting things ready. They were moving on to belly rolls tonight. It turned out to be hilarious and very tricky. At one point, while Maggie and Carla made their rounds between the women, Carla called out,

"Let's go ladies, God didn't give us all peaches if he didn't want us to shake our trees, did he!?!" Everyone laughed and tried their best to make their bellies do the wave. They were all comfortable in short shirts or sports bras, low hip hugging pants and belly dancing scarves or skirts, and feeling brave and confident with each other. Their laughter was at the challenge, not *at* each other, and they all realized this phase was going to take some time. They parted happily, everyone in good spirits from class and chatting excitedly about this year's fall gathering.

Maggie locked up and headed home, feeling very lucky and honored that so many different shapes, ages and walks of life had come together feeling safe and loved enough to learn alongside Maggie and Carla. She felt herself walking home proudly and joyfully as she thought about the group of women she was sharing an evening a week with.

Thinking about a number of things she wanted to do without Billy home, and hoping she'd have time before he got back, Maggie picked up her pace.

"Hi Maggie," Pat called as she passed.

"Hiya Pat!" Maggie smiled. "Everything good?" Maggie asked, still walking down the sidewalk. Pat nodded with a smile as she answered. "Gotta fly Pat, still got secret stuff left to do," she added with a nod. Pat nodded back with a half smile wink, then replied,

"All's well Maggie. See you tomorrow." Maggie turned and waved, stopping in at the grocery store to grab something quick for dinner. She decided to just grab some things to make subs, smiling to herself at the thought of a deli sandwich and when she liked eating one the most. Maggie chuckled quietly at herself as she thought of only having that craving after sex with Billy. *That man makes me hungry, in more ways than one!* Heading home with her groceries, happy and content with life, she wore a fulfilled smile on her face.

She spent the next forty minutes getting all the things ready for the dog, hiding stuff in the spare room closet. She had a bed, food, bowls, toys, leash, and collar. Smiling to herself thinking about her surprise for Billy, Maggie went into the living room and sat down at *her* gift. She played and played, Old Bill coming over, hopping up and sitting on the bench next to her. She was soon lost in the music. Her fingers doing their own thing and feeling so elated. She was playing one of her many favourite Blue Rodeo songs, "Head Over Heels," her voice resonating with the notes as she played, filling her heart. Maggie loved playing the lower notes, feeling the vibrations running up through her fingers, into her soul, then dancing her fingers up to the high notes, merrily smiling. She had almost finished the song when she heard Billy's voice joining hers and she grinned as he came up behind her; and their voices danced together. He sat down on the end of the bench with her and when she ended the song, he wrapped his arm around her waist and snuggled up against her.

"Sure love hearing you play again, Mag. I've listened to you in my memories for almost 30 years, but there really isn't anything like the real thing." Maggie smiled at him, a huge smile, and reached up to hold his cheek.

"Thank you, Billy," she said, then gently pulled his face closer, looking into his eyes, she gave him a soft loving kiss. Pressing together and breathing each other in.

"Hey, you're already showered!" she said suddenly, running her hand through his hair. He chuckled and she smiled, loving the crinkles around his eyes when he smiled at her.

"Ya, been listening to you sing and play for half an hour Babe." He kissed her again before getting up. She looked up at the clock, surprised to see it was already half past 6:00.

"If music be the food of love, play on," she said quietly, a tender smile on her face and a hand on her heart. Billy reached out to take her other hand and pulled her in for a hug.

"So, what's on the menu tonight Mag?" he asked, squeezing her tight.

"Well, let's see... there's me." She looked up at him with a cheeky smirk.

"Mmm, my favourite dish!" he said.

"And there's subs," she added.

"Oh, I see, so first you, then the subs?" he asked. Maggie giggled.

"No, we can eat first if you like. They're not *deli* sandwiches." Grinning, the two went over to the kitchen and made their subs, taking them over to the living room and watching TV while they ate. She knew Billy was beat, if he didn't attack her first. As they ate and watched a new cop show they'd never seen, Billy turned to Maggie and asked,

"You won't hate me if we don't have dessert tonight will you Mag?" she smiled and shook her head.

"No Lover, I know where you live, I'll get my dessert another night." He planted a big kiss on her, and they went back to their dinner.

***

Friday morning dawned sunny and hot for October. Beautiful for the gathering. Maggie was happy it was warm enough to be able to wear her favourite long green skirt with the big daisies on it, and a tank top with a little white sweater over top.

Maggie and Billy had gathered up a box full of things for the rummage table and had a couple chairs ready to take with them for the barbecue later. They were meeting Carla and Stu at 4:30, so they walked over to the town center just after four to add their things to the sale table and have a look around. There weren't too many people there yet. A few older couples in their chairs around the outskirts of the pavilion, and a number of ladies setting things up. Maggie and Billy went over and asked if they could help, and both got pulled in different directions. Billy was over helping set tables and chairs up and Maggie had been asked to help set things out as people came with the sale items. There was a beautiful table full of veggies, pumpkins and apples, from a number of surrounding farms, giving people a nice choice of fresh produce to buy, and Maggie noticed quickly that the baked goods table was already well stocked. *Best stay away from that table* she told herself, unpacking some knick knacks and setting them on the table.

"Hey Mags!" she heard Carla shout and looked up to see her and Stu coming over with a couple of their own lawn chairs, Stu already holding a beer.

"Hi Carla," she called back and headed over to give them each a hug.

"Where's Mr. Sweet Cheeks?" Carla asked her, looking around.

"Think he got roped into setting up more tables," Maggie answered, looking around for him. He wasn't much longer, and joined them as they walked around the tables looking at this year's goodies. Billy and Stu walked together, Stu grunting in his gruff way as he talked, Billy laughing. Maggie and Carla walked over to the knitting table where Maggie bought a lovely, crocheted blanket, and some knitted face cloths. A few tables down she bought a couple squashes and a basket of red potatoes. She was looking around for somewhere to put them, when Billy came over and said,

"Here Mag, why don't we just run them home." He took some of the items from her to carry and Maggie told Carla they'd be right back and they headed home. They dropped their things off, then turned back towards the door. They stepped out and Maggie locked up, Billy held her and spun her around.

"Hey Beautiful, how bout a quicky before we head back?" Maggie grinned at him, thinking he was just kidding around, but when she looked into his eyes, she knew it was no joke. He was already grabbing her breasts and pressing her against the front door.

"Billy, what's got you so worked up?" she asked through kisses and gropes.

"God, Mag, I don't know," he was still kissing her lips, her face, her neck, Maggie kissing back as he spoke, his hands squeezing her ass and her breasts and pushing himself tightly against her.

"I was just watching you walking around, talking and smiling and felt such a desire to jump you!" She laughed a little, but was now grabbing and pulling back. Their hands and lips almost frantic again.

"Billy," she whispered as he kissed her neck and ran his hand down the front of her body, pressing his fingers in between her legs. Maggie felt her legs go a little rubbery. He was kissing down the front of her body, still grabbing and squeezing, his breath heavy and hot through her clothes, and on her skin. He undid his pants and pulled himself free, then pressing Maggie against the door a little harder, he pulled up her skirt.

"Billy! Here?" He was breathing in her ear now.

"Everyone's at the gathering." His tongue was in her ear and his hand was now inside her underwear, rubbing her center. She was getting wetter by the second, and Billy was sucking on her neck, right where he knew she'd be putty in his hands.

"Mmmm..." her head falling back, "We might get caught," she breathed, her hands holding his hair, her mouth open and her body ready. He pulled her underwear down enough to slide between her legs.

"I know Mag," Billy replied with a husky whisper and a very intense stare. Maggie's body shivered at the thought and his rebellious desire.

"You're so hard," she whispered. He slid back and forth, sucking and licking her neck.

"Billy, I'm already cumming," she cried, and she felt him lift her and push inside. She wrapped her arms around his neck, pulling him in and kissing him hard, both with their mouths open and slipping their tongues in and out. He held her up, her legs around his hips as he banged her up against the door, over and over. The whole idea of someone seeing them amping up their arousal and Maggie was panting his name, Billy growling as he slid fast and hard. Maggie braced her hands on either side of the door frame.

"Damn Maag!" he groaned, and she felt his body convulse as he came. He was back to sucking and kissing Maggie's neck.

"Mmmm Billy," she moaned, her body shaking with her release. The two grinning and panting as they kissed. Then Maggie's legs slid down, and she touched the porch floor, her skirt dropping, and Billy zipped himself back up. "Bring on the sandwiches!" Maggie exclaimed. Billy burst out laughing, grabbing her face and kissing her hard. Maggie looked at the street and was thankful she didn't see anyone and surprised at how much she had enjoyed the element of getting caught. They went back in the house and freshened up before heading back to the gathering. Giggling like teens, hands all over each other as they walked back.

"Where've you two been?" Carla asked as they walked over to where her and Stu were sitting. Billy and Maggie smiled at each other as they held hands. Both of them had very rosy cheeks.

"Aw, gawd, you didn't?" Carla asked, and Maggie laughed. Billy tried to keep a straight face, but his smiling eyes gave him away. "Don't you two ever get enough?" Carla added, shaking her head.

"What time is the barbecue?" Billy asked and Stu laughed now too.

"Hungry eh! Better get yerself a drink there Billy boy, get yerself calmed down before dinner." Stu got up out of his chair and wrapped an arm around Billy's shoulder leading them over to the beer tent. They could hear Stu talking as they walked away. "Ya know, you and Maggie are like effing rabbits!" Maggie was grinning like she was practicing to be the Cheshire cat.

"Seriously Mags!" Carla said, looking at Maggie with her mouth hanging open. Giggling, Maggie said,

"What? I hadn't thanked him for my piano yet." Carla just shook her head again, then laughed.

"Well, all the power to ya Mags! Bout time you were get'n some eh!? Try not to wear'm out though!" Carla nudged Maggie, and Maggie laughed.

"I don't think that's ever going to happen Carla!" Carla pulled a face and pretended to gag, then shook her head with a laugh as they made their way over to the tent to grab drinks and join Billy and Stu.

While they sat enjoying their drinks, Maggie had to turn a few people away who were asking about the party. She'd smile and quickly talk over them, hoping Billy didn't catch on to anything. He did seem to be wondering, and asked why people were talking to her about it, but she'd shrug it off, and blame it on the beer or their old age.

The four friends decided to go back to Maggie and Billy's after the barbecue, with plans of playing a few rounds of Euchre. They walked along together, chatting and laughing. Maggie and Carla, cackling it up, walking together ahead of Billy and Stu. Walking into the house, still chatting and laughing, Old Bill was happy to hear people home, but jumped back into his window seat when he realized it wasn't just Maggie and Billy.

"Not feeling sociable tonight, Bill-the-Pill?" Carla asked, giving his head a little pat then walking away. They all sat at the dining room table, then Maggie and Billy grabbed drinks for all of them, and Carla grabbed the deck of cards to shuffle and dealt first.

"What are we playing Mags, couples or us against the men?" Maggie grinned, Stu grumbled.

"Us against You's!" Stu answered, pointing at her and Carla. Billy shrugged and winked at Maggie.

"Sure," he said, smiling at her. Maggie and Billy switched places, so they were across from their partners and the game soon started. Carla and Maggie were a good team. Being such good friends, having a strong women's intuitive connection, and playing against a pickled Stu, they definitely had the advantage. They played five rounds, and Maggie and Carla cleaned their clocks, winning every round except the first. Then, Stu, getting grumpier as the night went on, stood up and said he was taking a leak and Carla said they better head home.

"Thanks guys, see you tomorrow!" she called as Maggie and Billy stood at the front door waving goodbye. Closing the door and wrapping their arms around each other, they turned the lights off and headed to bed. Still feeling lovey and surrounded by a euphoric aura from their earlier escapade, they climbed into bed, kissing and snuggling, and soon drifted off to sleep, holding onto one another cozily.

CHAPTER 10

Ｔhey woke up still snuggled up and after taking turns in the washroom, they went down and cooked breakfast together. Dancing and singing along to the radio and hugging and kissing in between the eggs, toast and fried bologna. They were heading back to the gathering soon, so after they cleared up their breakfast dishes, they got dressed and made their way over. There were lots of games and competitions this year. Horseshoes in the field behind the grocery store, the biggest pumpkin wins a bottle of brandy competition, a dunk tank, and some random 'guess how many' of something were in each jar games. Most of the older men were playing horseshoes, while their grandkids were receiving lessons. The women were congregating around the baked goods and guessing games. Maggie and Billy went over to look at the pumpkins.

"Holy crap!" Billy exclaimed, pointing to one the size of a tractor tire. Maggie laughed at Billy's shock and newness to country life. He and his parents traveled a lot when he was growing up and he talked about how they would rent a cottage in the country every summer, but he was born a city boy and hadn't seen too much in the way of farm life. The pumpkins were quite funny looking, kinda lumpy and bumpy and there were lots that were strange shapes, and most of them were quite impressively large.

Maggie and Billy found themselves over at the dunk tank, and were quickly giving each other a look, like they were daring one another.

"Well, we know you'll be able to dunk me Billy, you used to play baseball," she said, and he grinned.

"Okay, Mag, I'm not too worried about you hitting that tiny target." Billy bumped gently against her arm teasingly.

"Oh, bring it on Sweet Cheeks!" she announced, trying her hardest to look tough. Billy paid $5, handed Maggie three balls and walked over to the tank and stepped inside. The two lovers grinned at each other, and Billy waved his hand like Mr. Cool, as he said,

"Good luck Babe!" he winked at her with an air of arrogance. *That's just what I needed* she thought to herself, *you think I can't, I will.* Maggie locked her eyes on the target and swung her arm once and threw hard. Bullseye! Billy went down with a surprised look on his face. Maggie threw her hands up in the air, jumping and laughing. As Billy came back up, water dripping down his face, T-shirt stuck to his body, and wiping the hair away from his eyes, he saw Maggie laughing, and all he could do was smile back, laughing along with her.

"Lucky shot Babe!" he called out, climbing back into the seat. She grinned at him as she got ready to take her second shot. He shook his head at her with a cheeky grin.

"Not this time Mag." And the ammo was loaded once again. "BING" rang out, Billy dropped, and Maggie laughed again as he came back up wiping water and hair from his face again, shaking his head at her.

"You've been practicing in secret haven't you?" he asked, laughing.

"Come on Billy, get back up there! I've still got one more shot." He chuckled at her in her attempts to be intimidating. She pulled her arm back and faked out her next throw, Billy looking triumphant, then she showed him the ball still in her hand.

"Oh, getting cocky Mag." She threw hard, another bullseye and down he went, his hands straight up in the air, laughing as he came back up. He climbed out of the tank still laughing and made a run for her. She wasn't expecting it and before she could run away, he wrapped his arms around her and picked her up, spinning them on the spot. Maggie laughed as Billy shook his hair and squeezed her tight, getting her all wet too. He put her back down, the two of them laughing and kissing.

"Seriously, do you *ever* leave each other alone?" They turned to see Carla headed for them grinning happily. "What happened to you Billy boy?" she asked him, laughing. "Look'n like a drowned rat." Maggie and Billy were still laughing.

"Oh, Mag had a couple lucky shots," he replied, and Maggie slapped him playfully.

"Ha! 3 balls, 3 hits!" she added proudly.

"I'll be back Mag," he told her, giving her a kiss and going home to change into something dry.

Maggie and Carla made their way around the gathering. Chatting with friends, making their guesses on the jars, and stopping to talk with Pat about the party later.

"Maggie, I got the cake finished this morning," she said looking a bit worried. "I hope you like it dear?" she added.

"Oh Pat, I'm sure it will be wonderful," Maggie assured her. They stopped talking when Carla cleared her throat suddenly and nodded behind Maggie, as Billy was making his way back.

"Hey, where's Stu, Carla?" he asked, joining them. "Hi Pat," he added, smiling at her and giving her arms a soft squeeze.

"Hello Mr. Stanton," she replied, patting his arm as she walked away and joined some other ladies at the craft table. Billy turned back to Carla.

"Oh, he's doing the chores. He'll join us later on." The three made their way around the other games together. Carla tried a ball in a basket game and won herself a skinny stuffed gorilla. "Good lord, like I need two gorillas! Looks just like Stu!" Maggie and Billy laughed at Carla's disgruntled face. After a few more games they found themselves back in their chairs where they sat and enjoyed some delicious baked goods. There were lots of choices made with apples and pumpkin; Tarts, cookies, muffins, squares, and pies, and they finished off their treats with some hot apple cider.

"What time is the barbecue tonight?" Billy asked, sipping his cider.

"5:00" Carla answered. "The dance'n starts at 7:00," she added, still munching on a pumpkin tart. After they stuffed their faces and sat relaxing for a bit, Billy went off to help the crafty ladies move a few tables.

"Think he suspects Carla?" Maggie asked her once they were alone.

"Nah," she responded, shaking her head. "Guys are easy to fool Mags." And she finished the rest of her apple cider. Maggie laughed inwardly, thinking, *not all guys Carla*. It was going on four when they decided to head home and change into their costumes.

"See you in an hour Carla," Maggie said as they went their separate ways.

Billy unlocked the door and went in, Maggie grabbing his butt as she followed him inside.

"So, am I Ernie, or Bert?" he asked her, smiling. Maggie laughed, but didn't reply. She gave his butt another squeeze and a slap before saying,

"I'm just going to feed Old Bill before we get ready, Sweet Cheeks." He pulled her back and gave her the look.

"Got time for another quicky, Mag?" he asked, kissing her passionately. Maggie kinda staggered as he stopped kissing her with a grin.

"Don't think so Lover, but I have a plan for later." She grinned at him seductively, trailing her hand down his back and slapping his butt smartly.

"Mmm, can't wait," he said grinning back. She fed Bill, then went up to the spare room and grabbed their costumes from the closet. She took them into their bedroom and started to take off her clothes thinking about how much she was looking forward to tonight, and hoped Billy would enjoy it too. She pulled on the beautiful Elena dress, put her hair half up, leaving some random curls falling around her face, tied her lacey locket choker around her neck and stuck a red flower into her hair. She left Billy's costume in the clothing bag on the bed and went downstairs. Billy was sitting out back and turned when he heard her coming, standing up and staring at her.

"Damn Mag, you look gorgeous!" he said, looking her up and down and then back again, smiling broadly at her.

"Thanks Babe," she replied and he came towards her.

"Mmm, sure we don't have time for a romp?" he asked, kissing her and rocking her in his arms.

"Believe me Billy, it's going to be hard for me to resist, especially once you're in your costume." and his grin grew, that cheeky glint in his eyes.

"Oh really, well, I better get into my costume then." He leaned down and kissed her.

"I left it on the bed for you," she told him, smiling up at him, eyelashes fluttering. Billy headed upstairs and after a few minutes she heard him call down.

"Really Mag? Really?" Maggie laughed to herself.

"Oh yes, really Babe!" she hollered back with a big grin. When he finally came downstairs, she was sitting on a stool at the island waiting eagerly.

"I feel a bit silly Mag," he told her, holding his hat and mask in his hands.

"Mmm, you look absolutely scrumptious," she purred at him. He stood up a little straighter and grinned at her.

"For real Mag?" he asked. Maggie stood up and kissed him, a long lingering kiss. She took the mask from his hand and tied it up for him, her hands running along his shoulders as she came back around to face him.

"Oh, yes, very much, really," she replied, her voice velvety and eager. He grinned at her and pulled her close, their lips brushing softly at first, then pressing together, Billy's hands sliding down to grab her waist, Maggie's sliding up to hold his head.

"Kay, we better get going," she said, breaking them apart.

"Oh, Mag, come on, just a few minutes upstairs won't hurt." Maggie grinned and grabbed his hand pulling him towards the front hall. She grabbed his boots and handed them to him, then grabbed her own and put them on, making sure to pull her dress up over each knee, just high enough to make him notice, then zipped each boot up slowly, with her head still bent down, her curls cascading down, and looking up at Billy with her emerald eyes twinkling.

"Gawd Mag, I won't be able to walk if you keep making eyes at me like that! You're giving me a chubby Babe!" She giggled at him and kissed his cheek as she walked to the door making sure to add an extra shake of her hips, with each step.

They walked hand in hand back towards the gathering. Well, mostly hand in hand. Billy's hands wandered quite a bit and between Maggie's giggles and his groping, his growls of lust were quite audible. He stopped them a couple times to embrace her and kiss her.

"Hey Babe, how about over there behind those hedges?" he suggested, trying to move her back towards one of the trees. Maggie giggled.

"Come on Billy, I promise it will be worth the wait." As they came around the corner and stepped into the town center, lights came on and an abundance of voices yelled "Surprise!" Maggie beaming at Billy looking truly surprised. Someone had hung a banner up above the stereo near the spot where the band was set up, that read 'HAPPY BIRTHDAY MAGGIE AND BILLY'. Billy looked at Maggie grinning.

"You did this Mag?" She smiled and nodded, and he leaned down and gave her a kiss, hugging her close.

"Happy Birthday Billy," she said in his ear. Billy looked around, now seeing everyone's costumes. He chuckled as Fred and Wilma walked over to them.

"Oh, you two look great!" he told them. Stu not looking quite as happy as Carla, but it just added to the effect of their characters. They saw Beetlejuice and Lydia. Leia, Luke and Han Solo, Elvis, Marilyn Monroe, Dorothy, a few scarecrows and a tin man and they lost count of all the cowboys and cowgirls. And of course, just as Maggie and Carla expected, quite a few Dukes of Hazzard characters. Each guest made their way over to say happy birthday to the two of them at some point.

There were a number of tables set up in a long row, covered in baking dishes and casserole pans. The beer tent was busy, kegs emptying quickly, and Maggie had bought a dozen bottles of champagne for them to toast with later in the evening. After many visits and happy birthdays, people were starting in on the food, finding places to sit and chat with one another. Snuggling up together in a corner, Maggie and Billy enjoyed a few minutes alone, grinning and smooching.

"Ah, Mag, this is great," Billy said to her, holding her cheek and giving her another kiss.

"Good," she replied with a smile and a kiss back.

"Well, I guess you were able to keep him on the right team after all." They heard a dry lazy droll and looked up to see Pauline dressed as Elvira. Maggie and Billy just gawked at her for a moment, then Pauline sauntered away.

"Oh good, she's back," Maggie grumbled, the grin fading from her face. Billy pulled her close again and kissed her cheek.

"She's harmless Mag. Nothing we need to worry about," he said and grabbed her hand. "Let's go get some dinner." They headed over to the tables. There was so much food and so many choices. Well, there was a whole table filled with a selection of lasagnas, but other than that, they had lots to choose from. Carla and Stu were sitting with a few others, already eating and Maggie and Billy went and joined them.

"Happy Birthday you two!" came Pats' voice as she walked up behind them and placed a hand on each of their shoulders. They looked up to see I Love Lucy smiling above them.

"Thanks Pat," they both replied, smiling back.

"You look lovely Pat," Maggie told her.

"Thank you dear." Just then the music started up. "All You Need Is Love" grew louder, and a few lights went out. People headed to the center to start dancing and Maggie grinned at Billy and nodded her head slightly towards Pat. He smiled at Maggie then stood up and held out his hand.

"Care to dance Lucy?" he asked, grinning at her. Pat looked at Maggie and Maggie smiled.

"All yours Pat." And off they went. Maggie saw Carla and Stu get up to dance as well. She looked around happily, watching everyone enjoying themselves. Then she heard someone behind her and jumped slightly when she turned around and saw The Phantom of the Opera standing there.

"Oh," she said, surprised. He didn't say anything and put his hand out towards her. She wasn't sure who it was, as he had a mask on, but she smiled and took his hand and was led out to the dance floor, "Superstition" now starting to play. He pulled her close, one hand on her waist, the other holding her hand in his as he moved them around the grounds, her dress billowing out as he turned them here and there. Maggie tried chatting with him, but he kept silent, pulling her close and dancing her in a sort of waltz. She still wasn't sure who he was after the song was over. Letting her go, the Phantom made a small bow, turned and walked away. She felt a hand on her shoulder, and feeling a bit creepy for some reason, startled a little.

"Who was that, Mag?" Billy asked and she softened again holding his hand in hers.

"No idea," she answered, wondering where the masked man had gone. While they were still standing there, "Mrs. Robinson" started playing and so the two grabbed hold of one another and started to dance, twirling each other about and laughing. Carla came over and the three danced together. They all danced to "Witchy Woman", "Legs", and "Looking Out My Back Door" before going and grabbing drinks and taking a break.

"Hey Sweet Cheeks!" Carla said after she finished a beer. "Let's say you show me some of your fancy moves." She jumped up and pulled Billy out of his chair. Maggie was laughing at the look on his face. She was thinking it looked more like Carla was leading as she danced him around to "Ain't Goin' Down Til The Sun Comes Up", then giving his butt a pinch and a slap on their way back making Billy jump a little. Carla went back to the beer tent and Billy sat down next to Maggie again.

"What's with Carla?" he asked, looking rather gobsmacked. Laughing at the expression on Billy's face, Maggie answered,

"Don't think she's been getting any lately. Think Carla's feeling a bit randy." Billy looked at her with more worry. Maggie laughed again and leaned over and kissed him.

"Just watch she doesn't get you alone." She giggled. When he looked truly anxious, she grinned and gave him a wink. "Oh, Billy, you're so cute," she told him, and he smiled at her cheekily. One of the cowboys DJing the music came over to Maggie at one point and said something in her ear. Maggie nodded and said something back to him, he nodded at her, then walked back over to the sound system.

"What's up Mag?" Billy asked, but Maggie just smiled at him.

"Alright folks, it's time we get our birthday couple up here for a special dance," came the voice of the cowboy who had visited Maggie. "Come on up here Zorro and Elena," he said, and everyone started clapping. Billy looked at Maggie, and although she couldn't see his eyebrows, she knew one was raised.

"Just dance your best tango with me Zorro. Like you have to win my heart." She smiled at him deviously, blinking her lashes at him. He chuckled and stood up, taking her hand and leading her to the circle. Playing their parts well, Maggie stood poised, with an air of regalness about her. Billy held out his hand and bowed to her as the music started. Santana's "Black Magic Woman" started playing and they smiled at each other. Billy began dancing around her, then as the vocals started, he came up behind her, grabbing her hand and spun her to face him and began dancing with her. She had never done the tango before, but Billy was an excellent lead and the two always had a way of working well together, feeding off each other and feeling out each other's next moves smoothly. Grinning broadly, he led her in the seductive dance, hearing a few people hollering happily and clapping as he spun her around, dipping her and grinning at each other. Maggie was undressing him in her mind as she found herself entranced by their tango. As the song came to an end, Billy dipped her and pulled her up slowly, smiling at each other and kissing as everyone clapped. Cowboy DJ was back on the mic.

"Wow, that was great. Let's hear it for Maggie and Billy!" Everyone hollered and clapped again. "Okay, we're going to take a break and have some birthday cake!" he added, and there was more cheering. Maggie and Billy turned to see two people carrying a huge cake over to the table nearest them, sparkler candles all lit up, everyone crowding around them, singing happy birthday, as they walked over to look at the cake. It was beautiful. Pat had managed to make two sidewalk tile sized red and gold walks of fame stars and added Maggie and Billy's names to each of them. She had stuck a movie slate into the center with the words "HAPPY BIRTHDAY TO OUR FAVOURITE COUPLE" written on it.

"Make a wish, you two," came someone's voice and Maggie and Billy, smiling, both thought for a moment, nodded, then blew out the two candles in the center of the cake together, to loud cheering and clapping. Billy picked Maggie up and hugged her, grinning broadly at each other, while kids suddenly appeared from every direction to get their dessert. There was plenty of cake for everyone. Pat had made it half chocolate, half vanilla, so everyone got what they wanted. After the cake, there was another announcement.

"Everyone grab a glass of champagne, as we toast to another happy trip around the sun to this beautiful couple." It took a few minutes for the glasses to be passed around, then everyone gave three "hip hip hoorays" to Maggie and Billy. After cake and champagne, people were up dancing again. Maggie caught a glimpse of The Phantom in the crowd, but then he was gone.

"Say Carla, who's The Phantom?" she asked as they sat and enjoyed their champagne.

"Huh, oh, don'know Mags, probably one of old farmer Bob's many sons," she said, finishing off her drink and pulling Stu back out to dance.

Billy came over and sat next to Maggie, reaching out and taking her hand.

"Great night, Mag!" he said, and she leaned over and held his face and kissed him softly.

"So glad!" Maggie replied with a big smile. He kissed her forehead and pulled her up to hug her. "Livin' On Love" had started playing and Billy pulled Maggie out to dance. She hugged him close as they swayed to the music, grinning contentedly with overflowing love.

"Say Mag, wanna sneak away?" he asked. She looked up into his hungry eyes and nodded.

"We should say thanks to everyone before we make a getaway though." Holding her hand, he walked them over to cowboy DJ, and Billy asked for the mic.

"Hello everyone," he said in his strong husky voice. A number of people looked over at him.

"Maggie and I just wanted to say thank you to everyone who helped make tonight happen and to all of you who celebrated our birthdays with us. It's been a great evening!" Everyone was cheering again, then right back to dancing and drinking. Taking advantage of the noise, Billy handed the mic back, and the two of them made their way to a dark corner, sneaking around the other end of the street and heading home.

"So, Mag," Maggie stopped and looked at him with a saucy expression. A grin playing behind her eyes. "Right, sorry, Elena, what did you have planned for tonight?" Billy asked grinning expectantly at her in the light of the streetlamp.

"Oh, Zorro, you must have patience." She turned to walk away, shaking her hips and looking back at him desirously. Billy growled playfully and ran towards her, wrapping his arm around her waist, giving her bottom a little squeeze, then back up to hold her waist with a grin and a wink as they walked down the middle of the street. As they reached the garden, Billy opened the gate and they strolled up the walkway and into the house. He started to take off his hat and mask and Maggie stopped him.

"Oh, no, I'm not done with you yet Zorro," she told him with a sexy grin. She started dancing sexily in front of him, making her way up the stairs, Billy grinned and followed her up. She turned and grinned at him when she reached the top, then walked down the hall and into the bedroom.

"Can I at least take my gloves off Mag?" he asked, and she gave him an intense stare.

"I don't know who this *Mag* is, I am Elena." He chuckled and pulled off his gloves. She bent over and unzipped her boots and pulled them off. Billy decided to do the same. Then he reached to take off his hat and mask again and she shook her finger at him. "No, no, not yet Lover." He grinned at her, loving her taking charge. She danced around him, running her hands over his body and each time she faced him, she stared intensely into his eyes. On one of her rounds, she took off his hat and threw it, stopping in front of him to grab his face and kiss him hard, then continued dancing. She danced in front of him again and undid his belt, slipped it from his pants and threw that aside too. On the next round she undid his shirt, slowly swaying and dancing her hips down with each button she undid, making her way back up and sliding her hands over his chest, pulling the shirt down his arms, kissing his neck softly, then back to her seductive dance, kissing him all the way around his body. Anytime Billy tried to touch her or hold her, she'd stop and say,

"No, no," grin and carry on. She undid his pants and pulled them straight down. Billy stepped out of them and kicked them to the side. Maggie danced to the back of Billy, and he felt her lips kissing between his shoulder blades. She reached up with one hand and softly grabbed his hair, holding on and squeezing as she slid her other hand around his waist to his stomach and straight down the front of his underwear. She felt him lift slightly, and inhale deeply. She stroked him for a moment, then danced around him again. Stretching up and licking his lips, biting his bottom lip, then grabbing his underwear and pulling those down too. Now, she stood in front of him and undressed herself. Still moving seductively as she stripped down to nothing. All she had left was the red flower in her hair, and all he had left was his mask. She kept dancing, shaking her hips and showing off some of her practiced belly dancing moves, then Maggie moved her body along his and around to press herself up against his back again, this time undoing his mask, but she kept it in her hand, making her way back to face him. He was very hard now, and she could see the longing in his eyes, turning her on incredibly. Placing her hands on his chest, she pushed him down on the bed. Billy grinned slightly, his eyes trailing over her curves. Crawling on all fours and forcing him to move up to the head of the bed Maggie smiled at him deviantly, then commanded,

"Close your eyes." It was Billy's turn to feel like he might burst with the loss of power and untamable arousal. He stared at her, a look of deeply impressed excitement on his face. "Close your eyes," she said again, and he did. She kissed him, starting from his chest, up his neck and then kissed his mouth softly. "Keep them closed," she whispered. Maggie took his hands and stretched them above his head using the mask to tie them to the headboard. She grabbed the scarf Billy had used on her during his ice cube tease, and wrapped it over his eyes.

"Mag?" he asked, and she grinned, knowing exactly what he was feeling. She whispered,

"Yes, Billy," back to him, then she slid down his body, running her hands from his shoulders, down, down, down to his thighs, squeezing them, letting her hair fall onto his body and trailing it along as she made her way back up. She ran her tongue up his neck and sucked on his earlobe, then kissed his mouth, making her way over to the other ear and sucking, feeling his body squirm with anticipation. She ran her tongue down his neck and kissed his chest, slowly, letting her lips drag open as she moved across from one side to the other, giving each of his nipples a lick, and nibbling softly. Maggie kissed every inch of his body she could get to, gently running her hands over him, tickling, and caressing him. Then sitting between his legs, near his feet she held both his legs gently, and ran her hands right up to the top of each one, and as she did so, she brought her face over top of his cock. She bent down and licked, feeling it move. She backed away and heard Billy breathe deeply. Enjoying his body and loving his arousal, Maggie kissed all around the top of his legs, over his center then down the insides of his legs and back up. She moved his legs apart and bending low, lifting, and holding him gently, she licked each of his balls, his hips moving with desire.

"Mag, you're driving me crazy," he called out to her. She grinned. Holding him at the base, she licked a very wet circle around the end of his dick, then ran her tongue over the very tip and flicked it a couple times, making sure he was nice and wet.

"Do you want me?" she asked in a hushed sultry voice, his hips moving as she held him and put the end of him into her mouth, moving the tip in and out ever so slightly.

"Gawd, yes, I want you!" he growled. She took him into her mouth all the way, deep and slow, sliding her tongue along him as she moved her mouth up and down. Licking and sucking hungrily. "Mag," he growled again, and she let him go, kissing up his body again.

"Do you want to watch me?" she asked him, sliding her body up his and reaching up to undo the scarf around his eyes.

"Maggie," he groaned, moving his body almost in agony. She undid the scarf and leaned over him, staring into his eyes. Then she kissed him, long and hard, and kissed her way back down his body. She moved herself over him, and Billy watched her longingly. She slid back and forth above his cock and then took him in, sitting down as slowly as she could, Billy's hands moving in an attempt to free himself. With her hands on his body, she rose up and down, now holding her own breasts and pinching her nipples, crying out with pleasure as Billy watched her, growing more animal-like with arousal. "Undo me Mag!" he growled at her. She grinned and kept riding him. "Gawd... Maggie," he moaned as she slid slowly and deliberately over and over.

"Oh, you feel so good," she cried with pleasure.

"Ohhh, God Maggie, undo me." But she was now sliding her hips back and forth quickly, making circles as she slid him in and out.

"Oh, Oh, Ohhh!" she cried, "Billy!" moaning with each movement.

"Mag! Oh God, Mag!" She made shorter, harder slides. "Oh my gawd!" he yelled, and she was so aroused with him cumming, that she was almost cumming too. She couldn't stop her body from moving, vibrating, her hips grinding him hard.

"Billy!" she cried out and fell forward onto his hot sweaty body. Finally reaching up and undoing his hands, Billy grabbed her almost aggressively, rubbing his hands up and down her body, kissing her with such intensity, then rolling them and still kissing her hard as he lay on top of her. Both of them growling as they kissed. "Zorro, you're so big and strong!" she said, and he bit her lip, then kissed her hard.

"My God Maggie, that was too much!" She grinned at him.

"I know right!?" she said with a cheeky grin. "I thought I would explode when you had *me* tied up Billy!" And he was back to kissing her like he might eat her right up. And suddenly, he was back inside her, sliding hard and fast.

"Ahh," she cried and reached up to hold the headboard as he basically pounded her, over and over. Squeezing her breasts and sliding faster.

"Maggie," he called out, exploding again, then bringing Maggie to climax, pinching her nipples and sucking her neck, holding himself inside her deeply as she moved into his body sensually. She was squirming now, and smiling as Billy watched her eyes roll back with hungry anticipation. Running his fingers along her center, feeling her cum and kissing her deeply as her body shook with pleasure. They could hardly catch their breath, and lay beside one another for ages, laughing and breathing heavily.

"Happy Birthday Billy," she finally said, and he gave a little chuckle.

"Happy Birthday Mag," he said back. They passed out, laying there, side by side, their naked bodies pressed together.

CHAPTER 11

They slept in the next day. Maggie finally got up to feed a very bossy and hungry Old Bill, then came back to bed and laid there until close to 10:30.

"You gonna put the coffee on Babe?" Billy asked her, running his hand across her body, turning towards her, and kissing her.

"Already did when I fed Bill, Lover." He kissed her cheek.

"You're the best Mag," he told her and she grinned.

"How are you feeling today, birthday boy?" she asked. "Oh, Mag, ask me again after a shower and a coffee.

"Okay, guess we'll skip our work-out today, eh Handsome?" she said, still grinning. He replied with a grunt and rolled over.

Maggie had a quick shower letting Billy lie in bed a little longer, then got dressed and went down to get herself a coffee. She brought one up to Billy and put it on his end table.

"Here you go my Lover," she said, kissing his face.

"Ah, thanks Babe." He opened his eyes and smiled at her. She went back downstairs and took her coffee out back to enjoy it in the morning sun while she waited for Billy. He took a little longer than usual, and looked incredibly sexy as he stepped onto the patio with his wet hair and twinkling blue eyes, and a smile that made her melt. He sat down with his coffee.

"So, how are you doing, Gorgeous Lover?" she asked again. He smiled at her.

"Perfect my sexy Mag." He winked at her.

"Yes, you are," she said, smiling back at him.

They had a very lazy day, spending most of it on the couch watching TV. Then, as it neared 4:00, Maggie got up and went upstairs to grab the things for Billy's surprise. She left everything in the front hall, so he wouldn't see them yet, then went back and sat with him.

"So, I have a birthday present for you," she told him, grinning.

"Wasn't the party my present?" he asked her. She shook her head. "What about the tie up?" he asked. She shook her head again.

"No, the tie up was just to return the favour, and the party was only the first part of your present, Lover." Just then, there was a knock at the door. She jumped up and grabbed his hand.

"Come on Billy, your gift is here." He looked at her in wonder and followed her to the front door, looking down at the dog stuff as they passed it. Maggie opened the door and there stood Mr. Crofter.

"Good afternoon, Maggie," he greeted her with a smile. "I have that delivery you were expecting." "Hello Billy. Happy Birthday," he said as he stepped out of sight, then back with a golden puppy in his arms. He handed it to Billy who stood there with his mouth open.

"Thanks Mr. Crofter," Maggie said. "I'll give you a call in a bit, and you can fill me in on any special instructions." He nodded and smiled.

"Ok, Maggie, that'll be just fine. Goodbye," he said, and Maggie waved and closed the door.

"You got me a dog Mag?!" Billy asked, looking at her like he might cry. She nodded, almost laughing with joy. "Oh Mag!" he exclaimed, holding the pup up and looking into its sweet face. Billy took it into the living room and sat down on the floor with it. "What is it, Mag?" he asked her, still looking at the pup.

"Boy," she answered.

"Oh Mag!" he repeated, and Maggie laughed.

"Happy Birthday my Love," she said and kissed the top of his head. She went and grabbed all the supplies from the hall and put them on the dining room table.

"How old is he?" Billy asked, still staring at the pup with an awestruck grin.

"Almost two months," she answered, coming over to pat him with Billy. She thought Billy might melt.

"Mag, this is just the best present!" he said grinning at the pup. He looked up at her, grinning from ear to ear.

"I'm so glad." Maggie grinned and gave him a big kiss.

"Thank you so much!" he said, giving her a hug, then turning his attention back to the puppy. They spent the rest of the day playing with the pup in the backyard and snuggling with him. Old Bill wasn't too sure about the new addition, but Maggie made sure to spoil him as much as she could, which suited him just fine. Billy called Mr. Crofter and was filled in on all he needed to know about his new friend. After he hung up, he walked over to Maggie and wrapped his arms around her in a tight bear hug, lifting her feet off the floor.

"Mag, thank you so much! I haven't had a dog since I was a kid; before I met you." Still squeezing her tight, she smiled and hugged him back. She felt her feet touch the floor again and Billy held her face in his hands and looked into her eyes. His eyes were full of love, as he gave her a long loving kiss. She grinned at him as he pulled away.

"I remember you worrying about leaving your dog when you told me about going into the military. I'm so glad you're happy Babe," Maggie said and Billy turned back and smiled at her again. "So, what are you going to name him?" she asked, and he turned to look at the dog, who was on the living room floor, chewing on one of his toys, Old Bill staring at him with a look of superior intelligence.

"Hmmm, well, we've got Mr. Bill, so how about... Mr. Bojangles." Maggie smiled.

"Ya, I like that." Billy bent down and crawled over to the puppy and rubbed his golden coat with both hands.

"Hey there Mr. Bojangles," he said. He chuckled to himself as the pup looked up at him with a grin, his tongue hanging out the side of his mouth. Once again Old Bill looking down at, now two creatures of lesser intelligence. Maggie giggled at Billy rolling about with the pup, and Old Bill's expression as he watched them. They set Bojangles' bed up for him in the front hallway. Maggie had bought a couple baby gates that they attached to the bottom of the stairs and at the end of the hall leading to the kitchen and living room. They left his toys out there for him, and his water and food bowls. Billy took him out in the backyard, Maggie fed Old Bill, and then the two of them headed up to bed. After they both got ready and were done brushing their teeth, Billy said he was just going to peek and see how Mr. Bo was doing.

"Ok, Babe" Maggie said grinning at his father bear love for their new addition. She couldn't help but think about what he might have been like as a dad. Knowing how loving, kind and patient of a dad he would have been. Laughing to herself as she suddenly envisioned a home full of far too many children, seeing herself very happily barefoot and pregnant most of the time. Billy came into the bedroom, a big smile on his face and sat down on his side of the bed, quickly rolling towards Maggie and grabbing her, rolling both of them about and kissing her everywhere it tickled.

"I'm so glad you like your present," she said as they stopped rolling about, and giving him a quick kiss. They laid in bed chatting for a while. In between their conversations, both of them had their noses stuck in a book. It was going on midnight when Billy put his mystery down, said he just had to have one more look and got up to go downstairs. A moment later Maggie heard Billy whispering.

"Mag, Mag, come here." She climbed out of bed and found him a few steps down.

"What is it Billy?" she whispered back. Billy pointed to the front hall. Maggie sat down on the step next to him and could just make out, Old Bill in his window seat sleeping and Mr. Bo sleeping underneath him on the floor. They smiled at each other and headed back to the bedroom. "Okay, that's pretty sweet," Maggie said as she pulled the covers over herself and Billy climbed in next to her. Billy looked so happy, which made Maggie just as happy.

***

They woke up to Bo barking and both Maggie and Billy ran downstairs quickly. He was barking at the front door. Billy pulled him close, reassuring him.

"It's okay buddy." But Bo kept barking at the door. Maggie came over and held him while Billy opened the door and had a look. No one was there.

"What is it boy?" Maggie asked, patting him, his barking calming slightly.

"Well, I guess he'll make a good guard dog Mag." She laughed.

"Well maybe. Wouldn't it be better if he barked when someone *was* there?" They both giggled.

"Come on Mr. Bojangles," Billy said, opening the hallway gate and taking the dog out back. Old Bill was up on the island looking like he wasn't too happy about the morning wake up call. Maggie picked him up and cuddled him.

"I know Bill, not the best way to wake up, but he'll get the hang of things eventually." Bill soon went from grumpy annoyance to pushing his head along Maggie's chin and purring at the snuggles.

"Here you go Bill," she said, putting him down and giving him his breakfast. Maggie went back upstairs and used the washroom. When she came down, Billy was still out back with Bo. She went to the back door and called out,

"Want a coffee, Babe?" Billy jogged back towards the door, Bo running along behind him, tongue lolling happily.

"Just going to jump in the shower first," he told her, and gave her a kiss. She walked in with him and grabbed herself a coffee, then went and sat out back, watching Mr. Bo chase his tail and sniff around the yard. By the time Billy came back down, joining her with his coffee, Bo was lying down at Maggie's feet, eyes closed, every once in a while his ears twitching as the occasional fly landed on him.

CHAPTER 12

It didn't take long at all for Mr. Bojangles to settle in. Even Old Bill was showing signs of liking him, or at least accepting him. On the days Billy had to work, Maggie stayed with Bo, and vice versa, until they had him trained enough that they could leave him on his own, gated, in the front hall.

One day when Maggie was home with Bo, she decided to go over to the farm. She hadn't had a chance for a couple weeks, taking care of their new pup, and she was really missing the horses. She put Mr. Bojangles' leash on him and opened the car door. Instantly he was smiling and sniffing around.

"Hey Mags!" Carla shouted, coming out of the cowshed.

"Morning Carla." Carla walked over and bent down to greet the dog. Bo walked over to her, still smiling, tongue hanging out. Carla laughed and said,

"Looks just like his dad Mags!" and Maggie laughed.

"Carla!" she said.

"What, that's what Sweet Cheeks looks like when he's gawking at you Mags." The two of them giggled. "So, what're you up to Mags?" she asked, still down patting Bo.

"Missed you and my horses," Maggie answered with a smile. Carla stood up taking the leash.

"Come on Mini Billy, let's go meet the animals," Carla told him, and he looked up at her still smiling away. Maggie grinned at the two of them and followed along behind them. Bo was very curious about the cows. They didn't seem to mind him at all, but the horses weren't too sure about him, and he wasn't too sure about them either, although he and Graze seemed to like each other alright. Maybe because she wasn't too big yet. He pulled Carla along when he saw the chickens, and they made an awful squawk running away from him. Maggie and Carla laughed at Bo bouncing along happily. After he met the pigs, who he tried to befriend but their snorts were just a little too much for him, Maggie took him back to the stable and tied him to the front door while she had a visit with Graze. She brushed her and snuggled with her for a bit, then went over to see Beauty. At first, he seemed to be a little cool with her.

"Ah, Beauty, don't worry, you're still my favourite stallion," she assured him, patting him and hugging him. He snorted, then rubbed his face along hers. She made her way over to Oatmeal and gave him a little rub too. She roped all three horses, then walked Beauty, Graze, Oatmeal and Bo out to the back field, where she let the horses run free for a while. Closing the gate behind her and letting Bo have a run around the field too. She laughed, hardly believing he could grin any bigger, running like the wind, tongue flying out beside his face.

"Come on Bo, come on," she'd call out to him, and he'd make a bee line for her, play fighting with him, then watching him run off again. They must have spent forty-five minutes doing this before he came and sat down at her feet, panting. Maggie grinned to herself as she thought, *you're a real goer. You are like your father!*

"Ok Mr. Bo, let's go get you a drink." She put his leash back on, and called the horses back, the five of them making their way back to the stable. Maggie showed Bo the water trough where he lapped it up urgently and thankfully. After she put the horses back in their stalls, she and Bo found Carla and said goodbye.

When she got home, Billy was in the kitchen, making himself some lunch. Maggie went over and gave him a hug and a big kiss.

"Hey Babe," he said, smiling at her. "Where have you two been?" he asked, bending down to give Bo some love too. Maggie told him all about Bo's farm adventure while the two of them ate lunch together. Bo slept for most of the afternoon. "Hey, Mag, maybe we could take him to the lake tomorrow?" Billy suggested while they tidied up their lunch dishes.

"Sure, sounds like fun. I'll pack us a picnic," she replied, kissing him on the cheek as she passed him. They both had Friday off, which hadn't happened for a few weeks now.

"It'll be nice to spend the day together Mag," Billy said, running his hand along her waist and kissing her on the forehead as he made his way to the back patio with his beer. Bo was now out back doing his afternoon yard patrol. Maggie grabbed her bubbly water and joined Billy at the little table.

"Yes, it seems like we haven't seen each other for weeks Lover." She smiled at him, and he winked at her. "I've been *missing* you Billy," she added, her gaze a little more intense.

"Well, neither of us have to get up and go anywhere tomorrow Mag," he said grinning. Later on, that day, Billy decided to take Bojangles for a walk and stopped into the b and b to grab dinner for him and Maggie.

"Say Mag, did Carla mention anyone new in town when you saw her this morning?" he asked as he sat dinner down at the island counter. Maggie got up from the couch and came over to unpack it with him, shaking her head.

"No, why?" she asked.

"Just curious. There was a guy sitting in the restaurant, never seen him before, but he looked strangely familiar. He was just sitting there watching me while I ordered and chatted with Pat." Maggie shrugged.

"Don't know Babe. Maybe he thought you were cute!" They grinned at each other and leaned in for a peck. "Maybe he just arrived. Carla usually keeps up with anything new." They soon lost interest in the subject, making their way over to the couch with their food while they watched Pulp Fiction, one of Billy's favourite movies. Maggie loved how he always sang along to the music in it. It was *kinda sexy and cute,* she thought to herself with a smile. After the movie, Maggie went into the kitchen to make their picnic lunch to take to the lake the next day. Then she packed up the small cooler with a couple cans of ginger ale and club soda, making a mental note to put the ice packs in before they left. The thought of ice sending shivers through her body with the tantalizing memory of Billy's ice cube delight.

The weather had started to become much cooler in the last couple weeks. Their warmer than usual summer had definitely turned to that brisk end of October feel. Maggie was in heaven with all the leaves in full poignant sunset coloured vibrance, strewn over yards and driveways, falling softly in the growing autumn wind. The smell and beauty of fall filled her with happiness. After their usual, walking hand in hand, playing with, and cleaning up after Bo, enjoying being outside with each other, take the dog out before bed, routine, they headed up to bed themselves. Both falling asleep before anything else could even be thought of.

Maggie awoke the next morning to a delicious, delightful

feeling. Billy's body on top of hers, his warm lips kissing her neck. She kept her eyes closed and reached her arms around his body.

"Mmm, morning Billy," she said, grinning. He kissed up to her ear and whispered,

"Good morning, Beautiful." Then he continued softly, slowly, kissing her neck, from one ear to the other, Maggie running her hands all over his back, with the occasional ass squeeze. He was just in his boxers, Maggie in an old well-worn, Bob Marley T-shirt of Billy's, that he soon pulled up over her head. Sliding it up slowly and softly sweeping the cotton over her breasts, giving Maggie shivers, then continuing his kisses down to each breast. Sucking and licking slowly, taking his time with each one. Maggie's hands in his hair, up and down his neck, purring with pleasure. Billy kissed his way back up to Maggie's face and they grinned at each other. Then he slid his boxers off and leaned down to kiss her again.

"Gawd, I love morning sex with you Lover," she said, and he chuckled.

"I love anytime sex with you, Beautiful." Maggie smiled and pulled his face to hers, kissing him hard. As they kissed, she felt him move her legs apart with his own and holding his ass as he pushed himself inside of her, she gave a quiet, drawn out,

"Ohhh." He was moving so slowly, both caressing each other's bodies with such love and kissing each other's necks and faces.

"Maggie, mmmm, you feel sooo goood." Billy slid in faster and a little harder, Maggie cried out with delight, then whispered,

"Slowly Billy." She moaned satisfyingly, as he made long, slow glides, Maggie grabbing his ass again and clawing at him, moaning with pleasure as she grew wetter and moved her hips into his. He ran his hands up her back, holding her shoulders and lifted her up slightly so he could kiss her neck as her head fell back, pushing himself a little deeper inside of her very inviting body.

"Mag, I'm close," he growled, and he moved a little faster again. She turned her head to the right, an invitation for Billy to suck on her neck, and as he did her arousal doubled.

"Oh Mag, Oh God Mag!" he yelled out, Maggie smiling with sheer enjoyment as she felt his body shuddering. He licked and kissed and sucked up and down her neck and she soon found herself very close to finishing too. Billy pushed deeply, allowing Maggie to slowly and sensually grind her hips into him, her legs wrapped tightly around him, as he sucked and licked, breathing heavily as he kissed her, into ecstasy.

"Ohhhh Billy," she moaned as she came. Maggie wrapped her arms around him, trailing her hands up and into his hair. Hugging each other for a moment as their bodies slowed their shudders. Lifting his face, Billy looked intensely at her, his eyes so deep and so blue. So full of love and mischief. He stroked the hair from her face, kissing her mouth softly. She smiled at him, rubbing his back gently.

"That was yummy Babe," she said, and he grinned.

"Mmhmm. Just gets better and better," he answered and kissed her again. They were pulled back to reality by Bo's barks.

"You really do look even more beautiful after we *dance* Mag," Billy swooned. Grinning at each other, they kissed once more, each with a hand holding one another's faces lovingly before Billy got up, pulled on his boxers, and ran downstairs. Maggie lay there smiling softly, enjoying the scent of Billy still lingering with her slightly sweat covered body. She felt slightly flushed and giddy.

Mmm, I really do love morning sex she thought to herself and grinned. Maggie had just closed her eyes again when she heard Billy coming back upstairs.

"Mag," he called as he walked into the bedroom, looking around for some pants and a shirt.

"What is it Billy?" she asked, a strange feeling of unease in her gut. Billy came over and looked down at her. She couldn't tell if he was worried or pissed off.

"Billy, what is it?" she asked, standing up, still naked.

"Better get dressed Mag. There's someone here to see you." She felt worried now.

"Billy, is anyone hurt?" she asked, pulling on her bra and underwear and grabbing a long cotton dress.

"No, nothing like that Babe." He realized he'd scared her. Pulling her close and hugging her against his body, he kissed the end of her nose.

"It's Pete, Mag." She felt her jaw drop.

"What!?" she whisper-yelled.

"He's the one I saw at Pat's. Don't worry Babe, just do what you have to do, I'll go back down while you get ready." He turned to leave, taking a couple steps, then came back grinning. "By the way, that was pure eff'n bliss Babe!" he said, grabbing her face and kissing her deeply. She grinned at him coyly, feeling her face glow, and smiled as he walked out and down the stairs. Maggie quickly pulled her dress on and used the washroom. *What the hell was Pete doing here?* She thought to herself, annoyed more than anything else. She just wanted to go back to bed, rewind about half an hour and lay there in Billy's arms. *Ok, Maggie, strap your balls on and go girl,* she thought to herself, thinking she wished her balls were a bit bigger. As she hit the last step, she heard Pete's voice and stopped to listen for a moment, unsure whether she wanted to see him. Then she heard Billy ask if he'd like a coffee, and her spirits lifted at his voice. *K, go on Maggie.* And her feet started moving again. *How freaking weird is this,* she was thinking as she came around the corner and saw the two of them standing there together. Pete turned to look at Maggie with a smile, she looked beyond him at Billy who was looking at her like he'd like to punch Pete in the back of the head.

"Maggie!" he said happily, walking towards her, and reaching out to hug her. Maggie was frozen to the spot, as Pete wrapped his arms around her. She just stood there like a tree.

"Pete," she finally managed as he backed away.

"Wow Maggie, you look great!" he said, still smiling at her.

"Pete, what are you doing here?" she asked, making her way over to Billy now, the two of them sliding their arms around each other's backs.

"Oh well, you know Maggie, just out for a drive, thought maybe I'd check out your part of the world," he answered sitting down on a stool. Maggie was gobsmacked.

"You were out for a thousand-mile drive?" she asked, Billy sipping at his coffee, still holding Maggie and pulling her closer.

"Well, yes, a long drive, but it was nice to get away, and it sure is beautiful here." He smiled, then had a mouthful of his coffee. Maggie looked up at Billy, his eyes grinned at her, but he didn't say anything. He looked back at their surprise visitor.

"So, how long are you visiting, Pete?" Billy asked, trying to break the tension radiating from Maggie and trying not to sound too annoyed himself.

"Not sure," Pete answered. "Don't know where I'm headed after this." Billy turned his back on Pete and looked at Maggie. He smiled at her and put his hand on her shoulder, giving it a little squeeze.

"Well, I'll let you two catch up then." He kissed Maggie on the cheek. "Just gonna have a shower, Babe. Bo's out back." Maggie nodded but wished he'd stay. Pete looked relieved to see Billy walk out of the room.

"Pete, what the hell are you doing here?!" Maggie asked, feeling very frustrated with him.

"Geeze Maggie, thought it might be nice to reconnect after, what fifteen years?" She shook her head in disbelief, thinking about how he certainly hadn't lost any of his arrogance over the years.

"I haven't talked to you since you ran off with another woman and we went through our divorce, and you think it would 'just be nice to reconnect'?" He nodded like that was perfectly normal.

"Ya, sure Maggie." He took another drink from his mug. "By the way, you really do look great. And you looked absolutely beautiful the night of the halloween party too!" She narrowed her eyes at him.

"What are you talking about?" she asked.

"At the birthday dance," he said grinning. "Like really gorgeous Maggie. The air up here certainly works for you." *Well, the tranquility, loving partner and great sex life did wonders too,* she thought to herself. She sat down at the end of the island, trying to calm down a little.

"How long have you been in town Pete?" He thought for a moment.

"Oh, I arrived a day or two before that party you all had."
Maggie stood up and started walking towards the back door.

"Just have to check on the dog," she said and walked out back.
Bo was busy digging in a corner of the garden. "Bo! Bo!" she called.
He looked up, stopped digging for a moment and tilted his head at
her. "Come on boy!" she yelled. He looked disappointed, and
hesitated for a second looking back down at the lovely hole he'd
started, then came running for her. "Good boy!" she told him,
rubbing him all over.

"Nice dog," she heard Pete say and Bo barked.

"It's alright Bo," she said, patting him and letting him run off
again. They sat down at the dining room table and Maggie lowered
her guard slightly.

"Pete, I am sorry to hear about Lucy," she said sincerely.

"Thanks Maggie. To be honest, that's partly why I came to see
you. Even after everything, there isn't really anyone else I could
turn to." Maggie felt her heart strings pull a little. Pete had hurt
her, and he had been an asshole, but they did have a lot of history
together, and no matter what, he was still a part of her story. She
reached out her hand to pat his without thinking, then pulled it
back, and gave him a consoling smile.

"By the way, how *did* you find me?" she asked.

"Oh, I was chatting with Mason, and he was more than happy to
give me your address." Maggie nodded, trying to hide her annoyance
with her brother. Pete and Mason had always got along well.

"So, how long did you say you're staying?" she asked. He
shrugged, looking a little lost and sad.

"Guess that depends on how things go with you Maggie." She
looked at him quickly, feeling her defenses coming back up.

"What do you mean by that Pete?" He shook his hand as he answered.

"Oh, nothing like that, I just mean our catching up." She backed down again.

"Have you eaten?" she asked him, standing up.

"No, not yet." She really just wanted to busy herself with something, feeling uncomfortable and anxious. Maggie walked around the island and into the kitchen. She opened the fridge, grabbed the eggs and cheese and the package of Billy's bologna. By the time she had started making breakfast Billy was back down.

"Smells good Mag," he said, coming up behind her and kissing her cheek. She turned and smiled at him. He whispered in her ear before moving away. "You alright Babe?" Maggie nodded at him with a slight smile. Billy winked at her, then grabbed another coffee and sat down on one of the stools. The three of them chatted for a bit, Billy being his kind patient self. Maggie looking to him whenever she felt herself tightening up again, his smiling eyes bringing her back down again. Pete ate breakfast with them, then Maggie said they had plans.

"Oh, ok, well maybe we could meet for coffee tomorrow Maggie?" he asked as they saw him to the door.

"Um, how about Monday Pete?" Maggie said, not wanting to give up her Sunday with Billy. He looked a little disappointed but nodded, and in his bullshit polite Pete way, said thank you for breakfast, nice to meet you Billy and goodbye.

Billy closed the door. Maggie was already headed back to the kitchen. "God. What does he think he's playing at?" Maggie said as Billy ran his hand along her shoulder and stood at the end of the island.

"Aw, Mag, didn't you know?" he asked, grinning at her cheekily. "You're very loveable." She looked up at him with a skeptical expression.

"Don't make fun Billy," she said, and he chuckled.

"I'm not Babe." He walked back over to her and pulled her in for a hug. "He's wounded and he knows you'll help him, because you're, well, *you*." She snuggled up to him.

"I don't want to help him Billy!" He laughed again.

"Okay, Mag, let's pretend you just had a weird dream, we just woke up, made sweet delicious love and now we're getting ready to go to the lake." She looked up at him and smiled.

"God, I love you!" she told him, with her big Maggie smile and, reaching up on her toes she kissed him.

"And I love *you*!" he said back, giving her butt a slap. "Now, let's go to the lake."

They packed up some towels for Bo, his leash, blankets, lunch, and themselves into the hatchback and off they went. Parking as close to the dock as possible, they unpacked their things before letting Bo out of the car. He hopped out and sniffed around for a few minutes. Maggie and Billy walked to the dock and put their things down. Bo followed them, then without any coaxing and no warning at all he made a run for it, right off the end of the dock. With a splash, Maggie and Billy ran to the end and looked into the water. In true Bo fashion, his tongue was hanging out, smiling, and happily swimming around in circles.

"Bojangles!" Billy laughed. "You *are* a funny guy." Maggie and Billy sat at the end of the dock watching him happily. After a bit, they thought they better get him out, so Billy laid down on his stomach and reached in to pull him up, Maggie ready to cuddle him up in a towel. He didn't stop smiling the whole time they were there. He jumped in a few more times, but happily came out to enjoy the sandwich Maggie had made just for him. The sun was on its way down in the sky when they packed up and headed home. Bo sitting in the back, his head peeking through the middle of the front seats, still smiling, his tongue lolling to the side.

They tried to keep him awake for as long as they could. But by 8:00 the poor little guy just couldn't keep his eyes open.

"Movie, Mag?" Billy asked as she approached in her pajamas.

"Sure," she answered and as she neared the couch he pulled her on top of him, the two of them laughing and kissing.

"Mmm, or maybe not a movie," he said grinning. They spent some time making out, but soon Bo was barking to go out, so Billy took him out back and Maggie joined them for a walk together. After they had spent some time outside, they were feeling relaxed and tired and headed up to bed for a snuggled night's sleep.

Carla called fairly early the next day. Billy was out back working on a doghouse and Maggie was inside doing her yoga, hesitating for a moment before getting up and grabbing the phone.

"Hey Carla, what's up?" she asked her.

"Mags, you'll never believe this!" Carla replied, very mysteriously.

"What is it?" Maggie asked giggling at the intensity in Carla's voice. She usually sounded like that when she had some juicy gossip on someone in town.

"You sit'n down Mags?" Maggie sat down on the stool nearest the phone.

"Yes, hit me!" Carla was quiet for a second, then said,

"Pete's in town Mags. *Your* eff'n Pete, Mags!" and Maggie couldn't help but laugh.

"Wow, you'll never believe *this* Carla? I already knew that?" Carla was silent. "You okay Carla?" Maggie asked, laughing again.

"What do you mean you knew Mags? You shit'n me?" Maggie was still laughing.

"No, he came by yesterday."

"No eff'n way Mags!?" she replied.

"For real Carla. Crazy huh?" Maggie had stopped laughing now.

"Wow. Well, what the hell is he doing here?" she asked her.

"He said he wants to catch up." Carla was quiet again, then finally spoke.

"Oh, Mags, he's trying to get back into your pants!" Maggie laughed again.

"Well, too bad for him eh?! My pants are well taken care of." Carla laughed now too.

"Hey Mags, wanna grab a coffee later?"

"Why don't you come over for dinner tonight?" she asked her friend.

"Really, you and Billy gonna be alright not ripping each other's clothes off for one evening?" Maggie rolled her eyes and grinned.

"I'm sure we can get a couple romps in before dinner!" And laughed as she heard Carla make a barfing sound.

"Ha ha Mags, good one!" Maggie chuckled. "See you around 5:00?"

"Ya, see ya then." They hung up.

"Hey Billy, Carla's coming over for dinner," Maggie yelled out back, noticing Billy was almost done with the doghouse.

"Cool," he called back, hard at work. "Stu coming?" he yelled as she walked in. She turned and shrugged.

"One never knows." They grinned at each other. Maggie went in to try to figure out what to do for dinner. They hadn't shopped for a while and things were pretty scarce. She walked back to the patio door. "Just going to run over to the grocery store Lover. Want anything?" He looked up with his cheeky Billy grin.

"Only you Beautiful," he said, and she grinned at him, blowing him a kiss.

When she got to the store, Maggie walked up and down the aisles, not really taking in what she was looking at. Her mind drifted to Pete's surprise pop-in. Carla was probably right. He was likely looking for some physical comfort, which she had no intention of fulfilling. She was starting her second round in the aisles now, trying to bring her thoughts back to supper. *Okay Maggie, focus,* she thought, now standing in the produce section. It was still early enough to make scalloped potatoes, remembering she still had lovely red potatoes in the cellar from the gathering. She grabbed some pork chops and some things to make a salad, paid and headed out the door. She had just started walking back when she heard someone calling out behind her.

"Maggie!" She turned to see Pete.

Oh, this guy! She said in her head, then laughed to herself.

"Oh, hey Pete," she replied, stopping. He had just come out of the b and b. Pete walked up to her, hugged her and gave her a kiss on the cheek in greeting. Maggie accepted but didn't return the affection. When Pete stood up straight again Maggie saw Pauline walking into the b and b, watching them. Maggie nodded and smiled, remembering something her mom used to say to her about being kind to everyone, even those who don't like you, "Magaret. It drives them crazy when you're nice to them!" she'd say. Pauline gave her a funny grin and walked inside.

"So, what are you up to Maggie?" he asked her hopefully.

"Oh, just headed home to make dinner for my girlfriend tonight, Pete." He looked a little disappointed. "We'll meet up tomorrow for that coffee though, right?" she added, hoping to bring his spirits back up.

"Oh, right, sure thing Maggie. 10:00 okay? Mugs & Saucers?" Maggie nodded and smiled.

"Yes, see you then." She turned and walked home. When she

got home, she was frazzled and apparently talking to herself, banging around in the kitchen getting things ready for dinner.

"Hey Babe, you okay?" Billy asked, coming in from out back.

"Fine!" she snapped. Then stopped and looked up at him. "I'm sorry," she said, walking over to him and putting her head down on his chest. "Just ran into Pete." Billy put his hands on her back and gave it a little rub.

"No worries, Babe. He pisses me off too." She looked up at him and he grinned at her. "Can I help with dinner Mag?" he asked, and she melted.

"You're so great Billy. How'd I get so lucky?" He kissed her forehead and walked over to the sink to wash his hands, then he started to take the groceries out of the bags. "Did you get Bo's house finished?" Maggie asked, happy to be in the kitchen with her man.

"Yep, he's in it right now," he answered smiling. Maggie went to the back door and looked out into the yard. There was Bo, laying with his face peeking out.

"Oh Billy, that's so sweet!" she said coming back in. Billy nodded with a smile. Maggie left and went down to the cellar to grab the potatoes. When she came back up Billy was washing the lettuce and tomatoes.

"So, what did Pete have to say?" he asked, feeling like she'd calmed down enough to ask.

"Not much, I tried to avoid him and managed to sidestep him coming home with me for dinner." Billy raised his eyebrow at her.

"Should I worry about this Pete fella of yours Mag?" he asked her.

"He's not my fella Billy, and even if you did have to worry about *him*, you don't have to worry about me Lover." Maggie leaned closer to give him a kiss. She'd never seen a jealous side to Billy before, and the feeling Pete had stirred up between them was not one she liked at all. "Billy, I mean it. You are my everything, and you have my heart, and body, completely." He looked into her eyes, and she saw them crinkle into a grin. Then he leaned over and kissed her.

"So, what's for dinner Babe?"

***

Carla arrived alone, grumbling about Stu as usual.

"Hey, you two love birds, smells great in here!" she said as she went to the fridge and grabbed a beer. She sat down on a stool to chat with Maggie, while she checked on dinner and Billy went out back with Bo. Carla waited till Billy was outside, then in a hushed surprised voice said,

"Mags, word on the street is that you and Pete came out of the b and b kissing!" Carla looked at Maggie with wide eyes. Maggie laughed.

"What are you on about Carla?" Carla was nodding quickly.

"Ya, earlier today!" Maggie stopped dead, holding a wooden spoon.

"Oh, good grief!" she half yelled. "Pauline!" Carla looked at her confused.

"Pauline, Mags? What's she got to do with it?" Maggie got the plates out of the cupboard and sat them down on the counter, Carla took them over to the table and sat them out.

"I came out of the grocery store, and Pete saw me as he came out of Pats. He walked over and gave me a hug and kiss, and

172

Pauline came up behind him and saw us. What a shit disturber she is!" Carla came back over and grabbed the cutlery.

"Ya, she's a piece of work Mags. I've warned you before you need to watch her!" Maggie shook her head annoyed.

"Pauline!" she said to herself again.

They ate dinner and listened to the many tales of Carla and all the newest town gossip. Billy mostly laughed and shook his head, Maggie nodding along with her.

"Hey Mags, what'ch doin' for yer birthday weekend?" she asked while Billy and Maggie cleaned up.

"Aw, nothing much Carla, already had our party," she answered, smiling.

"Oh, Mags, you gotta celebrate on your actual birthday!" Maggie shrugged, but noticing Carla was still waiting for a better answer, replied,

"Ok, well, I don't know...why don't the four of us have dinner then?" Maggie suggested, looking at Billy.

"Ya, sure, whatever you like my Love," he told her, and she smiled at Carla.

"Okay, Friday, dinner," Carla announced happily. Maggie and Billy had finished the dishes and were standing leaning against the sink with their arms around each other. Carla was grinning at them with a goofy look.

"You two really are the cutest," she said, Maggie laughed. "Gawd, barf-ola!" she added, walking over to them and hugging them at the same time.

"I'm gonna head home you randy love birds. Wouldn't want you two to miss a night rolln' about in the hay! Thanks for dinner you two!" Maggie walked Carla to the door. "You watch out for that Pauline, Mags!" she said as she pulled on her rubber boots and stepped onto the porch. Maggie smiled and nodded.

"Thanks Carla, I will." She watched her friend walk down the walkway to the gate.

"Have a shag for me Mags!" she called back before the gate swung shut. Maggie stood in the doorway for a minute, then went in and locked up. Billy was out back with Bo and she went out to join him. He was walking around the yard, and as she caught up with him she slid her hand into his and he grabbed it.

"Alright Lover of mine?" she asked, and he gave her a smile.

"Perfect Mag," he replied. They walked along behind the dog, Maggie resting her head on his arm.

"Do you have to work tomorrow?" she asked as they headed back toward the house. He nodded,

"Yep. Just half a day though." They went in and got Bo set for the night, turned off the lights and went up to bed.

***

Maggie woke up to her alarm at 7:30. She stretched and got up, headed to the bathroom for a shower, then dressed and went downstairs.

"Morning Billy," she said walking up behind him where he was sitting at the table with a book. Maggie wrapped her arms around him.

"Mmm, hey Beautiful," he said, reaching up and holding her arms.

"Sleep alright Lover?" she asked him.

"Yep, you?" she nodded and gave him a kiss on the cheek,

walking into the kitchen for her coffee.

"What time do you have to leave?" she asked and came back over and sat with him at the table.

"Not till quarter to twelve. Working the afternoon shift today." Maggie was taking a sip of coffee, then put it down on the table and looked at him disappointed.

"Oh, that's too bad. I'm heading out soon," she said looking at the clock, it was already just after nine.

"I was looking forward to spending the morning with you! Where are you headed?" he asked. Maggie looked at him for a moment.

"Coffee with Pete," she said, unenthused.

"Right," he said, "Pete." Billy got up and poured himself another coffee. "What time will you be back?" he asked in a slightly commanding tone, sitting down again. Maggie looked at him with her head tilted, hearing the slight edge to his question. When she didn't respond Billy added. "It's just that Bo will be alone." She watched his expression change from anger to his usual kindness before answering.

"Don't imagine I'll be too long. Actually, Bo will give me a good out." And she smiled at him. He smiled back but she could see he was annoyed. "Billy, it's not like I asked him to come." His face softened.

"I know, you're right Babe, sorry. There's just something about him I don't like. I mean besides the fact that he had you and I didn't, and he didn't even know what he had and treated you like shit." She grinned and stretched out her hand to hold his on the table.

"That he's seen your woman naked probably doesn't help?" she asked, trying to make him laugh.

"Well, that doesn't help me like him, no, but that's not the main reason. I don't know what it is, he just rubs me the wrong way." He looked at her and she squeezed his hand.

"Then I'll just have to make sure I rub you the right way later tonight," Maggie replied with a sexy smile. That got a grin and a chuckle out of him, and she got up from her seat and sat down on his lap, wrapping her arms around his shoulders, leaning in to kiss him. She held his face in her hands and grinned at him.

"I'll miss you today Lover." Billy squeezed her tight.

"Love you Mag," he said, kissing her. She hopped up and looked around for her keys. She grabbed some money out of the cookie jar on the side cabinet where they usually dropped small bills and loose change.

"I'm going to head out, Billy. Hopefully Pete will show up early too, and I'll get home sooner." She walked over and gave him a long kiss, then made her way to the front door.

"See you later," she called out, giving Mr. Bill a pat before leaving.

She was at Mugs & Saucers by 9:30 and grabbed herself a water while she waited. As she had hoped, Pete arrived early, and made his way over to her, smiling, leaning down, and kissing her cheek.

"Morning Maggie. You look lovely today," he told her as he sat down.

"Morning Pete," she said back, thinking he'd told her how good she looked more times in the last few days than when they were married.

"Can I grab you a coffee Maggie?" he asked, standing up again.

"Sure Pete, thanks." He started to walk away.

"Black?" he asked, turning to look at her. Maggie was a little surprised that he remembered.

"Yes, thank you," she answered, and he smiled then went to the counter. When he came back with their coffees they didn't talk for a minute. Then Maggie finally broke the ice.

"Look Pete, I know you just lost your wife and I'm so sorry… It must be really hard, but I'm not the answer to your problems." He stared at her for a moment.

"Maggie, I'm really sorry I hurt you. I wish I had made different choices all those years ago, but I can't go back. I'd just really like to make things okay between us. Maybe even find a way to be friends." He stopped and put his head down for a moment, when he looked back up she thought he might be on the verge of tears. "Maggie, I did love you once, you know that right? I am truly sorry for hurting you. I miss Lucy so much, Maggie." And his head was down again and in his hands.

"Pete, oh goodness, Pete. I don't know what to say, except I'm very sorry for your loss." She reached out her hand and touched his arm. She felt so bad for him. He looked up at her, his light brown eyes trying to pull her in. She let go of his arm and picked up her coffee. "Pete, I'm sure we can find a way to put things behind us, but I'm very happy here, away from my old life, and living with Billy." Maggie was quiet for a moment, then added. "I love Billy more than anything or anyone else I've ever loved." She couldn't help but smile a little thinking about him. Pete looked like the old Pete again. The air of arrogance and entitlement that Maggie wasn't "playing his game properly" look about him. But of course, that's not what came out of his mouth.

"I just want to be friends, Maggie, and hope you are able to forgive me for what I did to you?" She smiled considerately.

"Well, thank you Pete. I hope we can be friends too." He drank some of his coffee.

"Are you two married?" he asked her. She sat up straight, not liking the question she wished she could answer yes to.

"No, you asked me that when you called Pete," she replied, and he took another sip.

"Oh right. Engaged?" he asked. Maggie shifted awkwardly, hating that he still was able to make her feel controlled.

"Well, no, but we've been living together for a couple years now," she answered.

"Hmm," he said, "Sounds to me like a sure sign, Maggie, that this guy has no plans on tying himself down. Just enjoying the ride until he feels like moving on, is what I'd guess. A good ride too as far as I can remember." She ignored Pete's attempted segue into their intimate past. "Take it from me Maggie, it sounds like he's got someone on the side." Maggie looked up at Pete with shock. Her stomach flipped and knotted instantly. She was starting to feel angry with Billy now, having worried about the very same thing recently, herself.

"Well, we know we love each other, why do we need a piece of paper?" she answered using the very words she'd wilted with when Billy spoke them. Then rather defensively she added, "a piece of paper didn't help us any Pete." He smirked slightly, and she stood up.

"No Maggie don't go, I only smiled because I was thinking you obviously haven't lost your spunk," he said as she started to walk out. Pete followed her out of the café and out onto the street, grabbing hold of her arm. "Maggie please, I'm sorry, I didn't realize it was such a sore spot." Maggie stopped and looked at him, her eyes welling up. He was still holding her arm and she looked down at him as if to say, 'let go' and he did.

"Look Pete, I think I better go." She started down the street towards home.

"Maggie. Maggie!" he called but she kept walking. She was feeling very frustrated and angry. She hated feeling angry with Billy. *Why didn't he want to marry her?* She thought. *If it's always been me, why won't you make it official?*

When Billy got home later, Maggie was already in bed, stewing and hurting. When he asked how her day had gone, she started crying.

"Billy, why don't you want to get married?" she asked angrily.

"Mag, I told you, we don't need someone else announcing our love to know our love is real." She was out of bed now, grabbing her pillow and walking out of the room.

"Good night, Billy," she said quietly, and saw the stunned look on his face on her way down the stairs.

"Mag!" he called. By the time she was on the couch, he was walking down the hall and into the living room towards her. "Mag, what do we need an effing piece of paper for? You love me, I love you, what's the big deal?" She looked at him, so hurt, and although she was thinking a million things, she couldn't find any words to come out. They stared at each other for the longest time. Then Maggie quietly repeated,

"Good night, Billy." And laid down on the couch, pulling a blanket up over herself. She heard Billy upstairs a few minutes later, and she started crying again, which just added insult to injury, stirring up all those old wounds from so many nights with Pete, when she'd lay in bed wondering why he didn't desire her and all her thoughts of Billy and wishing she was with him. All she really wanted was for Billy to come and hold her now and tell her he'd marry her. But, instead, like countless memories with Pete, she cried herself to sleep.

When she woke up, she laid there for the longest time. Hoping when she opened her eyes, she'd be upstairs and find it was all a dream. She opened her eyes and found she was on the couch. Feeling her spirits drop slightly, she sat up and stretched. Maggie walked over to the coffee pot and saw a note. 'Mag, I'm sorry. I love you more than I could ever tell you. Love Billy. Ps. I'll be back around dinner' she smiled a little, but still felt a sting of rejection.

CHAPTER 14

Billy worked full days Tuesday, Wednesday and Thursday and Maggie was at the shop Wednesday and Thursday and back and forth from home and the farm the other days. They didn't see much of each other, and he had been called out to do some extra handyman work Wednesday and Thursday evening. Maggie was in bed both nights by the time he got home. Thursday, he snuggled up to her when he climbed into bed, but she surprised herself, and actually pretended to be asleep.

Friday, they were both home for the day. It was her birthday, and they had plans to go to the b and b with Carla and Stu. She got up and saw a vase full of daisies on her end table. Then she saw a trail of petals leading to the washroom and when she went in, "Daisy A Day" was playing quietly on her CD player. Maggie stopped in the doorway, her hand on her heart as she looked around the candle lit space with a tender smile. Hearing the song brought back so many old, happy memories. It was one of her parents' songs, and she thought of the two of them dancing in the kitchen together, looking at each other with grins, laughing as they moved each other around the room. She didn't even remember telling Billy the special meaning of the song, which made it even more special that he had picked it for her. She felt her eyes well up and her heart filled with love at the old memory and now the new one. Billy had run a bath for her and there was a message on the mirror that said, 'Happy Birthday Beautiful'. Her heart warming up a little, she slid into the warm bath and relaxed. Inhaling the oils he had thoughtfully added. Maggie let the hurt from the week wash away. She stayed in the tub for a long time, then got dressed and went downstairs. She didn't see Billy, so she got herself a coffee and was standing looking out the back door, realizing it was open. As she walked towards it, Bo started barking and she heard Billy trying to quiet him.

"Shh, Bo, quiet boy." She stepped out onto the patio and Billy was waiting with his guitar. He looked down at Bo and asked, "You ready boy?" Then he started to play and sing "Happy Birthday" to Maggie and at the end of each verse he got Bo to sing, well howl, "awooo". She grinned at the two of them. Billy sat his guitar down and smiled at her. "Happy Birthday Mag," he said, walking towards her.

"How'd you get him to do that Billy?" she asked.

"Oh, we've been practicing for a couple weeks, haven't we boy!" He bent down and gave Bo a good rub. "Had to teach Mr. Bojangles how to sing." Billy winked at Maggie. Maggie smiled again.

"Thank you for the birthday bath. And you have no idea what that song means to me Billy." She tried to say more but felt herself choking up. Billy moved closer to her, taking her coffee mug and sitting it down on the barbecue.

"You're welcome. I love you, Maggie." He held her and hugged her. She fell into his arms, and he wrapped his around her tighter.

"Happy Birthday," he whispered and then held her face and tilted it up towards his. His eyes twinkled cheekily, her legs turned to rubber, they grinned at each other, and he kissed her. Then without any warning, he bent down and scooped her up. "Come on boy," he called and when Bo ran in he carried Maggie inside and she reached out and slid the door shut. Placing her down, instantly grasping, and holding hands all the way back upstairs. Making soft eyes and smiles at each other as Billy led her into their room and laid her down on the bed. Kneeling on the floor beside her, he reached his hand up and moved her hair from her face, looking at her with love, brushing curls back and running his fingers through them, then kissing her face softly, then her lips. Looking into her eyes, and brushing his hand across her cheek, then kissing her softly again, then pressing harder, Maggie reached up and held his face in her hands. Billy climbed on top of her. They made love like it was the first time either one of them had ever smelled, tasted, touched, and experienced anything so pure and precious. Their hands like satin, on each other's bodies, looking deeply into each other's eyes, taking their time, and watching each move the other made, and following each curve they ran their hands over. Maggie felt like she was floating as his strong hands touched her with such tenderness. Their bodies moving slowly in a dance they'd never shared quite like this before. It was so warm and sweet and true; there was no doubt of their love or adoration of each other.

They stayed in each other's arms, holding and caressing one another, a beam of sunlight shining over them. Maggie didn't want to leave his arms.

"Let's just stay in bed for my birthday," she said, and he pulled her closer, kissing her head.

"Ok Mag, but aren't we having dinner with Carla and Stu?"

"Yes," Maggie replied.

"Well, do you really want Carla and Stu in bed with us?" She laughed. Billy chuckled along with her, hugging her tight. The two of them soon kissing again. Suddenly, they heard Bo barking, and looked at each other, both thinking something like *Oh shit, not Pete again* but when Billy went down, it was just to let Bo out back. Maggie jumped into the shower and had a very quick wash, waking herself again, and freshening up a bit. She and Billy didn't say a whole lot but did a lot of hugging and kissing for the next few hours. When it was time to get ready, Billy went up and showered while Maggie got dressed. She decided on one of her favourite long skirts, a jade green with black eyelet lace, and a black tank top with little frills on the tops of the sleeves. Then she grabbed her favourite emerald green sweater and looked in the mirror. "So, this is 45," she said to her reflection. "Well, so far, so good". She sat down at her vanity and opened her jewelry box, looking for a pair of earrings. Finding her long feathery silver ones Maggie put them on. Then she put her locket back on its silver chain and fastened it around her neck. She pulled half her hair up and clipped it, then went downstairs, fed Bill and Bo, and went out back to wait for Billy.

Billy came down about 10 minutes later. Bo was snuggled at Maggie's feet sleeping and looked up when he heard Billy at the back door. She looked over at him and felt warmth wash over her whole body. He looked so handsome, in his dark blue jeans and a light blue dress shirt. His eyes twinkling with love and kindness as he looked at her.

"Hello there, Handsome," she said with a smile. He walked out and stood in front of her and the dog.

"You look beautiful," he told her, holding out his hand to pull her up. Bo got up and looked at the two of them as they hugged, Maggie and Billy looked into each other's eyes and grinned.

"Mmm, you smell good Billy." He leaned down and kissed her

mouth, slowly moving them back and forth.

"You ready, Love?" he asked her.

"I'd rather stay home and take these clothes off with you Lover," she said, kissing him softly. He winked at her, his eyes crinkled with mischief.

"We'll have to wait till later for that, Beautiful." Billy kissed the end of her nose. They went inside, Bo followed close behind them, and Billy closed the back door. They gated Bo in the front hall and said goodbye to him. Billy grabbed his jean jacket, and passed Maggie hers and they walked out onto the porch. He locked the door behind them, then taking Maggie's hand and smiling at her again, they headed down the stairs. He kept sneaking glances at her as they walked to the b and b, grinning cheekily. She felt herself blush and finally asked,

"What Billy?" He shrugged and grinned a little bigger.

"Just thinking about how much I love you Mag." She smiled back at him, knowing there was more to it than that. "Oh and how much I love your succulent breasts!" he added with a cheeky smirk. Maggie laughed and stretched up to kiss his cheek and they walked along without another word.

Opening the door for her, Maggie stepped into the restaurant first, and Pat turned to see who it was, a smile spreading across her face.

"Maggie! Happy Birthday dear!" she exclaimed, walking over to her and giving her a hug.

"Thank you, Pat," Maggie replied, feeling Billy's hand on her lower back,

"Hiya Pat," he said.

"Hello Mr. Stanton," she replied, beaming at the two of them.

"Hey Mags! Happy Birthday!" Carla called out from a table in the corner, with a wave. Maggie and Billy walked over to their friends. Billy pulled a chair out for her, and she sat down smiling up at him.

"Happy Birthday Maggie," Stu said to her with a smile.

"Thanks Stu."

"So, how's your birthday been so far, Mags? Get yer paddy whacks yet?" Maggie and Billy both laughed, and Maggie shook her head at her friend.

"Oh Carla, wouldn't you just love to know." She gave her friend a little wink. Carla laughed heartily. Soon after, Pat came over with a bottle of champagne in a bucket and left it in the center of the table for them.

"Thanks Pat," Billy said before Pat left them again. Beatrice came over a few minutes later, sitting down four champagne glasses, and took their drink orders. Two beers, a ginger ale and a club soda with lemon.

"What're ya gonna order Stu?" Carla asked him once they had their menus.

"Think I'll get a steak," he grunted hungrily.

"Ya, that sounds good," Billy added. Maggie really didn't know what she felt like but finally settled on the chicken fettuccine alfredo and Carla ordered the fish and chips. The four ate and chatted away, laughing, and carrying on with each other. Every so often, Maggie and Billy would link hands under the table, and make eyes at each other, their feet gently rubbing together. When Maggie got up to use the bathroom, Carla went with her.

"So Mags, get lucky yet today?" she asked with a hopeful smirk. Maggie giggled.

"Yep!" she answered with a smile.

"Billy give you your present yet?" she added when Maggie came out of the stall to wash her hands.

"What present? He gave me a piano." Carla nodded but looked a little awkward.

"Right Mags," she added quickly, pretending to hit herself in the forehead adding, "Duh." Maggie looked at her and knew there was something she wasn't telling her, but Carla turned and headed for the door before Maggie could say anything else. When they got back to the table, they noticed Stu had moved over to sit next to Billy and the two of them were talking about cars and such. Billy looked up at Maggie with a look of love and pulled the chair out for her on his other side.

"Shall we toast to Maggie?" Stu said pointing at the bottle in the bucket. Billy took it out, dried it with his napkin and Pat came over with the corkscrew and handed it to him. He opened it with a "POP" and they all laughed as Maggie jumped a little.

"Pat, get yourself a glass," Billy said, pouring champagne into the other four glasses as it bubbled up. Pat came back with a glass and sat it down, and Billy poured some in.

"Oh, not too much!" she said, smiling at him. They raised their glasses and toasted,

"To Maggie! Happy Birthday!" Billy said, and the others repeated.

"To Maggie." They clinked their glasses together. Carla said she'd be right back and went out the front door, returning a minute later with a box, wrapped in green paper with a white bow on top.

"Here ya go Mags, from me and Stu." She handed it to Maggie with a big grin. Maggie took it, smiling at her friends.

"Aw, thanks, you guys," she said, pulling the lid off the box. She moved the tissue paper and looked in to see something that made her look up at Carla with a pink face. She grabbed it and pulled it out a few inches, not wanting to share it with the whole restaurant.

"Bit of a birthday present for you too Billy!" Stu said with a gruff laugh and a wink, his arm knocking into Billy's. It was a peach coloured, lacy, satiny, skimpy camisole with matching bra and panties.

"Carla!" Maggie laughed, dropping it back into the box.

"Like it, Mags?" she asked her, grinning.

"It's very pretty. I love it, thank you." And she felt her cheeks reddening.

"Mmm, that'll look gorgeous on you Babe!" Billy said quietly in her ear as he leaned close and kissed her cheek.

"Ha! For about five seconds eh Sweet Cheeks!?" Carla said, her and Stu chuckling.

Billy grabbed his jacket off the back of the chair and slid a long envelope out of the inside pocket.

"Here Babe, Happy Birthday," he said, smiling at Maggie with a huge grin.

"You already gave me a present Billy," she said looking at him, Stu grunting about getting lucky to Carla and Carla quieting him.

"Just open it," Billy coaxed. Maggie looked at the front. Billy had written 'Surprise Mag. One of many xo' on the outside. She carefully ripped open the envelope and found two plane tickets inside. Her eyes grew big, and she looked up at Billy, holding the envelope to her chest, surprised.

"Billy, these are tickets to Jamaica!" He chuckled.

"Yes, I know." Maggie stared at them again.

"We're going to Jamaica?" she asked, and the three of them laughed happily at Maggie's surprise.

"Yes, in less than two weeks." Maggie wrapped her arms around Billy's neck and pulled him close.

"Oh Billy, this is so exciting!" she said, holding him tight. He chuckled again and hugged her back. Then she looked up at him and gave him a big kiss.

"Alright, alright, gawd, get a room you two!" Carla joked. Maggie grinned the rest of the evening. She couldn't wipe the smile from her face if she wanted to. While they enjoyed the champagne, ate dessert, and talked about going to Jamaica, Maggie just kept on smiling, and every time the other three looked at her they couldn't help but chuckle at her shocked happiness. Billy said he couldn't wait to show her some of his old haunts and introduce her to his closest friends, the couple who owned the bar where he used to sing.

"Oh, but what about Bill and Bo?" Maggie asked suddenly, worried.

"Don't worry Mag, everything is taken care of," Billy assured her and he had another cheeky grin on his face. "Actually, that's another part of your gift," he added. She looked at him confused.

"Frankie's coming to stay at the house and pet sit for us, then he'll be there for a bit when we come home." Maggie's jaw dropped and Billy chuckled at her again.

"No!" she said. "Oh, wow, I can't believe I'm going to see my baby brother too." She hugged Billy again, thanking him about a hundred times over the rest of their evening.

The four friends left the restaurant, happily saying good night. Carla started the truck and Stu climbed into the passenger seat.

Then Carla waved and beeped the horn as they drove off.

"Good birthday Mag?" Billy asked as they started walking back home.

"Great birthday, thank you," she replied, resting her head down on his arm as usual as they walked home, arms wrapped around each other's waists.

CHAPTER 15

They had a quiet weekend together, most of it spent naked. By Monday morning, they both had perma-grins and well used muscles. Maggie and Billy had early appointments to see Dr. Trent and get their travel shots. Then Billy had to go into work. Because Carla and Maggie weren't going fishing, Maggie went home and relaxed for a bit after their needles. Then she went into town to grab some things from the grocery store. Before she got there, she saw Pete heading towards her.

"Happy Belated Birthday Maggie!" he said, smiling at her.

"Thanks Pete," she replied, and he leaned down to give her a kiss, she turned her face slightly making sure he got her cheek.

"What are you up to this morning?" he asked her.

"Just grabbing some groceries," she answered. He smiled at her.

"Can I buy you breakfast?" he asked, and she opened her mouth to say no and he added,

"You know, for your birthday." Maggie thought for a second, her stomach giving a little grumble, then answered,

"Ya, okay, sure, that would be nice, thanks Pete." The two made their way into the b and b.

"Morning Maggie dear," Pat called out happily. "Mr. Baker," she added politely as the two sat down at a table together. "What can I get you?" Pat asked.

"Coffees to start please Pat," Maggie said smiling. Jane, Beatrices' younger sister, came over with the coffee. She seemed a bit nervous and a little clumsy, and Maggie smiled at her reassuringly.

"Thanks Jane, could we please have some water too?" Jane smiled at her, and nodded. Maggie had just had a sip of coffee, Pete was adding his cream and sugar, and then... Jane was back with the waters, tripping on the leg of Pete's chair and spilling the water all down the front of Maggie.

"OOOH!" Maggie yelled jumping up. The water was quite cold and was a bit of a shock.

"Oh, Maggie, I'm so sorry!" Jane was almost in tears. Maggie laughed a little and reached out her hand to touch Jane.

"It's okay Jane, it's just water." But Jane already had tears streaming down her face.

"Oh, but Maggie, your shirt," she said pointing at Maggie's chest. Maggie's pale mauve T-shirt was now very see-through. Pat was walking over with towels.

"Jane, what on earth, child?" Maggie grinned again.

"Pat, it's okay," she said. Pete was shaking his head, but Maggie gave him a little kick under the table making sure he didn't say anything that might really upset the poor girl.

"Here Maggie," Pete said, standing up with a disgruntled look on his face and reaching into his pocket. He handed her his room key. "Why don't you grab one of my shirts. Room 3." Maggie took the key and thanked him, then came back and gave him a look, bending down and whispering in his ear, she said,

"Don't be a jerk to her Pete." He shrugged like he was saying "as if" and she went up to his room to find a shirt. Maggie found a T-shirt and quickly changed into it. She held hers in her hand, and opened the door to go out, the door across the hall opened and at the same time, out walked Pauline, grinning at Maggie.

"Well now, you do seem to get all the good one's don't'cha darling? That strapping man of yours isn't enough for you eh!?" She waved her pointer finger at Maggie and made a clicking sound with her tongue. "And people say I'm friendly," she added and sauntered down the hall, down the stairs and right out the front door. Maggie stood still, feeling her blood pressure rising.

"Great!" she said out loud going back down and joining Pete at the table again.

"This okay?" she asked, and he nodded with a smile.

"Sure thing, Maggie." Pat came back over and took their orders.

"Sorry about Jane, Maggie." Maggie waved her hand and replied,

"Oh Pat, don't worry about it. Please let Jane know it's no big deal." Pat grinned and walked to the kitchen. Pete proceeded to talk about Pete over breakfast. Maggie nodded and smiled as they ate. She thanked him and said goodbye to Pat and Jane. Pete walked along with Maggie, then she turned to say goodbye and go into the grocery store, and he opened the door for her and followed her in. Still talking about all the places he and Lucy had been, and the sights they'd seen. Going on about not being sure if he'd sell the house and get a little place somewhere warm. Maggie walked along with the cart, shopping, and nodding. Then he started reminiscing, and they shared a few laughs and old family memories as they walked the isles. It was nice to go back in time to their families and the farms and times gone by. After a bit, Pete was becoming a little too friendly for Maggie's liking, with his arm draped over her shoulders every so often, leaning against her as they walked the aisles. She realized it probably felt natural to him, as they had grown up together, and whether their marriage had been good or bad, they had a familiarity with one another, but she tried to keep to herself as much as possible. When she paid, he took some of the bags for her and offered to help her home.

"It's no problem, Maggie," he insisted, so they headed back to her house, Pete now asking Maggie about what she'd got up to in the last few years. She actually preferred not talking about herself with him, so asked him another question that led him down another rabbit hole of Pete's adventures with Pete. He carried the groceries right into the kitchen for her, then she walked him back to the front hallway.

"Thanks a lot for breakfast Pete. It's been nice catching up," she said with a smile, hoping to be rid of him.

"Yes, it's been great seeing you, Maggie. Say, I'm probably only staying for a few more days. Maybe we could have dinner before I head off." Maggie nodded, feeling relieved that he was leaving.

"Sure Pete," she replied, and he went to give her a hug. "Oh, just a second," she added, looking down at the shirt she had on. She ran upstairs to change out of his top, and as she pulled it off and took her wet bra off too, she turned to grab another shirt just as Pete walked into the room.

"Pete!" she yelled in surprise and irritation. Pete looked around the room then back at Maggie.

"Sorry Maggie, didn't mean to startle you. Really nice place you've got. You've done well for yourself." Maggie stood there, holding her shirt against her body, staring at him in disbelief.

"Do you mind?" she asked. Pete smiled and waved her comment off.

"Oh Maggie, it's nothing I haven't already seen! Still gorgeous by the way!" Maggie walked towards him and pushed him out of the room ahead of her and down the hall towards the stairs. The front door closed and she heard Billy say hello to Old Bill. Pulling her own shirt over her head, they made their way back downstairs.

"Hey Babe!" Billy called out. Maggie and Pete continued down, and she finished pulling on her T-shirt.

As Maggie stepped off onto the floor she looked up at Billy who was looking behind her at Pete, then back at her with hurt, and anger in his eyes.

"Hey, you're home early," she said, smiling at him, handing Pete his shirt back.

"Thanks for a wet, reminiscent morning, Maggie. It was fun reliving some old times together. And wow, you're still a hottie Maggie. See you for dinner," he said grinning, and leaned close to her, his hand holding her close, Maggie not quite quick enough to turn her head this time as he planted a kiss on her lips. She felt like punching him. He just grinned at her as he let her go. Billy was staring at Maggie with a look she'd never seen on his face before.

"Bye," Pete said as she pushed him out, walking past Billy to close the door. Maggie walked over to Billy to give him a kiss, and he glared at her.

"What the hell Mag?" he asked. She stepped back, not used to Billy being angry with her, well, with anyone really.

"I had to borrow one of his shirts because Jane spilled water on mine," she answered, looking concerned with his obvious annoyance with her. "Billy, it was nothing." He walked down the hallway and dropped his things off on the island. Then came back, passed her, and went upstairs.

"Taking a shower," he called, and she heard the bathroom door close, a little harder than usual.

Maggie went and sat in the window seat with Bill, patting him absentmindedly, Bo now on the floor at her feet, feeling sick to her stomach. She wasn't sure how long she sat there, but it seemed longer than he usually took to shower. When he came down, she tried to talk to him, but he pulled his boots on, grabbed his leather jacket and opened the front door.

"Going for a ride." And out he went, closing the door behind him. Maggie fell back against the door, her heart thumping in her throat. *What just happened,* she thought. *Everything's gone wrong.* She heard his bike skid down the road and could hear "She Sells Sanctuary" blasting. Walking to the kitchen, she fed Bill and Bo, then picked up the phone and called Carla. There was no answer. She went and sat in her chair on the patio. Tears now rolling down her cheeks. "Shit Maggie," she said to herself. She sat out back, just staring at nothing for the longest time. Bo coming and going, sitting at her feet, then sniffing around the yard again. She was starting to get cold and went back in, realizing she'd been out there for hours. Maggie didn't know what to do with herself. She wished Billy had let her explain. She wished Pete had never come. She awoke to the sound of the front door, the TV still on, sitting up in the big chair in the corner.

"Billy?" she called and saw the clock on the wall read two something. He came into the kitchen and looked over at her. "Billy?" she said again and got up and started walking towards him.

"Mag, I don't want to talk about this right now." She reached out to put her hands on his chest and he held them, slowly lowering them and looking at her. She'd never seen his eyes like that before, almost grey with...defeat.

"Billy, please," she begged, starting to cry.

"Look Mag, I don't want to play games alright. If you and Pete have some old flame still burning that you want to explore, I'll step back." He turned to walk away.

"Billy!" Maggie cried. "There's nothing between me and Pete." He stopped for a moment, then walked away.

"Goodnight Mag," he said, leaving Maggie standing there breaking.

He was gone when she got up. Maggie decided not to go into the shop. She had spent most of the night crying. When he came home that evening, he seemed angrier than the day before.

"Billy, can we please talk about this?" she asked pleadingly. Billy turned to look at her. He looked so angry.

"Maggie, you were seen coming out of Pete's room, then you brought him back here!" he said, and he looked like he'd been crying too. She ran over to him and wrapped her arms around him.

"Billy, I was in his room alone to get a dry shirt." Billy wouldn't even look at her.

"That's not what I was told. You two were seen cuddled up nice and cozy while you shopped together too. And, I had a chat with Pete. He told me you didn't think we'd make it Mag. That you couldn't be with someone who didn't want to marry you. He said he was glad to be able to comfort you like old times." Maggie was shocked. "Why was he upstairs with you? Changing in front of him is okay to you? Did you sleep with him, Maggie?" He turned his back as he asked the question. Maggie's mouth fell open in disbelief. Feeling her heart fracturing at his words.

"Billy no, of course not. I have no desire to sleep with anyone but you. And, that's bullshit! I never said anything like that. And oh my God, we were not cuddling!" Billy was already walking away.

"I'm going to stay at Pats for a bit, Mag. I just need some time to think, and let you and Pete work things out." Billy went upstairs and came down five minutes later with a packed bag. He bent down and gave Bo a rub, kissed Maggie's forehead, looking at her with such hurt, mouthed I love you, then he left.

"Billy!" Maggie yelled, tears streaming down her face. "Billy!" she said again but she knew he was already out the front gate. She dropped to the floor and sobbed. This couldn't be happening. The phone rang, but she couldn't get up. She could hardly breathe. Bo was nudging her, whimpering, but she just kept crying. Time sped up and slowed down all at once. She couldn't stop sobbing and had no idea how long she was on the floor. Then there was a frantic knock at the door.

"Mags! Mags!" she heard Carla but didn't answer. "I'm coming in, Mags!" The door opened. Carla saw her on the floor, closed the door, and dropped down beside Maggie, wrapping her arms around her. "Mags, what's happened?" she asked, holding her. Maggie couldn't even speak, she felt so drained, so empty. "Mags, Pat said Billy checked back in? She said he and Pete were yelling at each other about you and Pete getting back together? What's going on?" Maggie just shook her head. "Okay Mags let's get you up." Carla picked her up and walked her to the living room, sitting her down on the couch and bending down in front of her. "Mags, talk to me," she pleaded. Maggie was almost hyperventilating. Carla jumped up and went to the kitchen. Cupboard doors opening and closing frantically. "Geeze, haven't you two got any hard liquor?" she complained going through the cupboards. "Aha!" she yelled and came over with a glass and a bottle of rum someone had given Billy for their birthday party. "Here Mags." Maggie took it and drank it. It only took a few minutes for her breathing to calm down, and the sobbing to subside. Then she looked up at Carla and started to cry again, falling into her arms. After another shot, Maggie was able to tell Carla all the goings on, Carla sitting gobsmacked as she listened. "Well, what in the effn' hell Mags! Billy needs to hear this!" she said, pissed right off.

"He won't listen, Carla. I don't think I can bear losing him again." Maggie started to cry.

"Okay, Mags, Okay. We'll fix this, don't worry." Carla stayed with Maggie until she fell asleep, then headed back home.

CHAPTER 16

Billy met Carla out front of the b and b a couple days after she'd found Maggie on the floor.

"Billy, I don't think you should go!" Carla told him, taking the bags he handed her to put in the back of the truck. "Maggie doesn't want Pete. She wants you." Billy didn't say anything, pulling his helmet on and doing up his leather jacket.

"I think it will be better if I just go Carla." And he walked over and climbed onto the bike. Carla stared at him for a few seconds, then hopped into the truck and they drove to the farm. Billy parked the bike in her shed, then helped her in with his few things and his helmet that he was leaving behind. "I'll wait outside for the taxi Carla, thanks again." Carla looked at him, a pained expression on her face.

"She loves you more than life ya know?" He tried to smile, then turned his face away.

"I love her too," he said, his voice cracking slightly. Carla walked closer and gave him a hug. At first, he just stood there, then leaned in and hugged her back. "You'll watch out for her for me, eh Carla?" and he attempted a grin.

"You got it Sweet Cheeks." They heard a "beep beep" and saw the cab pull up. "See ya Billy," she said. Billy picked up his suitcase, backpack, and guitar, and without turning back, he waved as he walked away.

It was a long ride to the airport, and Billy stared out the

window in a hazy kind of numbness the whole way. Time seemed to stand still and fly by in the blink of an eye. Billy's thoughts fading in and out of reality. His mind replayed conversations with Pete, and Maggie. A few Tamarack locals had had lots to say about seeing Maggie and Pete together and he felt himself growing more angry and hurt. He was brought back to awareness with "Dancing In The Dark" playing on the radio, and he felt himself wilting, trying to zone out as much as he could. Before he knew it they were outside the airport stopping at the drop off. He paid the driver, thanked him, and grabbed his things. Feeling like he was just an empty translucent orb floating along, unseen, as he made his way through the airport. Able to swap his flight to one a week earlier than his and Maggie's original flights, Billy would soon be on a plane, alone. He walked over to the gatehouse. *What am I doing? What the hell am I doing!? How has it all gone so horribly wrong?* Were the thoughts popping into his head. He sat down, his elbows resting on his knees, holding his face in his hands. His heart was aching and trying to pull him back towards Maggie, but his head and his ego were telling him to go to Jamaica. He could hear music coming from the headphones of someone a couple of seats away from him. They were listening to "By Your Side" and it was making Billy's heart ache even more. *Of course, an eighties song to tug a little harder on my heartstrings!* He took a deep breath. *Maybe a break would be good? Maybe giving her space is what she needs?* He rubbed his forehead with both hands. *Maybe I'm being stupid* he thought, rubbing his forehead harder.

"Flight 404 to Montego International Airport, now boarding," was announced. Billy stayed put. *What are you gonna do?* He thought to himself, sitting there for another minute; his whole being pulling him in opposite directions. His ego winning the tug of war with his heart. Billy grabbed his bags and guitar and gave the woman at the boarding gate his ticket. She smiled and handed it back.

"Have a good flight Mr. Stanton," she said as he took it in his hand and started down the jetway towards the plane. Sitting down in his window seat, he couldn't help but hope Maggie would use her ticket and come in a week.

***

The next few days were like a foggy nightmare for Maggie. She dragged herself from bed to the washroom, fed animals, sat like a lump staring into nothingness, then back to bed again. By day four she spent the whole day sitting on the couch, except to use the washroom and let Bo out. She had the TV on the music station, and if she'd had any tears left to cry, she'd still be crying as she listened, lost in "Cedar Lane", "Everybody Hurts", and "Power Of Love" laying on the couch in her fog. Day five Carla stopped by and said she'd met with Billy before he left.

"He wanted me to give you this Mags." Carla said, handing her an envelope. It was the one from her birthday, with just one ticket in it now. "He's gone to Jamaica on his own Mags. Thinks you don't want him. Thinks you want to be with Pete." Maggie felt her heart breaking some more.

"Carla, what am I going to do?" Carla put her arm around her and rubbed her back.

"Well, I'll tell you one thing you're going to do Mags, take an effn' shower! Girl you are ripe!" And Maggie actually managed a giggle. So, she went up and took a shower. A long shower, and it felt so good bringing herself back down to Earth. She still felt like she was in a nightmare, but the water washing over her snapped her out of it a little, renewing some of her sanity. Carla was waiting downstairs and had made coffee.

"Thanks Carla," Maggie said, getting herself a mug full and sitting with her at the island. Carla stayed and made dinner for the two of them. Scrambling some eggs and making toast as she talked about things on the farm, in an attempt to take Maggie's mind off of things. Maggie just picked at her food, not feeling hungry, but it was nice to have company.

After Carla left, Maggie walked over to the piano and opened it. She felt a wave of sadness creeping up again at the thought of Billy but shook it off and placed her fingers on the keys. Her body instantly becoming part of the piano as she started to play "What Is This Love", singing and crying. Her fingers running up and down the keys, tears dropping down into her lap and onto her hands. She still felt like hell, but playing the piano always made her feel better. It helped her release a lot of pain. She went out back with Bo and enjoyed some fresh air, then ended up eating a little of her dinner before going to bed instead of crashing on the couch. She had both Bill and Bo in bed with her now. She'd just not been bothering with the gates, and they found their way up to her on the first night she was alone. The three of them snuggled up together and fell asleep.

The next day, Maggie woke up, and rolled over to wrap her arm around Billy, forgetting he was gone. She lay there staring at his pillow for a moment and felt like staying in bed and crying. Instead, she got up and had a shower right away, hoping to clear a little more of the fog. Carla stopped by again, dropping off mail and checking in with her.

"So, Pete's gone now Mags. Left yesterday." Maggie was glad to hear it, but it didn't bring Billy back. "Mags, I think you should go to Jamaica!" Carla told her before leaving.

"What, why?" Maggie asked her with some annoyance.

"Well, whether you and Billy work things out or not, a couple weeks away, somewhere sunny and warm on a beach would do you good. It was *your* birthday present Mags." Maggie shook her head.

"No, I don't think so Carla." Carla shrugged. Then Bo started barking and ran to the front door. Maggie went to see why, hoping it was Billy. Carla followed, and when Maggie opened the door, Frankie was standing there with a big smile on his face.

"Magster!" he said, beaming and wrapped his arms around her with a big hug. Maggie hugged him back, smiling so big as her cup filled up.

"Frankie!" she said happily. "Come in come in," she told him and they stood looking at each other. "This is my friend Carla," she said. Carla smiled and held out her hand to shake his.

"Hullo there Frankie, nice to meet ya!" she said with a smirk. "Look Mags, I gotta get going, I'll call ya later." She waved and walked out the door, pulling it closed behind her. Standing there grinning at her, his wavy honey brown hair all tousled just right, wearing a creamy cotton T-shirt and slim fit jeans, with a long dark multi coloured scarf around his neck and a dark grey Gatsby on his head.

"Wow, you look so great Frankie!" Maggie said, grinning at him.

"Maggie, what's wrong?" he asked, taking her hand, and making her look right at him.

"Nothing, you're here, and I'm so glad!" But as they walked into the kitchen, he stopped her again.

"Maggie, it's me... Frankie. You can't lie to *me* sis!" and she felt her eyes well up. They sat down at the dining room table together and she told him all about the last few weeks, he listened intently, then when she finished, he said. "Pete! What an idiot he is!" shaking his head angrily. "Maggie, you *have* to go to Jamaica!" he told her, holding her arms and looking right into her eyes.

"But now you're here Frankie, we can visit." He shook his head at her and held her arms tighter.

"Listen to me sis, you have to go find Billy." Maggie gave him a funny look, narrowing her eyes at him.

"Why Frankie, Billy won't listen to me. He's gone." He stood them up, gave her a big hug then looked at her seriously again.

"Magster, we've never lied to one another, we've always had each other's backs, I need you to trust me. You just *have* to go Maggie, you just have to!" His eyes seemed to be pleading with her.

"What aren't you telling me Frankie?" she asked, feeling a little frustrated now.

"You just have to trust me, Magster," he said again and gave her another hug. "Come on," he said, taking her hand and walking them back to the front hall. "Your place is absolutely gorgeous by the way," he said admiringly, looking around with a big smile. "Way to go big sis!" Maggie smiled at him. He opened the front door and picked up his duffle bag and Maggie grabbed his backpack. Frankie led the way upstairs. "So, where's my room?" he asked, giving her a mischievous grin. Maggie nodded her head to the right. He looked towards Maggie's room, then turned right at the top of the stairs and walked down the hall at the opposite end.

He dropped his bags off in the spare room, Maggie following closely, then pushed her back out into the hall. "Now, you!" he said as he coaxed her down the hallway, past the washroom, to her room. "Let's get you packed. You're leaving in 2 days!" She tried to argue with him, but he was packing things she didn't want, so she had to butt in and pack properly. After they got her packed, they went back down, and he asked her everything he needed to know about the house and the pets. Writing down numbers of people and where they lived, finding out where things were in town and such. They stayed up late, eating, laughing, crying and catching up. She loved seeing him again and hadn't realized just how much she'd missed him. He told her all about the different countries he'd been to, and all the interesting people he'd met, and all the weird food he'd tried. Maggie complimented him on his hat with a grin and he told her it was from his trip to England a few years back and how he had quite a collection now. Maggie had inadvertently started a tradition when she brought him back his first hat from her mountain vacation cabin trip where she met Billy. He always bought a hat in every new country he visited. Talking long into the night, they finally headed to bed around 2:30.

Maggie and Frankie enjoyed the next day together. Although Maggie was still so heartbroken, having her favourite little brother with her was filling her with joy again. She took him around Tamarack, showed him her bookshop, proudly introduced him to Pat when they went into the b and b for lunch, then enjoyed the afternoon talking more about Frankie's travels. Carla stopped by later that evening to make sure Maggie was still going to Jamaica, and to let her know what time she'd pick her up the next day.

"You all packed Mags?" she asked her, the two of them at the front door, while Carla pulled her coat on.

"Yes. All packed. But…" Carla cut her off.

"Say Mags, just gonna run up and use the bathroom before I head home." And she ran up the stairs. Maggie went back to the kitchen and saw Frankie was out back with Bo, playing fetch with a stick as big as the pup. She was just thinking Carla was taking a while when she heard her call out.

"See ya tomorrow Mags." And the front door closed.

The next day, Maggie was feeling like backing out again. She heard voices downstairs and grabbed her housecoat and went down to see who it was. Carla and Frankie were in the kitchen drinking coffee and chatting.

"Morning sunshine!" Carla said happily. "Let's get you ready to go!" Maggie shook her head at her.

"No, I'm not going to go you guys."

"Mags, we need to head out soon, it's starting to rain, and they say it might turn to freezing rain later on." Maggie put her hands in the air and added,

"All the more reason for us not to drive in it then Carla." Carla gave her a look.

"Mags, that old bugger of a truck and I have driven through worse than some November rain. Get a move on, would'ya." Frankie jumped off the stool, poured her a coffee, then walked straight for her, handed it to her, turned her around and marched her to the stairs.

"Magster, go shit, shower and shave and get that cute fine ass of yours back down here so Carla can take you to the airport, kay." As she turned back to look at him, he nodded at her and gave his best Frankie pleading face with his big grin and batting his long eyelashes at her. She laughed and went up to get ready. After her shower, she came back into her room and sat down on the bed for a while, feeling empty and lacking any motivation to go off on her own. She didn't want this to be a trip alone. Feeling defeated, but knowing she wouldn't get away with staying put, she dressed, pulled her hair back and braided it, and then catching a glimpse of herself in her vanity, she sat down in front of it and looked at her reflection. Her eyes still showed signs of all the tears she had shed. Then she noticed a glint of silver and she looked up at her locket, hanging on the edge of the mirror. She picked it up and put it on, holding her hand to her heart and taking a deep breath in.

"Okay Maggie, off you go. Go find your Billy," she said to herself, and grabbed her things.

She came back down, plunked her two suitcases and her carry-on at the door, and grabbed her small wrap-around purse and threw it over her shoulder.

"Now, here's a coffee for the road sis, and a kiss." Frankie kissed her cheek and gave her a big hug.

"Frankie, there's close to $200 in the cookie jar in the kitchen, for whatever you need okay. And I'll call and let you know when I get there. You sure you'll be okay?" she asked, and he laughed.

"Magster, quit stalling." She smiled at him.

"Okay, just one more thing." She walked over to Bill and picked him up, giving him a hug and some kisses on his head. Then she knelt down to Bo and loved him up too.

"You three have fun," she said, giving Frankie another hug before he pushed her out the door with her carry-on, Carla loading her suitcases into the truck.

"Ticket? Passport? Credit card?" he asked, and she nodded.

"Bye Frankie. Thank you," she said, and he smiled.

"Bye big sis. Love you." He gave her another little push and closed the door.

"You coming Mags!?" Carla hollered from the truck, and with another feeling of chickening out, she walked over reluctantly, and climbed in.

"Carla, I really don't know about this!" Maggie was saying anxiously, about five minutes out of town.

"Mags, go and enjoy your two weeks on the beach. Relax, get tanned, drink champagne," she said, smiling at her. Maggie looked out the window, thinking about how different this month had been 27 years ago. It was almost the same date as when she and her friends headed to the cabin, so many years ago. They had been so excited. Oh, how she wished she could go back to that week. It had been one of the best times of her life. Except for the last few weeks, all her time with Billy had been wonderful. As she stared at the trees flashing by and the rain starting to hit the window, she noticed the tears falling down her cheeks. God, I miss you Billy she thought to herself, feeling her heart tugging, and somehow feeling Billy's embrace.

They arrived about an hour before Maggie's flight. Carla helped her check her bags, then stayed with her to make sure she got on the plane, more importantly, to make sure she was okay. The time seemed to drag on and Maggie kept having the urge to run away. She was glad Carla was with her. They made their way to the gatehouse, with the coffee Carla had grabbed them, and they sat sipping quietly as they waited. It was another fifteen minutes before they announced Maggie's flight.

"Let me know when you get there, Mags," Carla said as the two of them hugged.

"Check in with Frankie for me Carla?" Maggie asked and Carla nodded.

"You betcha! Safe flight Mags," Carla told her, and she watched Maggie walk to the plane. She waited until the plane pulled away, then bee lined it to a phone, calling one of the numbers Billy had given her months ago, at the place where he used to play his guitar. It rang and rang and she was just going to hang up when she heard,

"Yello."

"Hiya, ya, is there a Billy Stanton there?" she asked eagerly.

"Billay, no, him not inna right now love, I can take a message for him though." Carla wasn't sure what she should say. She wasn't even quite sure what the man had said.

"Um, okay, can you just tell him Maggie's coming?" The man was quiet for a moment, then spoke again.

"Right, Maggay is coming." Carla nodded as she responded,

"Yes. That's very important." She hung up and made her way out of the airport and back home.

CHAPTER 17

aggie had a very long flight ahead of her. At least 12 hours, if all went well. She hadn't been on a plane since the cabin, and that had only been a few hours and with six friends, so she was feeling very nervous, wishing she hadn't decided to go. *Where do I go when I get there?* She wondered. There was a confirmation receipt for a hotel in the envelope with her plane ticket, called Coral's Cozy Cottages, booked for the next afternoon, but she wasn't sure if she'd go there, and wondered if Billy had checked in. She put her headphones on and listened to Blue Rodeo, closing her eyes, and pretending she wasn't thousands of miles in the air.

***

"Billay!" The man at the bar called out. He was thin and tall, had his long dreads pulled up into a half bun, at the back of his head, and had one of the biggest friendliest smiles, which he was producing now as he called out to his friend. Billy was sitting over in a dark corner, playing his guitar, singing quietly to himself, "Long As I Can See The Light" and nursing a drink. He looked up but didn't answer. "Billay!" the man repeated.

"What is it, Del?" he called back.

"Bowy, that Maggay of yours, she's coming for yuh!" Billy sat his rum and ginger down.

"What are you on about Delroy?" Billy asked gruffly. The man laughed a hardy laugh right from his gut.

"Yo, she's coming. Your Goddess, she's on'er way!" Billy picked his drink back up and finished it, then walked over to the bar.

"Why are you saying that Del?" and the man laughed at him again.

"Cuz, thats what some lady called tuh say! She's on'er way Billay bowy." He reached out and gave Billy a pat on the shoulder. "Looks like you're inna for a good time after all my bredren."

***

Maggie woke up to an announcement that there was only about an hour left for their flight. She was stiff and sore from sleeping curled up in her seat and glad to hear she'd be able to stretch her legs soon. They were going to be landing in Montego Bay's Sangster International Airport at 1:40 pm. She stretched as much as possible in her spot, then looked out over the water. It was so blue and clear.

After getting her bags, she hailed a cab and gave the driver the address to the hotel. She figured she'd at least go and see if Billy had checked in, and if he hadn't, *she* might as well. The drive from the airport to the hotel took about an hour and a half, and when Maggie arrived and was greeted by the bellhop, and made her way to the front desk, she was tired and very hopeful she could go straight to her room.

"Reservation for Stanton," she told the woman at the computer. The woman smiled and typed something, looking at the screen.

"Yes, Madam, your room is ready for yuh." She smiled at

Maggie and gave her the key.

"Excuse me," Maggie said. "Did Mr. Stanton check in yet?" The woman looked back at the computer screen, still smiling, she looked back at Maggie.

"No, Miss, Mr. Stanton has not arrived yet." Maggie felt a mix between disappointment and relief.

"Okay, thank you," she said and picked up her carryon bag, the bellboy leading the way with her suitcases. He took them back outside and along a boardwalk leading through dense green leaves, and beautifully vibrant coloured flowers sprinkled throughout.

"Only about a five-minute walk from the main beach house Miss," he told her as she followed him, looking around in awe at the mix of aquamarine water, white sand, huge twisty trees, and green mountains. They passed a few other villas, colourfully painted, all about twenty feet apart from each other, with lots of trees and vegetation between them. Then he turned and led her up to one painted bright yellow and turquoise, with a darker yellow sun painted on the front.

"This is the Sunshine Villa," he said, holding out his hand for her key, taking it and opening the door for her. Maggie walked in and couldn't help but scan the space in awe. It was lovely. An open concept, huge windows, an open staircase and landing above, and she could see a complete windowed wall at the back with a private pool beyond its sliding doors. "If there is anything you need Miss, just dial 1," he told her, and put her key down on the kitchen counter by the phone.

"Thank you," Maggie replied with a smile, and he bowed a little and left. She spent the next half hour wandering about the villa and taking it all in, feeling happier about coming now. *This place is so beautiful.* She thought, taking her things upstairs and starting to unpack. As she got to the bottom of her suitcase, she found the birthday present from Carla and Stu. "Oh, very funny Carla!" she laughed to herself, feeling a little sad Billy wouldn't get to enjoy it. She went into the washroom and was instantly in love. In one corner was a huge standing full glass shower. Along one wall was a beautiful double sink vanity, toilet of course and against the back wall, there was a big soaker tub, big enough for three, built into a platform with a few steps leading up to it, overlooking the most beautiful view of the beach and the mountains. She was torn between having a bath and gazing at the view or going for a swim in her private pool. Deciding on a swim, Maggie stripped down to nothing, grabbed a towel and headed downstairs and out to the private patio. She dropped her towel and dove in. The cool water an elixir of blissful serenity as she broke through the surface with a splash. The sun shining, the air hot with a lovely breeze and the water just cool enough to awaken her stiff muscles. After a bit of a swim Maggie placed her hands on the deck and pulled herself out. Then laid on her towel on a lounge chair in the sun for ages, drying off. When she went back inside, she dialed the main building.

"Yes, how can I help yuh?" came a friendly voice.

"Oh, hi, I was just wondering what I do for meals?" she heard the woman typing on the keyboard.

"Your inna the Sunshine Villa, yuh have the all-inclusive package miss, so yuh can come down to the dining room for meals or yuh can have full room service." Maggie felt like a queen.

"Ok, thank you so much," she replied, then hung up the phone. She picked it back up and dialed home. Frankie didn't answer so she left him a message letting him know she had arrived safely and left the name and number of the hotel. Then she called Carla, not getting an answer there either, and left a similar message. Maggie went upstairs and got dressed, then headed to the main building. She found some information on mealtimes, and some recommended tourist attractions, then went through to the dining room for dinner. The room was like a huge patio, overlooking the water, with a bar to one side, and many tables scattered around. There was quiet reggae music playing in the background, and a few couples were sitting together, eating. A family of six at another table chatting and laughing together happily. Maggie found a small table away from the others and sat down looking out at the view. A waiter came over immediately and took her drink order. He soon brought back a club soda with a little umbrella and a lime wedge. She enjoyed her curried chicken, then had some mango ice cream before heading back to her villa, where she was soon climbing into bed and falling asleep.

***

"What should I do?" Billy asked his friend, as he sat deflated and broken at the bar. He looked and felt horrible. Scruffy, rum and tequila pickled and feeling lost. Putting his head in his hands on the bar, Billy spoke again, lifting his face up slowly. "I've hurt her, Alvi. I had no right hurting her." Billy shook his head frustrated with himself. "I can't believe I left her. Damnit, how could I leave her? How do I fix this?" Billy slammed his hand down on the bar looking back up at the woman pleadingly. Alvita looked at him with compassion. She was very beautiful and almost as tall as her husband. She also had long dreads, but hers were hanging down her back, loosely pulled together with a red elastic. Alvita and Delroy were the couple who owned the bar he was sitting in, and this had been where he used to play his guitar when he lived there. They were very good friends to Billy. Like the family he never had.

"Oh, Billay, yuh have to do what yuh heart tell'n yuh," she told him with a smile, patting his hand from across the bar.

"Another shot Del," he called to his friend.

"Come'n right up," Delroy replied, filling it halfway with tequila and sliding the shot glass back towards Billy. Billy grabbed it, threw his head back and finished it, then hit it on the bar.

"Once more Del," he said. Alvita patted his hand again.

"I know one ting my bredren, this isn't the answer." And she walked off.

***

When Maggie got up the sun was shining in through every window. She called for coffee and decided to do some yoga while she waited. She hadn't practiced for a while and within minutes she was feeling less tense and a little more peaceful. When room service arrived, she took her coffee up to the bedroom balcony to enjoy it. Then she went for a swim, got dressed and headed out to the main street to have a wander around the shops. It was fairly busy, and everyone she passed smiled happily. Many people approached her trying to sell her things. She smiled and laughed and continued walking, graciously declining. Music was playing everywhere, and she found it hard to feel sad. The energy was just so laid back and friendly. She went into a few different shops that sold typical touristy things, bought herself a few colourful dresses, a pretty bright coral bikini, a disposable camera and some knick knacks to take back to Carla and Frankie. Then she walked along the beach for a while, stopping to grab some lunch at a little hut. She took a few random pictures here and there, ate some kind of fish she never heard of, but really enjoyed, then made her way back down the beach to her villa.

Maggie hadn't been back long when the phone rang. It was Carla.

"Hey Mags, how's things?" she asked in her usual happy go lucky way.

"Actually, it's really nice here Carla," she answered, smiling as she looked around her getaway for the next twelve days.

"Yer not sitting and moping, are ya Mags?" she asked with an air of motherliness. Maggie laughed.

"No, not really. It's hard to mope here. It's so beautiful and warm and colourful and full of music Carla."

"Yer not thinking of moving on me are ya Mags?" she asked, laughing, and hoping the answer was no.

"Course not. But I'll definitely come back." They didn't talk long, as the charges were pretty steep, but Carla said everything at the farm was fine and that she'd checked in with Frankie earlier and everything was fine there too.

"He said to say have fun and he loves ya Mags," she told her before they said their goodbyes and hung up. Maggie went for a swim, then she changed into one of her new dresses. It was turquoise with a white and sandy coloured shell print. It had wide straps, and the skirt came just above her knees. She put her hair up in a clip, it was still quite warm for what she was used to in the evenings and wanted her hair off her shoulders. Then she made her way to the main building. There was music playing, and as she entered the dining room, she saw there was actually a band at the open end of the patio, playing steel drums, guitars and singing. A few people were up dancing, others were enjoying their dinner at their tables. It was lovely, but Maggie suddenly felt very out of place and didn't really want to sit amongst the couples tonight. She walked back out and decided to stroll the beach walking in the opposite direction to what she had gone before and found that end of the beach to be much quieter. There were a few people spread out, and some people smiled and greeted her happily along the way. Eventually she came to what looked like an old cottage, on the end of the beach, and nestled up in the trees with a boardwalk from the beach meeting a tall staircase that took you up to its front patio, was another small house. There was a long dock at that end of the beach and a decent sized houseboat was docked at the end of it. Written in dark green, along the side of the boat was the name 'Emerald Pearl'. She could hear music playing in the boat. It sounded like someone playing a guitar which of course made her miss Billy more than she already was. She stood and watched the sun starting to set for a short time then looked at her watch; it was 6:30, so she decided to head back to her villa. She had a long bath, singing "Listen To Your Heart" softly as she relaxed, then just laid in her towel on the bed for the longest time.

She'd ordered dinner when she first climbed out of the tub, and heard a knock now, and went down to answer it, still in her towel.

"Room service," a voice said.

"Just a moment," she replied and opened the door to see a happy looking woman with a big beautiful flower in her hair and wearing a brightly multi coloured dress. The woman pushed a cart over to the dining area and set things up for Maggie. Maggie thanked her and she left smiling. She sat down and enjoyed rice and peas, callaloo and finished it off with sweet potato pudding. It was all so delicious. She washed it down with a drink called Ting that tasted like bubbly grapefruit.

Maggie sat on the balcony until pretty late, listening to the steel drums and the chatter and laughter at the main house. The waves washing up onto the beach were relaxing and she stared up into the sky thinking about how much she wished she was sitting next to Billy.

***

"Wah gwaan!" Del called as Billy came in. "Bring them trays Billay," Delroy called out, pointing to a spot in the corner. It was early in the morning and Billy had just walked into the bar looking like an old raggedy blanket.

"Sure thing," he called back and saw a stack of them on the table. He picked them up and put them down on the bar in front of Del.

"So, feel'n rough by the looks my bredren?" he said smiling at Billy. Billy shrugged.

"You got any coffee on yet?" Del nodded

"Help yuhself Billay bowy," he offered, moving his head towards the kitchen. Billy went in and got himself a cup full. Alvita came down and saw him standing there.

"Gud morning Billay," she said, patting his arm as she grabbed herself a cup too.

"Morning Alvi," he replied, giving her a half smile.

"Aw Billay, yuh got to go make tings right," she said, waving her finger at him. "Yuh love her don'cha?" Billy smiled and nodded at her. "Well then Billay bowy, go get her!" Billy took another drink of coffee.

"Ya, you're right. Think I might wait till I'm not so hung over though." He rubbed his head as she laughed.

"Aw, yuh need a Del Special, dat's all!" Alvita walked towards the front. "Delroy, make our Billay one a yuh specials won't cha?" and she laughed.

"Gud thinking Empress," he answered and started mixing up a concoction. Alvita pushed Billy back out to the bar and sat him down.

"Now, don't'cha tink on it there Billay, just swallow'er down inna one," she told him, patting his shoulder as she sat next to him with her coffee. Del sat a tall glass in front of him. Billy looked at it for a second with a disgusted expression. It was green, foamy and had a cracked egg floating in it. "Now Billay, I told yuh, just drink'er down bowy!" Billy picked it up and chugged it.

"Aargh!" He complained, putting the glass down. "That tastes like shit!" he informed them, looking up at Del. Both Del and Alvita started laughing.

"Yuh right Billay, but yuh wait ten minutes, an yuh be right as rain." He and Alvita laughed some more.

Not more than ten minutes later, Billy felt like a million bucks again.

"Say, mind if I use your shower, Alvi?" he asked her.

"Not at all, gorgeous bowy," she replied with a grin.

"Thanks, I'll be back in a few." Billy headed out the front door and down to the beach, walked about twenty feet along, then made his way down the long dock and onto the boat that used to be his. He'd left it to Del and Alvita when he moved from Jamaica. He was using it again while he was here, hiding out, but he didn't have anything hooked up, so he still had to use their bathroom. He gathered up some clean clothes, then headed back into the bar and upstairs to their apartment above the bar. After he showered and dressed he headed for the hotel, not finding Maggie anywhere in the main buildings, he tried the villa, but she didn't answer. He walked up and down the strip popping into shops, then along the beach for a while, and after five hours of looking, he still hadn't had any luck finding her, so he headed back to The Robinson's.

CHAPTER 18

Maggie got up and went down to the pool for a very early swim. Then, wearing another one of her new dresses, long and light blue, pink, and green, she went to the dining room for breakfast. The family of six were there already, laughing and talking as they ate. Maggie smiled and sat down at the little table she had used her first night.

After breakfast she went for a walk on the beach, heading up to the main strip and buying herself a hat to keep the sun out of her eyes, grabbed a coconut iced coffee and headed back down to the beach. She had her new bikini on underneath her dress and the beautiful water was calling to her. Carrying her sandals so she could enjoy the soft white sand under her feet, Maggie soaked up the beauty of her surroundings. She had her camera with her and took a number of shots of the water. She asked a nice elderly couple in beach chairs if they'd take a picture of her with the water behind her and they did, chatting with her for a little while before moving on.

She walked for hours and decided to go back on to the main strip in search of lunch. Realizing she was well past the familiar colourful shops, she headed back down to the beach and started walking back towards her hotel. Maggie walked for half an hour then tried the main road again, finding a place to grab some sort of jerked chicken wrap, and a coconut water and went back down and sat at the edge of the water to eat it. She finished her lunch, then sat enjoying the water rolling up over her feet. It was getting quite hot, and the beach was filling up, so she started walking again. When she got far enough along to recognize some places, she pulled her hat and dress off, put the camera and her key under it and her shoes on top, and went in for a swim. The water was like crystal clear magic. *What a glorious place this is,* she thought to herself, as she enjoyed a quick swim. *I can understand why Billy loved it here so much.* The thought made her ache for him again. She came back to the beach and put her dress back on and carried her hat, shoes, key, and camera, and started walking again.

It wasn't long before she saw her villa and started towards it, still walking along the edge of the water on the beach. She stopped once more and sat down in the sand. Running her hands through it and watching it pour from between her fingers, the waves washing up over her feet. She felt something behind her, sensing something she couldn't quite place, but a feeling of familiar energy. She looked behind her, but no one seemed to be bothered with her. She looked up and down the beach, but everyone was doing their own thing. Maggie picked up her things and walked on, deciding to walk to the other end where she'd seen the cottage and the boat at the dock. She liked how quiet it was and felt herself drawn to it. There wasn't any music coming from the boat this time, but the house at the top of the long staircase seemed to be some sort of restaurant or pub and she could see colourful lanterns lit outside and hear music coming from within. She was tempted to go up, but didn't have any money left with her, so she went back to Sunshine Villa to grab her purse and head back out. Maggie took the main road this time, walking along past a few different pubs and restaurants, people going by on their bikes and out walking together. She got to the end of the stretch of shops and wondered if she'd passed it, but walking just a little farther, she saw a sign at the top of a very long staircase that read "The Robinsons Rockhouse" and saw that the staircase led all the way down to the beach and to the house she had seen. She walked down, the music getting louder as she neared the bottom of the staircase, and took the boardwalk leading to the front patio. There was a couple out front with their drinks, leaning against the banister.

"Yello Lovely," the man called out when he saw her.

"Hello," Maggie said back with a big smile. The woman had turned to look at her, her eyes narrowing, then growing bigger.

"Say gyal, yuh look familiar to me." Maggie shook her head.

"Oh, I doubt that. I've only been here a few days and it's my first visit." The man and woman looked at each other, the man didn't seem to be connecting any dots, but the woman slapped his arm playfully and said, in a very hurried Jamaican accent,

"Delroy, go an get our Billay." Maggie wasn't quite sure what she had said to him. "Come on gyal," she said looking back at Maggie. Maggie walked up onto the patio, and into the bar, following along behind the woman closely, wondering why she was letting herself be led by perfect strangers. There were a few men sitting at the bar, a couple sitting at a table in the back and two people playing pool. Maggie stood waiting for a moment, then the man she'd seen out front came out of the back kitchen from behind the bar, followed by Billy. He wasn't looking up yet and hadn't noticed her. The woman was watching Maggie's face and started to grin, knowing her guess had been right.

"Billay, this be yuh goddess?" the woman asked him, and the man started pulling Billy out in front of him. Billy looked up and stopped dead in his tracks.

"Maggie?" His lips moved but no sound came out. Maggie felt like time had stopped, unaware of her movements as her feet moved her forward. Billy started to walk towards her, his face looked shocked.

"Mag?" he said again, this time she heard him. They were only a foot away from each other now.

"Billy!" Maggie said, and she was crying. They both had their arms stretched out and closed the gap between them quickly, meeting with an impactful embrace.

"Billy, I've missed you!" she cried, her face under his chin, nestled tightly against his chest. Billy was holding her so tight, one hand in her hair, holding her head close.

"Mag, I'm so sorry!" he said, and they looked at each other smiling, both with tears running down their faces.

"Aw Delroy, tis his goddess!" Alvita said, and Maggie and Billy looked at them and smiled.

"Mag, these are my dearest friends, Delroy and Alvita," he told her, his arm around her back, walking them over to the bar.

"Billay, she be hot my bredren!" Del exclaimed, smiling at Maggie. Alvita gave him a smack.

"Down Del," she said.

"Maggay, I feel I already know yuh. So nice to meet yuh," and she took Maggie's hand in both of hers and gave it a little squeeze. "Billay, you go'on. Be with yuh woman," Alvita said smiling.

"Aw, what about tonight Alvi?" he asked her.

"No, go'on gorgeous man, this be more important!" She grinned at the two of them, waving her hands at them to go. Alvita hugged each of them then pushed them out without much convincing. Billy and Maggie stared at each other as they left the bar and walked down the steps onto the beach. They stopped when they got to the dock and Billy turned and held her arms looking at her with shock, excitement, surprise and love.

"Mag, I'm sorry I didn't believe you. I'm sorry I let my own insecurities hurt us. I'm sorry I hurt you, my Love. I'm so sorry. I'm so glad you're here. Oh, I'm so sorry Mag!" He pulled her close and held her, running his hands up and down her back, hugging her and holding her face as she cried and smiled, and he kissed her head and her face and her lips and her hands. His face was wet with tears too, and she held his hands as he cradled her head and kept kissing her. She felt like things had somehow made a complete circle between them. He had been pulled towards her and found her; now she had found him. A force bigger than them had been pulling them together, over and over, for a very long time.

"Billy, I'm sorry I hurt you too. I never thought about how things might look, because I knew my intentions with Pete were zero. I'm sorry, Babe." And she was kissing him back. Maggie crying, the two of them smiling and holding each other's heads, kissing one another's faces all over. They stood holding each other, little kisses, soft kisses, looking at each other dreamily.

"I think we just had some kinks and milestones to accomplish that we probably would have done a lot sooner... if we'd been fated those younger years together." Billy leaned close and pressed his lips to hers and hugged her. Maggie pressed into him and let him swallow her up in his arms, holding him tight.

"Come on Mag," he said, holding her hand and walking her down the dock to the boat. She stopped suddenly.

"Oh my God, it *was* you?" she said, looking from the boat back to Billy.

"What was me, Babe?" he asked her.

"I went for a walk and stopped here and heard someone playing a guitar. It was you." She smiled at him, Billy pulled her along again, stepped onto the boat and held out his hand for hers. Hopping down with his help, Maggie followed him and he unlocked the door. There was a table with bench seats on the back deck that they walked past, as she followed him below, into the cabin where she looked around as he gathered his things up. The glow of the hanging lantern shining cozily as he lit it. The inside was all maple wood, and Maggie was instantly in love with the warmth and the scent. *It was so, Billy*, she thought with an affectionate smile. There was a kitchen, a table, a couch, and she could see a bedroom at the end of the hall.

"Nice place you got," she said grinning.

"Ya, thanks. I spent a lot of time on this boat when I lived here," he responded.

"I thought you lived in a shack?" she asked him.

"Oh, I did Babe, just down the beach a little further. I'll take you over tomorrow if you like. It's not what you'd call livable anymore, but it worked for me back then, although I did spend most of my time here, especially in the last few years." He shoved his clothes into his suitcase, grabbed his guitar and backpack and they climbed out of the boat and back onto the dock.

"What did you mean when you mentioned 'tonight' to Alvita?" she asked as they walked back towards the bar. He waved his hand.

"Oh, I was going to play tonight, that's all." Maggie grinned at him.

"Really?" she asked with an air of yes please, but he shook his head.

"Ya, but now you're here Mag." She stopped him and hugged him, stretching up to kiss him.

"I'd love to hear you play in your old bar Billy." His eyes twinkled cheekily and he kissed her, a long pressing kiss, then grinned at her.

"Okay, Mag, but after I play my set, I play you!" Billy nuzzled his face into her hair, kissing her neck, tickling her. She giggled, squirming playfully, looking forward to *later*.

***

"Billay!" Delroy said as they walked back into the bar. "Yuh still play'n for us tonight bredren?" Billy nodded. Alvita came over and scooped Maggie away from Billy.

"Now Billay, I better get to know yuh gyal." Maggie smiled as she was led away. The two went and sat at a little table near the bar together.

"Maggay, what yuh gonna drink goddess?" Delroy asked her with a big smile.

"Just a club soda, thank you, Delroy." He quickly brought over her soda and a colourful drink for Alvita.

"Tank yuh Love," Alvita said as he walked away. "So, yuh tell me all about yuhself gyal." Maggie laughed.

"What do you want to know?" Maggie asked, feeling like she'd probably find it very easy to tell Alvita anything. The two chatted away for ages. Maggie soon discovered Alvita knew a lot about her already. Starting from 27 years ago. Maggie got Alvita all caught up on her and Billy finding each other again, after he left Jamaica. Billy had apparently mentioned her often over the years. Alvita had a picture of her and Billy from the cabin Maggie had never seen, and that's how Alvita had recognized her.

"It was yuh big grin baby gyal, an those sparkling eyes," she told her, reaching out and holding her face for a moment, the two smiling at one another, then sitting close while Maggie learned more. Alvita talked about how fuzzy and long haired, *gorgeous bowy* got while he lived there. How he stayed on his own or with The Robinson's most of the time. Billy and The Robinsons became good friends within the first month of Billy arriving in St. Ann. She also discovered Delroy, Alvita and Billy considered each other family. They were like an aunt and uncle to him, and she knew his loss of job and position as well as the loss of his parents were things he'd worked through with them. Maggie felt so honoured to meet such amazing friends who shared another piece of Billy's story, and who cared about him as much as she did. She felt an instant love from both Delroy and Alvita, the connection had already been there for them. Because of Billy's love for her, they already felt they knew Maggie. And now, they were getting to see how much Maggie loved him. They finished their drinks laughing about old stories of Billy in Jamaica. Shortly after that, the bar started filling up. Alvita patted Maggie's hand then got up and headed back to work. The usual night crowd, plus a few people who had heard Billy was back and was going to play, had come out to visit and listen. It was loud and joyous, and Maggie couldn't stop smiling. It was also nice to see Billy surrounded by his friends. His kindness and love seemed to grow around these new people she already felt such a bond with. He went up on the low stage built into the front end of the bar, sat on a stool, looking right at home, and looked up with a smile. His gaze falling on Maggie. Everyone started hollering at him.

"Ya Billay, sing sumting good for us!" Feeling his cup filling up, being back on his old stage, he happily played. Maggie thought he looked more gorgeous than ever, in his element. His playing and singing made everyone in the bar sing along happily. A few of the songs he played, Maggie didn't know, and he sang and played lots of reggae and then some of his own favourites. People were dancing and singing, they even pulled Maggie up to dance with them too. She and Billy would make eyes at each other and grin every once in a while. So many people she'd never met before, dancing and talking with her like she was their long lost relative. When Billy took a break, he came over to Maggie and gave her a long kiss. She wrapped her arms around his neck and kissed him back, grinning her huge Maggie smile at him.

"You look so damn good tonight Billy Stanton!" Maggie told him with a crooked sexy grin. Billy chuckled, his head falling back, making Maggie smile even more.

"Are you enjoying yourself, Beautiful?" he asked her, and she smiled at him again.

"I'm with my Love again, listening to him weave his beautiful voice right into my soul. What could be better." Billy smirked and pulled her hard, and close. Their hips pressed together tightly and he winked at her.

"Mmmm, yes that would add to the 'what could be better' for sure." Maggie added hungrily, her eyes flashing. Billy chuckled again, sliding his hand down and holding hers, they walked over to the bar, grinning goofily at one another. Billy got them drinks, and he sat with her for a few minutes while they enjoyed them.

"I'll do one more 15-minute set Mag, then we can head out if you like?" She nodded and gave him a kiss before he headed back to the stage. He played a couple more songs she didn't know, then "No Woman No Cry" and "One Love".

"Sing us yuh boat song Billay!" Delroy yelled out with a huge smile on his face. The whole bar yelled their agreement. Billy chuckled and started strumming. "Something 'Bout A Boat" was a house favourite that Billy used to finish all his sets with. Everyone, including Maggie sang along, all of them moving together in one big dance. Alvita was standing with Maggie, the two of them smiling as they danced and sang. Billy finished playing, then announced,

"Ok my friends, one more before I'm outta here!" And people started yelling out their complaints.

"No, Billay! Keep'm coming." He laughed and got up and grabbed another stool and sat it next to his, then he started strumming. He locked eyes with Maggie, dropping his gaze sexily, and with his finger, motioned for her to come up to the stage. Her smile faltering slightly, people looking around to see who he was summoning. He grinned at her, and she felt someone give her a little push. It was Alvita.

"Best go baby gyal, yuh man wants yuh." Maggie slowly walked towards him and up onto the stage. He patted the stool next to him and she sat down.

"Billy!?" she said, and he winked at her.

"Just one Mag?" he pleaded and gave her a kiss, everyone cheering and hollering. Maggie's heart lifted, as she realized he was strumming, "All I Have To Do Is Dream". She grinned at him, and his smile grew. And they sang. Their voices harmonizing like two beautiful silky ribbons of love twisting and tangling together. Smiling as they sang, everyone else fading away as they looked into each other's eyes. They finished the song with a kiss. Everyone in the bar was yelling and clapping.

"Come on Babe, let's get out of here," Billy said looking at her with that look that made her legs turn to jelly. He held her hand as they walked through the crowd to the bar, where he grabbed his bags, hugged Del and Alvita and said goodnight. Alvita smiled broadly at the two of them, knowing they had some making up to do.

They walked toward the villa along the beach, both still smiling, Maggie carrying Billy's backpack, Billy carrying his suitcase and guitar.

"Billy, our oasis is so lovely," she told him as they made their way along the boardwalk to Sunshine Villa. "And the name is perfect, Lover of mine," she added. He smiled, pulling her close for a kiss. Maggie unlocked the door, and they walked in, putting Billy's things down just inside the front door. As soon as their hands let go of the bags and Billy sat his guitar down, they attacked each other. Billy lifted her off the floor a few inches, kissing her hard, Maggie's hands in his hair, holding him tight. He put her down again, and they continued their passionate kisses as they moved together towards the stairs. They could hardly stop kissing and caressing long enough to make it up the staircase, grinning at each other between kisses. Maggie pulled Billy towards the bedroom. Stopping and hitting walls along the way, Billy kissed Maggie's face, neck and chest. Maggie was grabbing and squeezing his body and running her hands up and down his back, as they pressed each other against the wall. Drawing closer to the bedroom, they began pulling each other's clothes off, still walking and attacking each other. They couldn't get their things off fast enough. Maggie held Billy around the shoulders as he picked her up and dropped her down onto the bed. Her heart was racing deliciously as he climbed on top of her, kissing her neck and shoulders, then moving down to her breasts, licking and kissing each one, then back up to her mouth. Maggie slid her tongue into his open mouth, as he moved nearer, their tongues dancing around each other, then deep kisses and rubbing each other's bodies. As Billy lowered himself, Maggie wrapped her legs around him and both of them moaned as he glided in, kissing each other deeply.

"Billy!" she cried as he moved in and out, fully and slowly dancing with her body, kissing down her neck. She was holding his hair, squeezing her fingers gently, moving her hips sensually and Billy kept a steady rhythm with his glides. Maggie grabbed his ass and pulled him in deeper, holding him tightly for a moment, and squeezing his butt as she grinded in slow, deep circles. Billy groaned with pleasure, then returned to his rhythm.

"Damn, I missed you," he breathed in her ear, goosebumps running all over her body.

"Billy, you feel amazing," she breathed back, and he slid in and out harder. Their kisses becoming more intense as Maggie started crying out.

"Ohh, faster Billy, Oh God...Billy." Her hips rose as her body burst with pleasure, Billy's head, snug against Maggie's neck, his movements faster and shorter, then his head lifted, and he slid in with one hard glide, Maggie holding his ass and squeezing.

"Maggie!" he yelled, and she felt him cumming. They smiled at each other and started kissing deeply again. Billy, still inside of her, his hands in her hair, Maggie rubbing his back.

"I love you," she said between kisses. He held her face and looked at her with a grin.

"I love you more," he replied, kissing her pressingly, his hands playing with her hair. Embraced so lovingly, holding on tight and tenderly touching one another's bodies.

The next morning, waking up in the sunshine together, in a beautiful villa in a beautiful part of the world, felt like heaven. They snuggled and ran their fingers all over each other, kissing and cuddling. They ordered a big breakfast, and along with coffee, Billy ordered Mimosas, which Maggie enjoyed as they reminisced about their first week together, so long ago, and the mimosas they shared then too. They had plans to go out and see the sights, but ended up staying in all day, mostly naked, swimming, eating, bathing each other in the huge tub, having sex again, and again, throughout the day, then repeating and laying with each other happily. They ordered dinner in, and in just their little house coats, ate out on the bedroom balcony, playing footsies, feeding each other, kissing and smiling, then relaxing, watching the stars and listening to distant music. They decided to go out the next day and Billy would show her some of his old favourite places, maybe check out his little shack and go for a swim at the beach.

***

"Good morning, Beautiful," she heard Billy say, and she opened her eyes to him leaning over her, then kissing her nose.

"Mmm, morning Handsome," she replied, smiling up at him.

"Feel like a swim to start the day?" he asked her, handing her a coffee.

"Mmm, sounds lovely Babe, after my coffee." Billy winked at her.

"I'm just going to run out for 20 minutes or so Mag."

"Your jog?" she asked.

"Nope, already did that," Billy answered walking away. She looked a little disappointed. "You enjoy your coffee, do what you gotta do, and I'll be back." He walked back over and leaned down and gave her a kiss, then started to leave.

"Where are you going my Lover?" she asked, and he turned back and grinned mysteriously at her.

"Just to see Del and Alvi, won't be long my Love." She smiled at him, watching his cute butt as he left the room. Maggie got up and took her coffee to the washroom. Then headed down for a swim. She was upstairs and in the shower when Billy came back. The shower was wonderful. It had to be 5 square feet, and the shower head was so big it was like standing out in the rain. She was standing under the water, daydreaming when she heard the shower door open, and blinking, looked just in time to see Billy's cheeky grin before he wrapped his arms around her and joined her under the water. Kissing her and pulling her body up against his, running his hands down to grab her ass.

"Mmm, this takes me back Mag." She grinned at him seductively, Billy's hands now running over the front of Maggie's body, water cascading down as he kissed her, and she pulled his body tighter against hers. Their bodies slippery and pressed together, Maggie kissed Billy's neck and squeezed his deliciously tight ass. Billy slid his hands all over her body, squeezing and grabbing along the way. She pressed him against the shower wall, kissing him hard and reached down to stroke him.

"Mmm," he moaned happily as she slid his hard, slippery, cock in both her hands, sucking on his earlobe and sliding her tongue along and into his ear. He grabbed her and pushed her against the other side of the shower, grasping her breasts and squeezing them as he pushed her body harder against the wall, frenching, their mouths opened wide now, water running down over their bodies, as he squeezed and pinched her wet nipples.

"Aah!" she cried and he pulled and pinched a little harder. She kissed him hard, pushing him back again, his body against the glass wall, and she slid down to kneel in front of him. She put her hands on the floor at his feet and looked up at him. Water running down her face, her green eyes lustful and hungry. Billy watched as she took him into her mouth, sliding her hands to the back of his legs, squeezing. And then she licked and sucked like a hungry animal, still looking up at him. She slid her mouth up to his body, then all the way to the tip, licking, then sliding down to the base of his very hard cock, devouring him enthusiastically. Billy's head fell back against the wall.

"Maggie," he growled, his hands braced on the wall as she reached up to hold his ass and slide him in and out of her mouth, licking along the way, steadily moving her head back and forth, squeezing his sweet cheeks and taking him in as deeply as she could, twisting her head and moving faster.

"Damn Mag!" he yelled and tried to move her up, she kept going, sliding him in and out faster, one hand still squeezing his ass, the other playing gently with his balls and she felt his body tighten, his pelvis moving with her and then he came. She looked up at him, watching him as his body shuddered.

"Ohh God," he breathed, Maggie held him at the base, licking right to the tip of him again as he finished. The water was washing over him, Maggie still holding him in her mouth as he looked down at her, and his body quivered. She let him slide out of her mouth slowly, and let the water wash over her face, her mouth still open slightly, still looking up at him provocatively, then she kissed and caressed her way back up his body. His eyes were still rolling back as she kissed his mouth.

"Mag," he said, and it came out in a low growl, as he kissed her and pressed her back against the other wall. He looked into her eyes, looking like he might swallow her up, and started sucking his way down her body. She was so aroused from going down on him, and she could feel the intense electric energy coming from him too. He sucked on each one of her breasts hard, squeezing them and gently biting her nipples, his hands on her ass, one squeezing and pulling her cheeks apart and sliding his finger in and out of her center. He was sucking her breasts as he fingered her, then he moved down to his knees and stuck his tongue right between her legs and started lapping her up. His tongue moving strong and deep, inside her and around her clit, then back inside her as he squeezed her ass hard. Now flicking his tongue quickly over her clit, sliding a finger in and out, she was finding it very difficult to stand up.

"Billy," she whispered softly, and he kept licking, faster and harder.

"Oh God, Billy." He looked up at her and grinned as her eyes rolled back and her head fell against the shower wall. Her legs shaking as she cried out with an elated "Awww." Her whole body vibrating as she came. Billy licked her center with a hungry growl, then kissed his way up her abdomen, up between her breasts, and standing up, he growled a whisper in her ear,

"Mmm, you taste so good Maggie." The two of them wrapped

their arms around one another, and kissed frantically again, pressing their mouths deep together, licking and pushing hard. She already wanted more and was almost growling herself. They stayed in the shower holding each other as the water ran over them. Kissing slowly, faces wet. Then they finally turned it off and got out.

"That was fantastic, Lover," she said, pushing him down on the bed in their towels. He hugged her and rolled on top of her grinning.

"Deliciously fantastic," he replied, kissing her softly.

"Maybe, we'll go see some sights tomorrow?" she suggested, grinning at him. He chuckled and they were back to kissing and rolling about the bed.

They were still in bed at lunch, still not feeling like going anywhere.

"Why don't we get room service and then maybe go for a swim and try to leave the room for dinner?" he asked as he ran his fingers up and down her naked body. She lay next to him, fingers in his hair, with a relaxed satisfied feeling running through her body.

"Ok Lover," she replied softly. It was a little bit before he got up and ordered them something, then coming back to the bedroom, letting his robe fall to the floor, he climbed back into bed. She watched him with dancing eyes, giving his whole body the once over.

"You are a beautiful hunk of man Mr. Stanton," she said, licking her lips.

"Maggay, my goddess, I think you're purring," he teased and landed playfully on top of her, kissing her, the two giggling and groping one another. They heard a knock, and Billy jumped up, threw on his robe, and went down to answer the door. After a moment she heard "Mag", and she grabbed her robe and went to the top of the stairs.

"Yes, Lover?" she asked, smiling.

"Lunch," he answered, motioning in a sweeping bow, at their set table of food. She walked down to sit with him at the table with a big smile. They ate patties and boiled plantains, mangos, and pineapple slices. Billy drank an ice-cold Red Stripe and Maggie sipped on a virgin Caribbean Delight.

They lounged out on the pool patio in the sun after lunch, then Maggie dropped her robe and dove into the water. She did a couple laps before looking up at Billy who was still sitting in his chair, happily watching her swim, with a goofy grin on his face. She was treading water and grinned at him.

"You going to join me, Lover?" and he shook his head.

"Nah, I get a better view from up here, and let me tell you, it is one fine view Babe!" She splashed water at him. He jumped up, dropped his robe and jumped in next to her, the two of them laughing, going under, coming up and laughing some more, then swimming to the shallow end and hugging each other, kissing sweet kisses as they talked about what they might do the next day, if they actually left the villa.

They started fooling around in the pool, things getting pretty intense, and they tried completing their intentions in the water, but ended up climbing out and making their way back up to bed where they delighted one another multiple times, deciding between romps, that they were going nowhere.

CHAPTER 19

The sun shone in, across their faces the next morning. Billy rolled over and wrapped his arm around Maggie, pulling her up close and softly kissing her neck and cheek. She woke up smiling and snuggling into him.

"Morning my Sweet Lover," she said, turning and kissing him tenderly.

"Mmm, morning Beautiful," he said back, grinning at her.

"Okay, let's get up and steer clear of one another until we get out the door," Maggie said, smiling at him.

"Oh, Mag," he said, his face moving into her hair and kissing her with hot, gentle lips on her neck.

"Let's not go out today," he said softly, still kissing her neck.

"Mmm, that does feel really good," she moaned, nestling into him, then pushed herself back, Billy grabbing her again and pulling her up close.

"Come on Mag." He was trailing his tongue down her neck now, his hands running all over her body. "Just a quicky," he whispered in her ear, and licked his way back down again. She tried to resist, but all she could think was, *God, he smells so good, he feels so good, oh God oh God* and she grabbed his face and started kissing him intensely.

"Mmm, that's what I was hoping for Babe," he growled as she started running her hands down to grab his ass, and pulled his body towards hers, feeling his already very hard dick between her legs as

Billy moved on top of her and pushed himself inside.

It didn't end up being much of a quicky, and after a wonderfully drawn out workout between the sheets, she finally managed to send him for a shower, staying put until he finished and went downstairs. Then, closing the bathroom door behind her, she had her shower. When she came out to get dressed, she decided to wear her bikini, and put on her last new dress, looking in the mirror and thinking it was probably her favourite of the three. It was long, right to her ankles, and the most beautiful coral colour. It had wide straps, was cut low with buttons down the front, and was so light and cool and flowed so nicely when she walked. She rolled some vanilla oil over her neck and shoulders, scrunched some lavender oil into her hair and went downstairs. Billy was sitting out at the pool when she came down and turned in time to see her walking towards him. He smiled and got up to come back inside.

"Mag, you look gorgeous!" he told her, hugging her and kissing her passionately. She kissed him back, then gently pushed him away.

"Billy, we'll never get out of here if we keep doing that." He winked at her and grinned.

"I know!" he replied, Maggie smiled.

"Okay, here's the plan, I'll go out first, and wait at the main building. You wait a whole minute before following Billy." She pointed a finger at him playfully. He gave a little growl and tried to grab her again, but she laughed and jumped back.

"See you soon Sweet Cheeks," she said, backing out the door.

She was surprised she actually made it to the building, and Billy strolled in nonchalantly, grinning at her with his eyes twinkling.

They went onto the patio and sat at a table overlooking the beach and had breakfast, smiling at each other often, feet rubbing together under the table.

"So, where to, my Love?" he asked her as they finished their coffee.

"I don't know Babe, you know the area, where would you like to take me?" He grinned mischievously and she laughed.

"Wrong choice of words!" Billy chuckled.

"Hmm, well, there's a place where we could swim with pigs." Maggie looked at him with a funny expression.

"What?" she asked and laughed.

"Ya, never did that when I lived here, but now that you've broken me in on the farm a bit, I'd try it with you Mag." She smiled.

"Kay, what else?" she asked.

"We could rent some jet skis and go out for a few hours." She took a drink of water and smiled.

"Always lots of tours to go on. Or we could, I don't know, have a shower or something." Maggie giggled.

"Why don't we walk the beach, and you can show me around all your old favourite places." She reached out and held his hand.

"Ya, sure Babe, that'd be nice. Ready?" Maggie nodded, and they thanked the staff as they left for their day out together.

They stopped in at a couple of bars and restaurants, Billy introducing Maggie to some old acquaintances. They grabbed some drinks at a little beach hut and sat in the shade, wrapped around one another. Early in the afternoon, they went in for a swim, Billy saying he'd have to stay in the water a bit longer after seeing Maggie in her bikini, and swimming out deeper. Maggie laughed as she walked out and sat in the sand to dry off. Billy followed a few minutes later and laid down in the sand next to her, both smiling happily, soaking up the sun for a while. Picking up their things they continued along the beach hand in hand.

As the sun started to drop, Maggie pulled her dress back over her bathing suit, Billy pulled his light button T-shirt back on, and they decided to turn around.

"Hey Babe, there's a little food truck that makes the best jerk chicken just a little way up." He pointed to a boardwalk that left the beach. "If it's still there," he added and she nodded.

"Sure, sounds good," Maggie replied, so they made their way out to the street, hand in hand. They didn't walk far before Billy happily exclaimed,

"Yes, it's still there!" They walked over to a green, yellow and red truck parked on the side of the road, music playing from speakers on the roof, a couple tables on one side of the truck and laughter coming from within. "Might want to stick close, Mag!" Billy said with a big smile. Maggie looked a little concerned. "Don't worry Babe, these two just...appreciate a fine woman," he added, winking at her admiringly. Still hand in hand, they approached the side with the window, a small counter running along the outside, with a little awning above. They couldn't see anyone, but Billy smiled broadly when he heard voices inside.

"Wah gwaan?" he said loudly, it was quiet for a split second, and then they heard a reply.

"Yello, can we help yuh with sumting?" Soon they saw a man's face peek around the window. He stared at Billy for a moment, then beaming said "Bless! Tis Billay!" And someone else's voice was speaking quickly and happily now too.

"Wadup Billay bowy!?" the other man said, and both came out of the truck, grabbing Billy, hugging him and clapping each other on the backs.

"How'ave yuh bin?" the first man asked. Billy smiled and nodded.

"Good boys, how about you?" Maggie tried to follow their answers, but they were speaking too fast, and she just stood there smiling.

"Ahh, who dat Billay?" one of them asked, whistling and smiling at Maggie and walking towards her. Billy walked over and pulled her close.

"Barkley, Marland, this is my Maggie." Both men beamed and gave her big, very friendly hugs grinning from ear to ear as she leaned back against Billy again, and he slipped his arm around her waist.

"Noo, Billay, not yuh Maggay?" Barkley said, both men looking at her like they were seeing a ghost. "Lord 'ave mercy," he said, clapping his hands together, and he leaned back towards Maggie and held her face and gave her a big kiss on the forehead.

"She very criss Billay!" Billy laughed, hugging her tighter.

"I know!" he smiled. "You boys still make the best jerk around?" he asked them, and they headed back into the truck.

"Yuh betta believe it Billay! No question!"

"Two a dum Billay?" Billy smiled at Maggie.

"Please Barkely, thanks." Billy and Maggie sat down to wait for their food. It only took a few minutes and then they called them back up for their orders. "Thanks boys, see you around." Billy said, as they walked back down to the beach to eat.

Maggie was grinning at Billy, and when he noticed he smiled at her, then asked,

"What is it, Mag?" She shrugged and kept grinning as she answered,

"Just enjoying seeing you with your friends." He chuckled at her. "I feel like I'm famous or something though," she added grinning again.

"Well, I lived here for ten years Babe, and I might have mentioned you once or twice," he told her, winking cheekily. They found a spot right near the edge of the water and ate their dinner, watching the sun setting right down into the sea. Then they walked back, wrapped around one another. Maggie carried her shoes in her free hand and walked right along where the water met the beach. Once in a while they would stop and kiss, look out at the water, then walk along again.

"So, what are our plans for tomorrow, Lover?" she asked as they headed up the boardwalk to the villa.

"Thought maybe we could stop by and see Del and Alvi for dinner Mag," he answered, opening the door for them. "But other than that..." and he closed the door behind her, giving her one of his hungry Billy looks. She giggled and ran for the stairs,

"You'll have to catch me first!" she called out, and Billy took off after her, scooping her up before she made it to the bedroom. Maggie laughed as he carried her and dropped her down on the bed, jumping next to her and tackling her, rolling around laughing together. They were huffing and puffing between giggles, hugging and looking at each other.

"I'm so glad you're here." Maggie kissed his nose and smiled.

"Me too!" Billy replied very thankfully. He stood up and reached out his hand to pull her up, walking them over to the balcony and stepping out into the softly lit night. He sat down in one of the lounge chairs and pulled her down in front of him. Maggie leaned back against his body, and he wrapped his arms around her, snuggling his face up to her cheek, and Maggie held his arms. He started to quietly sing "Ain't No Sunshine", rocking them gently as they sat watching the stars, enjoying the warm Jamaican breeze snuggled together. She closed her eyes and listened with such love. She never tired of his voice. She loved him so much, and she knew he loved her with all of his heart. The more she learned about him, the more she discovered how similar their lives had been, in very different ways, their stories had always been one, and, even in their years apart, the likeness of how those 25 years had played out was beautifully connected. The impression that week together so long ago had made on both of them, and the flame they had both carried for one another after almost three decades was unbelievable. They stayed on the chair for a long time, almost falling asleep. Then they dragged themselves inside and got ready for bed sleepily and climbed in, holding each other close.

Maggie got up and went for a swim, while Billy was still sleeping. She didn't wake him when she came back in, instead she called room service, requesting coffee and breakfast to be sent in half an hour, then went upstairs and sat down on the floor next to the bed. She sat staring at Billy for the longest time, the sun shining across his tanned strong body, still so muscular and taught, the white sheet draped over his lower body and his feet peeking out the bottom. She reached up and ran her fingers through his hair, moving the soft dark strands away from his face, smiling as she watched him, thinking how handsome he was and how lucky he made her feel. Maggie sat up and leaned over to kiss his mouth softly, lingering for a moment. She felt Billy's hand slide up the back of her head, then his fingers sliding into her hair holding her and kissing her. They both held each other's heads and kissed soft warm, long kisses. Then, Billy moved his face back and smiled at her.

"Morning Beautiful. You coming back to bed?" she smiled back but shook her head.

"Not yet Babe, breakfast is on its way." He was completely quiet for a moment, just looking at her, then,

"Oh ya!?" he said and with a big surprised "Whoop" from Maggie, he pulled her up over him, rolled on top of her, and started to tickle her and kiss her.

"Billy!" she laughed, her face tangled in her wet hair. He bent down and kissed her again, then got up and went to the bathroom. She lay there smiling and feeling her heart beating quickly. She heard him turn the shower on, so she got out of bed and went back down to wait for room service.

Maggie was waiting at the table when Billy came downstairs. Their food was already set out for them. He was grinning cheekily at her as he walked over to her, bent down in front of her and pulled her robe down, kissing each shoulder softly, and only touching her with his lips.

"Billy, breakfast is going to get cold," she said, her breathing becoming faster as he stood up and walked behind her. Softly with his fingers, he ran them up and down her arms a few times, then lifted her hair and kissed the nape of her neck and across her shoulder blades. Her body shivered with delight, his hands holding her shoulders now as he kissed her neck and her ears, then he whispered,

"I've got quite an appetite this morning, Beautiful Lover." Maggie reached up with one hand and held his head, fingers in his hair, as he continued to kiss her neck, his hands wrapped around the front of her holding her breasts and slowly massaging them.

"Mmmm," she moaned softly, his tongue running along her shoulders.

"Want me to stop Mag?" he breathed in her ear, making her more aroused.

"Gawd no," she whispered. He squeezed a little harder, then rubbed his hands over her nipples softly, Maggie's head falling back onto his body. Then he slid one hand down the front of her body and down between her legs and teased her with his fingers, Maggie's body aching for more.

"Billy, you're making me crazy," she breathed. He was sucking and kissing, all over her neck, breathing heavily in her ear, a finger sliding along her wet center, and pressing all the right buttons. He walked around to face her. Maggie pushed her chair away from the table and Billy moved closer. She undid his belt, and ran her hands under his robe, sliding from his hips to his ass, face to face with a very excited breakfast guest. Looking up at Billy and grinning, she began kissing just below his navel, then from one hip bone and across to the other, massaging his ass. Then she slowly stood up, and kissing his body along the way, slid his robe down, watching it fall to the floor. She pulled him close and holding his ass again, kissed his chest and stomach, Billy's hands in her hair, Maggie kissing her way up to his neck, giving his ear a little nibble. Then she undid her belt and let her robe fall to the floor too. Billy softly ran his hands along her waist to her ass, then holding her firmly he turned to sit on the chair, pulling her on top to straddle him. She held his head, her hands in his hair, his face right in front of her chest and she felt his hands move up her back and into her hair as he looked up at her with desire, Maggie's eyes deep and inviting. His hands moved back down her body and he held her hips, lifting her up, as he pushed himself inside of her, pulling her down hard, Maggie moaned, lowering herself all the way down against his body, rocking her hips back and forth gently. Billy held her and lifted her up and down. She held his head, and they were kissing deep, open kisses, as she moved up and down, their bodies tightly pressed together. He held her face, growling with pleasure. Maggie steadily and sensually moving up and down, looking into each other's eyes with a lustful stare.

"Faster Mag," he breathed, and letting her head fall back and holding his arms she rose up and down, adding speed, Billy held her hips and pushed her down hard each time she landed on his lap. Faster and shorter now, Billy licking her breasts as they bounced in front of his face.

"Mag, Ohh Maag!" he groaned, and she looked at him, knowing he was about to explode.

"Billy, you're sooo big," she purred, and he moved her quicker still, Maggie landing harder with each thrust he was now adding.

"Billy, kiss my neck," she called out, and she felt his warm lips kissing and sucking, making his way all over her neck on her left side. Maggie started to feel herself close to orgasm now too.

"Don't stop Mag!" Maggie was holding his face as he kissed her neck, his tongue hot and wet against her skin.

"Mag... Oh gawd... You're so sexy!" he was saying with each movement she made, and she was cumming, smiling as her body shuddered.

"Billy!" she cried out. Now looking at her intensely, his mouth open, his eyes fixed on her, Maggie traced her fingers down to his chest, across his nipples and back up his neck into his hair, squeezing and pulling softly.

"Ahhh gawd," he groaned with a long breath, pushing inside her deeper as he finished. His face back on her chest, their arms wrapped so tightly, their bodies were practically glued together. Maggie held his face and lifted his head, looking at him with a smile, then kissed his lips with constant pressure, hardly moving, both of them inhaling suddenly and holding each other snuggly.

"I didn't realize I could order that with room service," Maggie said grinning. Billy grinned back.

"Mmm, yes, and it's 24-hour room service Babe." They smiled

and kissed again. Maggie gave him one more kiss before she stood up and grabbed both their robes, passing Billy his and putting hers back on, then sitting in the chair next to him. They poured some coffee and snacked on some sweet cinnamon buns, and fruit. Kissing deeply every so often, hands still touching one another and grinning at each other.

"What time are we going to see the Robinsons, Billy?" she asked as they finished up their breakfast.

"Should probably aim for 4:30 I guess," he answered, standing up and stretching. She reached out and ran her hand down his body.

"You're a gorgeous lover." Billy winked at her.

"You make me that Mag." Maggie stood up and hugged him, Billy hugged her back.

"Think I'll go for a swim Mag, cool off a little." She grinned at him.

"Okay Billy, I'm going up for a quick shower." And she gave him a kiss before heading upstairs.

***

"So, what will we do for the next few hours?" she asked when she came down and found him in a lounge chair by the pool.

"This," he answered, grinning. She sat on the edge of the chair, and he held her hand. And they pretty much did just that. They laid around in the sun at the pool for a while, then went down to the beach and laid there in the warm sand, taking a few swims, then drying off on a blanket, sipping their coconut and lime drinks together. It was close to 4:00 when they finally went back to the villa. Maggie wore her long blue, pink and green dress again, and swimming in the slightly salty water and letting it dry in the soft breeze had made her curls even tighter than normal, so she left it down, bouncing around her shoulders and down her back. Billy walked over to her with a smile, moving her hair off her shoulders, and playing with her curls, then he held her face and kissed her softly before saying,

"Mag, you look absolutely beautiful." She grinned. He kissed her again, Maggie holding his wrists and looking at him lovingly.

"Ready to go Babe?" he asked. Maggie smiled and nodded.

They walked out into the warm evening air, the sun still shining brightly, both of them smiling broadly, walking hand in hand along the beach to the bar. Before they started up towards the cottage, Billy stopped Maggie and held her arms.

"What is it Billy?" she asked, thinking something was wrong. Then, a huge smile spread across his face, and he shook his head.

"Just love you Maggie." He gave her a kiss. "I love you with every beat of my heart, you know that, right?" he added with another kiss. Maggie smiled softly, placing her hand on his cheek and nodding. They rubbed noses with a grin before they carried on up to the patio.

They went inside. The only lights on were the ones behind the bottles at the bar and it was quite dark. Maggie turned to Billy to speak, but before she could say anything, the lights came on and a whole bunch of voices yelled,

"Surprise!" Maggie jumped slightly, and Billy slid his arm around her waist. She didn't realize who they all were at first, then as the initial shock lessened, she recognized... Bridget? Tina? Becky? Justin? Carla, Stu! She looked at Billy, her hands over her mouth, Billy was grinning watching her. Maggie's face was that of shock and happiness. Oh my God, Jon? Sam? She couldn't believe it. Everyone from the cabin was standing there, and they were all coming over to say hi to her and hugging her. Then Carla and Stu came over, Carla was almost bouncing.

"Carla! What the heck?" Maggie asked, and Carla laughed, pulling her in for a hug.

"We're here for the week Mags!" she replied, her excitement tangible. Maggie beamed at her.

"Billy!" Maggie said, turning to ask him what was going on, but he wasn't there anymore. She couldn't stop staring at everyone, her smile growing as she stopped and smiled at each one of them in turn. Chris, Gwen, Tammy, Dave, Kim, Cindy, Adam, she couldn't believe it. She was in shock and still moving from one happy face to another, hugging each person tight, when she suddenly heard music from somewhere, first someone playing on the piano in the bar, then a guitar starting to play from somewhere outside. As she walked back outside, Billy started singing "Always Remember Us This Way" standing at the bottom of the steps, the patio lights lit, and shining all around him. Everyone slowly came out and stood behind Maggie. Billy was staring at her as he sang, his eyes so misty and blue. She felt the girls behind her, and someone's hand squeezed her shoulder, and she looked to see Carla smiling at her. Maggie smiled back then she turned back towards Billy quickly, his voice pulling her right in. She couldn't stop smiling at him as he sang, loving how he sang the song like he was telling *his* story of his love for her. She was rocking back and forth, feeling like she was in a dream listening to her man happily. The others happily moving to the beat around her. Maggie's head was tilted to one side as she swayed with the beautiful music Billy was sharing and she found herself loving him a whole lot more than she already did. His voice grew stronger and more husky as he sang. Maggie's heart overflowing and stretching the distance between them, beating along with Billy's. The magnetic pull between them, stronger than it had ever been. A single tear ran down Maggie's cheek, as she smiled at him, thinking *Sexier and more Beautiful than ever*. Singing right from his heart, with so much emotion and feeling, more tears running down her cheeks, her heart bursting. Then as he sang the last of the song, he walked up the steps, and sat his guitar down. Stopping about a foot away from her, he knelt down on one knee, reached into his pocket, pulled out a little green velvet box, and smiled up at her. Her heart was racing. She put her hands over her heart, smiling at him, shaking, and feeling tears welling up in her eyes again, as he spoke, in that deep husky voice that made her turn to jelly.

"I don't really know what I'll do if you say no, so damn Babe, save us both the trouble, and say yes." Billy opened the box as he continued. "Will you marry me, Mag?" He took the ring out and held it in front of her. She reached out her hand, tears running down her face, her big Maggie smile growing, and he pulled her down in front of him as she answered,

"Yes, oh my God, Billy, YES!" He slipped the ring on her finger, and they wrapped their arms around each other and kissed, a long smiley wet kiss, both of them crying joyfully. Everyone clapping and yelling around them.

"Ya, Billay bowy!" they heard Delroy call out and Billy stood up, pulling Maggie up off the patio and kissed her over and over hugging her tight.

Once they had a few minutes embracing one another, everyone was suddenly around them, in the biggest group hug ever. Maggie and Billy were still hugging in the center of everyone, smiling and looking around at all the faces and bodies pressed up together, calling out their congratulations and smiling happily at them. After the love huddle broke, they spread out again. Maggie grinned at Billy as he took her hand and pulled her over to the railing.

"Happy Birthday, my beautiful Mag," he said, kissing her.

"Thank you Billy. This is so amazing! I can't believe you found everyone!" He smiled, his eyes twinkling.

"It took a while! I've been working on this for months now." Maggie's smile faded slightly.

"What is it? he asked her.

"God, you were planning all of this and we were fighting and dealing with Pete." He pulled her tighter.

"Mag, it's alright, it all worked out." Billy gave her another kiss, their hands rubbing and sliding over one another. "And I will never doubt what we have again, my Love."

"Hey dudes! See things haven't changed much over the years!" came Jon's voice and Maggie and Billy laughed as they broke apart and looked at him. "I'm sure we could find you two a closet!" he added, then, The Jon Chuckle.

"Jon, how are you?" Maggie asked.

"Ah, you know, same old me." He was rocking a tie-dyed shirt and although he was a little thicker around the middle and his hair a little thinner on top, he still had his long ponytail, hanging all the way down his back, and he still looked like he'd been at the bong all day.

"So, dude..." he said to Billy, "...when's the party man?" he asked. "Oh, and you think you could hook me up with some bud dude?" he added hopefully. Billy chuckled at him.

"Ya, I'll introduce you to Barkley and Marland, think you three will get along nicely." He gave Maggie a grin.

"Be back in a few, Babe," he told her and led Jon over to his friends. Carla, Becky, Bridget, Tina, Kim, Gwen, Tammy, and Cindy all walked over to Maggie, closely followed by Alvita. All of them grinning at her. Maggie couldn't stop smiling at them. She still couldn't believe they were all there.

"You ready Mags?" Carla asked, linking her arm with Maggie's.

"Ready for what?" she asked, confused.

"We're having a girl's night back at your place Maggie," Bridget said happily.

"Ya baby gyal, this yuh night," Alvita said, linking her arm through Maggie's, opposite Carla. They started walking her to the bar entrance. "Billay, yuh gorgeous bowy, get yuhself out here!" Alvita called as she walked inside. A moment later, she came out with a beach bag and Billy.

"What is it Alvi?" he asked, smiling sheepishly as all ten women stared at him, grinning.

"We're taking Mags now, Sweet Cheeks!" Carla told him, walking up next to him and giving him a pinch. Billy laughed.

"Good to see you too, Carla," he replied, giving her a one armed hug, then he walked towards Maggie, pulling her free from the ladies.

"Have fun with the girls tonight, Babe. I'll see you tomorrow." Billy held her face, his fingers stretching into her hair as he gave her a kiss, Maggie held his hands and smiled at him.

"Won't I see you tonight?" she asked.

"No, the guys want to have one of our old all-night parties, then they're taking me out somewhere for the day. We'll all meet up again tomorrow for dinner." He gave her a long kiss. "I love you with a never-ending fire, Beautiful," he told her, their faces almost touching, looking at each other.

"I love you too, Gorgeous Lover of mine." They hugged. Then the girls started pulling Maggie away again and she smiled at Billy as she was backed away. He gave her a wink and a cheeky Billy grin before she headed down the stairs to the beach.

The party of ten was chatting and laughing all the way to Sunshine Villa, and stepped aside to let Maggie open the door. As she walked in, she was greeted by fairy lights and coloured lanterns strung everywhere, big beautiful tropical flowers floating in bowls of water, bottles of champagne here and there, and sitting on the coffee table in the living room was a big white box with a big white bow on top. She stood there in awe, then remembered everyone behind her, and she turned to see them all smiling at her.

"Go on Maggie," Tina coaxed her. She went right in, everyone following her.

"Wow, it's beautiful," Maggie said as she walked over to the box on the table, looked back at the group and a few people shrugged but they all still had big grins on their faces. She knelt down and pulled the lid off and looked inside. On top of the white tissue paper was a note.

'My Dearest Mag. Happy Birthday. Just a little something from me to you. I hope you like it. The girls picked it out so I wouldn't see it. Can't wait to see you tomorrow my Love. Love always, Billy xo P.S. I picked the daisies for you.' She looked at everyone again, and they seemed to be holding their breath, watching her pull back the tissue paper. First, she saw a beautiful silk daisy crown, and her heart started melting. She pulled back another layer of tissue paper and saw a white dress.

"Ohh my goodness," she whispered in awe, pulling the dress out and standing up. It was absolutely beautiful. Long, completely lace, soft and flowy, the top was like a bodice, with daisy lace around the low off the shoulder neckline, with thin decorative straps that were also daisy lace. She turned it around, to look at the back and saw that it was cut very low.

"Do you like it, Mags?" Carla asked, all of them waiting expectantly. Maggie looked at them, her eyes full of tears. All she could do was nod. She heard a bottle of champagne pop and some of them hollering.

"Let we party!" yelled Alvita and Maggie put the dress back in the box and the lid back on. She took the box upstairs and left it on the bed, noticing a number of bags along the wall that must have belonged to the girls, then smiling she went back down to join the happy sounds in the living room.

"Maggie, come and sit!" they called out to her.

"Maggie, you look great!" Becky said grinning. Maggie smiled and shrugged,

"Oh, well, a little thicker and greyer than I once was." A couple of them laughed.

"Aren't we all Maggie?" Kim said giggling.

"Tell us how Jamaica has been so far," Tina said smiling.

"Oh, but I want to hear all about you girls," Maggie replied, beaming at all their faces. And so, they all took turns catching up.

Becky and Justin had bought *The Cabin* and carried on with the tradition of renting it out, living in a house at the top of the hill in town, overlooking the mountains. Kim and Adam were married a few years after their week at the cabin, now living in Quebec, and had three kids. Cindy was single, recently divorced.

"No, not from Dave!" she added, to multiple questioning looks. She and Dave had gone to different colleges and eventually lost touch. She was a vet and kept herself very busy. Bridget was married and had a son. Tina lived in the same town as Bridget, also married and had a daughter. Tammy and Gwen had been together for about 26 years now, happily running a flower shop in Florida.

"Wow, I just can't believe you're all here," Maggie kept saying.

"Ok Maggie, tell us about you and Billy," they implored. She gave them the condensed 25 years apart, then with many "awes and oohs" she told them about how they found each other again, then bringing them right up to date on the past week in Jamaica. They finished off a bottle and opened more champagne, ordered room service and spent time reminiscing and looking at pictures of people's kids and spouses. Then, Alvita announced it was time to give Maggie her presents! They all brought over bags and boxes and sat them on the coffee table in front of Maggie.

"Wow you guys!" She smiled, picking up a red gift bag.

"That's from us," said Tammy and Gwen together. Maggie pulled out the black tissue paper and reached in, pulling out a very sexy black and red lace bodysuit.

"Oh, this is gorgeous!" Maggie smiled. "Thank you, ladies," she told them.

"That will look sweet on yuh Maggay!" Alvita said whistling. Maggie felt her cheeks going a bit red and reached for another gift, which was a little box from Tina. Inside was a pair of drop pearl earrings.

"Oh Tina, these are so pretty, thank you!" Tina grinned at her sweetly.

"They can be your something new Maggie. And Maggie means pearl, did you know?" she added, grinning again. Maggie smiled back and nodded at her. Then she was given a bigger box from Becky, and inside was a matching set of onesie pajamas and slippers for her and Billy. Maggie laughed, remembering Becky and Justin in their matching set all those years ago.

"Oh Becky, these are too cute, thanks so much." Becky smiled and said,

"I'm sure you two keep each other... warm, but for those extra cold nights you might want some cozy pjs, you know when you're already into the deli sandwiches!" Becky laughed at the surprised look on Maggie's face. Maggie laughed along with her.

"Mine next!" Bridget called out, passing Maggie a flat box. Inside was a silky, sheer teddy. It was a beautiful jade green with silver flecks running through the lace.

"Ohhhh," they all cooed as Maggie held it up against herself and looked down at it.

"Very pretty Bridget, thank you." Maggie picked up another box that was quite heavy. The tag read *from Kim*. She took the lid off and looked inside. It held a set of four candles, black with gold lace around them, the biggest candle said, "Two hearts, one flame" and in the box under the candles was a golden snuffer.

"Oh Kim, these are so lovely. Thank you."

"You're welcome, Maggie," she replied, smiling at her. "There's one more thing though." Maggie looked back inside the box and saw tissue paper on the bottom and found a blue garter. "That's your something blue," she said grinning.

"Thanks Kim!" she said. Maggie reached over and grabbed another gift bag. She looked up and Cindy smiled at her,

"That one's from me Maggie." Maggie looked inside and pulled out a little tin of champagne flavoured gummy bears, a silver picture frame that said just married on the bottom, a his and hers hand towel set and a half dozen disposable cameras.

"Thanks so much Cindy, these are great." Tina grabbed one of the cameras.

"Should we use one for tonight?" she asked, already taking it out of the packaging and snapping shots.

"Excellent, thanks Tina," Maggie replied happily. Tina smiled at her.

"Here Mags!" Carla said, passing her a wrapped gift.

"Carla, you already gave me a birthday gift. You know, the one you snuck into my suitcase." Carla laughed.

"Well, it needed to come to Jamaica with you Mags! This is just a little something extra." Maggie pulled the paper off the present. She laughed as she looked down at the title of the book she was holding, and read "Date Night; cookbook and saucy activities for couples." It had a slightly out of focus picture of a couple getting busy on the kitchen counter in the background.

"Oh, a woman after my own heart!" said Alvita, grinning at Carla.

"Thanks Carla." Maggie smiled.

"Well you and Sweet Cheeks seem to like hanging out in the kitchen, so..." and she laughed, the others laughing along with her.

"Ok, gyal, now for mine!" Alvita handed Maggie the biggest box yet. Maggie sat it on the table in front of her. She unwrapped it and opened it up and looked inside. It was full of all kinds of goodies. A board game called Anti Climaxing, a set of naughty dice, fuzzy handcuffs, beautiful long soft feathers, a book titled

Tantric Sex Techniques, and an oil set with six different rollers. Carla grabbed them and read them out loud, the girls giggling and commenting as she read their names, "Golden Arrow", "Tarzan", "Pep In Your Step", "Sensational Nights", "Joyous Occasions" and "Vanilla and Lavender Forever". There was also a body butter that was vanilla, coconut, lemon and lime named after the drink "Caribbean Delights".

"Keep look'n baby gyal," Alvita instructed her, grinning, and Maggie realized there were still a few more things in the box. Edible body paint, a small whip, a blindfold, two different sized vibrators, and a coupon book, for things to do to each other. "From what me know Maggay, yuh two don't need any help, but there is no harm inna having a little extra fun is there gyal!" and she smiled broadly at Maggie and winked. Maggie giggled.

"Thanks Alvita." Feeling her cheeks go red again as everyone checked out Alvita's bag of tricks.

"Oh, here is one more ting," she said, handing Maggie a dime. "For luck an prosperity. Keep it with yuh on yuh special day."

"Thank you." Maggie went around to everyone giving them all a hug and thanking them again.

"Alright ladies let's go for a swim!" Kim said, and they all headed up to get into their swimsuits and were soon back down jumping into the pool. It was getting quite dark, but the lanterns and fairy lights had been strung up at the pool and made a lovely glow. Becky came out last carrying a CD player and turned it on before jumping in. "Just Like Heaven," started blasting, "Like A Virgin", "Wake Me Up Before You Go Go", "Take A Chance On Me", and "Come On Eileen", everyone was singing and swimming, visiting and talking for ages, before they started getting out of the pool to go back in and enjoy more food and champagne.

"Alright, I say it's time for truth or dare without the dare!" Becky proclaimed, sitting down next to Maggie once everyone was dry and back in the living room.

"Ya, ask the bride-to-be questions time," yelled Kim, Gwen and Tammy raising their arms and cheering their agreement.

"Oh boy," Maggie replied, smiling. "How about we *all* answer these questions ladies?" she suggested, grinning.

"Okay, let's go," coaxed Bridget, smirking at Maggie. "How old were you your first time, with who and where?" All of them looked around at each other grinning.

"Bride goes first!" Maggie gave her a look.

"You already know the answer, Bridget!" and she grinned back at her. Maggie grinned sheepishly, then answered, "Ok, well, 18, Billy and at the cabin." There were hoots and whistles.

"But where, Maggie?" Bridget pressed.

"The cabin," she answered, grinning.

"Hey Maggie, it didn't happen to be near some snowshoes, did it?" Becky asked, laughing.

"Ha ha, ok, in the shed next to the cabin," she added. They each took turns giving their answers, laughing and carrying on. Tina, just like she used to be, was still rather timid, and went very red when she said,

"Twenty-four, my husband, his bedroom."

"Wooo, way to go Tina!" Bridget chimed in. There were a couple of 16s, a 17 and one other 18. Cars were the most popular place for the first time, and besides Maggie and Tina, everyone else did it with someone they no longer had anything to do with. Well, Carla's was in the back of a truck of course, and she wasn't sure if his name had been Ned, Ted or Rick.

"But he kept his cowboy boots on and he had a lovely big...."

"Okay, that's great Carla!" Maggie yelled with a laugh before her friend could finish.

"Ok, next question," Cindy said, "If you could have sex with anyone, who would you pick?" Of course they made Maggie go first.

"Hmm, I don't want anyone else except Billy," she said, and she meant it, but the girls wouldn't accept that.

"Come on Mags, gotta say someone else!" Carla yelled out.

"Ok, ok, ummm, Antonio Banderas." A few of them "Mmmm'ing" their agreement. There was Jason Mamoa, Sean Connery, Johnny Depp, Gordon Ramsay, Cher, Elvis, Farrah Fawcett, Shemar Moore, and Tina said, her pharmacist. Everyone was quiet for a moment then burst out laughing.

"What, he's really nice and has really big hands," she answered with a dreamy guilty pleasure look on her face. Everyone burst out laughing again.

"Here ladies," Carla brought over another bottle, and they passed it around topping up their glasses. Maggie filled her glass with orange juice avoiding any more champagne.

"Next!" Becky yelled. "Where's the best and/or weirdest place you've done it? Maggie go!" Maggie smiled her huge Maggie smile.

"Come on Maggie, gotta tell us!" Becky said.

"Oh, I will, I just can't decide, there are so many good choices." They all "oooohed" and laughed.

"Well now!" said Alvita, grinning at her. "That Billy an his gyal really don't need the box." Everyone laughed again.

"Ok, come on Maggie," someone said.

"Best place..." her face went red now as she had thought of a few places at the cabin, but then remembered some recent events and answered, "Best...Here, in the shower, or at home on our front porch and weirdest, toss-up between closet, a bus and against the banister of the stairs." Someone was clapping, more laughter and "whoop whoop" from Bridget, Kim and Cindy. "Oh, and a floating dock. That was pretty awesome!" Maggie laughed as she looked at Carla's face.

"Aw shit Mags, no!?" she said with a disgruntled look on her face. Maggie laughed harder. There were some interesting ones in the group. A phone booth, the back of a bakery, a few showers, on a blanket in the woods, on a toilet, in a confessional, in a tree house and for Tina, in the living room, in the middle of the day.

After their truth or dare without the dare, they chatted some more, mostly laughing and enjoying each other's company. They had plans to take Maggie out the next day and do some girly things before meeting the guys for dinner. Slowly people started disappearing to their sleeping bags, and Maggie went up to bed. She had more champagne than she had planned on and was very ready to sleep. Carla and Bridget climbed into her king size bed with her, and the others were scattered around the villa. The last they saw of Kim, she was on a lounge chair in her sleeping bag, out on the balcony, Tammy and Gwen following suit.

The next morning, lots of coffee was brought to them and lots of coffee was consumed. After ten women shared the bathroom, it was going on eleven before they were ready and headed out. They took Maggie for lunch, then Alvita took them to a spa where some of them had their hair and nails done. Maggie got a mani-pedi with Carla and Alvita, while the others had some extra TLC.

"Hey, I saw a place down the street that reads palms Maggie!" Kim said when they were finishing up at the spa.

"Ohh, that sounds like fun," a few of the others chimed in. Maggie was a bit reluctant but in the end thought, why not. Only half of them had a reading, but they all sat in with each other to listen and watch. The palm reader was very beautiful and very large. She had a very strong Jamaican accent and was very enthusiastic. When she took Maggie's hand in hers, she looked right up at Maggie's face and deeply into her eyes.

"Oh, m'dear, you're a very lucky gyal." She smiled at Maggie as she nodded her head. Then looked back at Maggie's palms, turning her hands and moving them, looking intently, then said, "Yuh have seen heartbreak, an hard times, but yuh heart have found it's true love, an yuh future bright an long m'dear." She patted Maggie's hand, looking back into her eyes deeply. "Him will neva hurt yuh angel, an yuh will love him an him will love yuh with all yuh heart till the end of time. Dis is in all yuh lives. Dis is a soul bond. Yuh no worry m'dear, yuh will neva part. Yuh souls are old and have been together for time out of mind." She gave Maggie's hand a little squeeze and smiled at her, then said, "Bless." Letting go of Maggie's hand. Maggie smiled at her, and she felt like the woman was still reading her.

"Thank you, Miss Dell," said Maggie as she stood up, and she and the others left the table and went back out into the sunshine.

"Wow Mags, that was pretty cool!" Carla said, walking along with her.

"Yes, it really was," Maggie replied. "Kind of intense! I'm just glad it was a *good* reading," she added and the two linked their arms together and walked to the beach with the others. "I'm going to go for a swim, ladies." Maggie announced. "Anyone want to join me?" The few that hadn't had their hair done joined her, the others got drinks and sat on the beach.

It had been a lovely day out and there were many stories and laughs shared between them. By the time they got back to the villa, it was after four. A few of them went up, washed up and got dressed, in very nice clothes, fixing their hair, and making themselves up.

"Maggie, are you going to get ready?" Becky asked, taking her hand, and leading her up to the bedroom.

"Wow, everyone's getting so dolled up for dinner," Maggie said smiling. Becky looked around the room and spotted the big white box.

"Here Maggie, better put this on," she told her, grinning. All the others were now in the room with her grinning at her. Maggie looked at them dumbstruck.

"*What*? No, I don't want to wear *this* for dinner!" she replied, sweetly laughing Becky's suggestion off. Carla stepped forward,

"Mags, I think you might like to wear your wedding dress for your wedding day." Maggie's chin dropped.

"What?! Today?!?" They were all beaming at her now. Tina was walking around them taking pictures.

"Hey Maggie, we didn't come all this way just for a birthday surprise!" Kim laughed.

"Ya, Maggie, we're here for your wedding silly!" Tina added, smiling at her, starting to look a bit teary eyed.

"Better get ready Mags," Carla said, grinning at her. Maggie was in shock. It was totally surreal. She freshened up, put on a little peach lip gloss, the kind she had always loved, rolled on her vanilla and lavender oil, and wore the peach bra and undies Carla gifted her. Then a few girls helped her pull on her dress, Tina taking pictures, the others watching happily.

"Oh Maggie!" they all said, staring at her with huge grins, "you look beautiful!" She put on her silver locket, her new drop pearl earrings and pulled her hair up, very loosely, with lots of curls falling here and there. Pulling on her blue garter belt, she slid the dime into her bra and then placed the daisy crown on her head. She was suddenly feeling very much the part, smiling broadly at her friends. She slipped on some white sandals and turned to look in the mirror. She smiled at her reflection, suddenly feeling very eager to see Billy again. Carla and Maggie headed down first. When they got downstairs there was a knock at the door. Carla opened it and Maggie heard her say thank you, then she turned and handed Maggie a bouquet of daisies and she was holding a little box in her hand.

"Billy's ring Mags," she said, grinning at Maggie. She and Carla beamed at each other.

"Is this for real Carla?" Maggie asked, her smile so big it was almost hurting!

"You bet your cute bridal hiney Mags." The others were all downstairs now too, waiting behind Maggie and Carla. Maggie turned to look at them and saw them all smiling just as much as she was.

"Alright, let's get this show on the road!" proclaimed Becky, leading the group.

"Where are we going?" Maggie asked Carla.

"Not far Mags," Carla answered, grinning at her again and waiting for her to go out, closing the door behind them. Taking pictures, they made their 10-minute walk down the beach towards The Robinson's. The sun was starting to drop, the colour of the water transitioning into a beautiful blue turquoise with coral bursts reflected in it. As they neared the end of the beach Maggie's heart was bursting. That end of the beach had been roped off and there was an arbor just before the dock, so you could look through it down the length of the dock and into the water. There were long sheets of white fabric loosely draped over top, like a tent, leaving space between each one and hanging down onto the sand, blowing softly in the gentle breeze. Fairy lights and ivy had been strung around the poles and at the end, just on the first couple feet of the dock, was a pulpit, with a white carpet leading up to it, someone who Maggie assumed was the Pastor was standing waiting, and standing together beside the arbor on one side of the dock were Delroy, Stu, and all the guys from the cabin, and Billy. Her beautiful, strong, kind, romantic Billy. How was it possible, after so much life and heartache, that her 30 year old dream was coming true? There were about a dozen seats spread out on either side of the carpet and a number of people were already sitting in them. Maggie didn't know most of them, but recognized Barkley and Marland and saw people she'd met when she and Billy had walked the beach together. The girls were blocking Maggie so Billy couldn't see her yet, but Maggie was watching *him*. He was in sandy coloured pants and a light linen white button-down T-shirt, and sandals. He looked so peaceful and handsome. When he turned, she saw he had a daisy pinned to his shirt, and he smiled when he realized it was time. The guest's all looked towards the group of women now, and Billy's expression was full of anticipation. Carla was with Maggie and turned to her smiling. She reached into her bra, fished around for a moment, then grabbed Maggie's hand.

"Mags, this was my Gramma's, and she wore it on *her* wedding day." Carla dropped a little horseshoe pin into Maggie's hand. "She had it pinned to her dress for good luck, and my grandparents were married for 67 years Mags! This is your old and borrowed." Maggie smiled as Carla carefully pinned it on the back waist of her dress for her.

"Thank you, Carla," she said, giving Carla's hand a squeeze.

"You ready Mags?" she asked her, and Maggie, still unable to stop smiling, nodded. "Ok Mags, we're all going up first, then you follow. I'll be ahead of you." Carla gave Maggie a big hug. As she watched the girls walking up, one at a time, she felt like she might float right off the beach. She couldn't wait to get to Billy, knowing he'd hold onto her, and keep her from floating away. Carla was the last to walk up, all nine girls sitting in the first row, the men joining them. And then, suddenly, there was no one else in the world, but her and Billy. Their eyes met, he smiled at her, and she felt so much love coming from him, and had so much love pouring from her as she walked towards him. She saw him reach up and wipe his cheek, still smiling at her, his eyes dancing. Maggie was beaming at him, and as she came close enough, he reached out his hand and took hers, whispering,

"You're breathtaking Mag." She smiled softly, then Maggie passed her flowers to Carla and turned back to Billy. Maggie and Billy held one another's hands, looking at each other so lovingly. The Pastor started talking, looking around at everyone there with them.

"Dear friends, we have gathered here today to witness and celebrate the union of Maggie Ashberry and Billy Stanton. In the years that they have been together, and over the many they have spent apart, their love for each other has grown, blossoming into the loving couple you see before you. Now, they are ready to spend the rest of their lives together as husband and wife. A true marriage begins well before the wedding day, and the efforts of marriage continue well beyond the ceremony. A brief moment in time and the stroke of the pen are all that is required to create the legal bond of marriage, but it takes a lifetime of love, commitment, and compromise to make marriage everlasting." Now he looked at Maggie and Billy and continued, "Today you declare your commitment to each other before your friends, family and God. Billy would now like to say something to Maggie. Billy..." he finished and smiled at him. Billy looked back at Maggie, he was so calm, his eyes smiling, so deep and blue as he began to speak.

"Maggie, in you, my life is complete. With you by my side, each day is filled with light. In your arms I want to lay, tonight and the rest of my life." Maggie's eyes were now so full of tears she could hardly see his face, and he reached up and wiped them away, smiling at her and taking her hand again. The sun was setting, beautiful purples, reds, yellows and oranges, glowing beside them, melting into the water. The Pastor smiled at them and continued on, looking at Carla and Stu.

"May I have the rings please?" He held out his hand and they placed them into his open palm. Then he turned to Billy. "Do you William Matthew Stanton, take Margaret May Ashberry, to be your wife; promising to laugh with her, dance with her and cherish her, to always be faithful to her in good times and in bad, in sickness and in health, promising to have many adventures, as you grow old together, and to love her and honour her, all the days of your life?" Billy's grin becoming cheeky, eyes twinkling, he looked at Maggie and answered,

"Without a doubt! I do!" Maggie grinned, her heart soaring, Billy winked at her and they linked fingers, holding tight. The pastor smiled and turned to Maggie.

"Do you Margaret May Ashberry, take William Matthew Stanton, to be your husband; promising to laugh with him, dance with him and cherish him, to always be faithful to him in good times and in bad, in sickness and in health, promising to have many adventures, as you grow old together, and to love him and honour him, all the days of your life?" She was smiling so much, and she could see Billy's eyes welling up, as she squeezed his hands in hers and answered,

"Oh yes, I do!" A few guests couldn't help but hoot and cheer. The Pastor smiled, then went on.

"Billy, please repeat after me," he said, handing Billy the ring. "Maggie, with this ring, I gladly marry you, joining my life to yours, completely and unconditionally." Billy repeated the words as he slipped the ring onto her finger. They were both smiling and crying now.

"Maggie," the Pastor said, handing her Billy's ring "Please repeat after me. Billy, with this ring, I gladly marry you, joining my life to yours, completely and unconditionally." She spoke the words, feeling so overwhelmed with love for him, slipping the ring onto his finger. They were both more than ready to seal the deal, and the Pastor laughed as they suddenly pulled each other close. "And so, before these two get any closer, and by the power vested in me, I now pronounce you, husband and wife." Maggie and Billy, nose to nose and grinning at one another, held each other tight. "You may now, oh, alright then!" He laughed again, watching with a smile as Billy and Maggie held each other's faces and kissed before he could finish speaking. Then, Billy dipped her and brought her back up, holding each other and smiling as they kissed again. Everyone clapped and cheered.

"Ya Maggie and Billy!!!" They kept kissing.

"I love you Maggie Stanton," Billy said, looking at her with a big grin.

"Oh, I like the sound of that!" she replied. Then, with a mischievous smirk, added, "I love you too Mr. Ashberry." Billy's head fell back, and he gave a husky chuckle, then another long kiss.

"Ok yuh two! Time to partay!" came Delroy's voice, along with happy agreement from all their friends. Maggie and Billy came up for air, still nose to nose as they grinned broadly. They stood at the pulpit and signed their marriage license, followed by another happy kiss, then walking back up the carpet, smiling hand in hand, with all their friends around them, they made their way to The Robinson's Rockhouse, stopping for a few pictures from their friends. All the coloured lanterns were lit and they had added some fairy lights all around the awning and patio railing. Tables covered in white tablecloths were spread out on the patio, and on each one a vase filled with fairy lights and little daisies. There was a makeshift dance floor on the beach in front of the patio, and a band with steel drums, guitars, and some instruments Maggie didn't recognize, were set up next to it where they were playing reggae music as the group walked towards the Rockhouse. Billy and Maggie could hardly stop hugging and kissing. Staring at each other with huge smiles. Everyone who passed them, giving them hugs and words of congratulations. Delroy and Alvita came over and gave them both hugs, welcoming Maggie to the family.

"Now yuh two, let's eat!" Alvita announced, grinning and walking them to the tables. There was so much food! The restaurant was closed to the public for the night and Delroy and Alvita's staff were serving. They kept a steady serving of food coming to all the tables. Jerk chicken, curries, coconut chicken, shrimp and seafood pasta, fried fish fritters with spicy fruit salsa, fried plantains, breadfruit, and an open bar. Of course, there was a bottle of champagne at Maggie and Billy's smaller table facing all the other tables, with the beautiful sunset glowing behind them. Billy popped the cork and poured two glasses, toasting to Maggie, his beautiful wife, and they wrapped arms and drank together to many cheers. Laughing as people clinked their glasses, Maggie and Billy had to kiss each time, which was already happening frequently anyways. The happy couple didn't eat much. They kissed and smiled for most of the meal. A few people got up and made toasts throughout dinner. Jon stood up and toasted,

"To the coolest and nicest Dude and Dudette ever! It's about freak'n time!" And then, his chuckle. And through much laughter, everyone raised their glasses and yelled "Dude and Dudette", Maggie and Billy grinning and hugging. The music played in the background, with so much laughter and visiting between all the old friends. There was such an abundance of happiness all around them. Becky and Justin both stood up at one point, glasses in hand and smiled up at the bride and groom. Then Becky spoke,

"Billy, we have known each other since you were a toddler, and you really are like a brother to me. I have seen you grow and change, and watched you go through many phases of your life, and I have never known you to be more fulfilled or happy, as you are when Maggie is next to you. You two are such special souls and the love you share overflows infectiously onto anyone lucky enough to be nearby. I'm so glad you found your way back to each other. Here's to your happily ever after!" Together Becky and Justin raised their glasses high and yelled out, "Maggie and Billy!" Everyone raised their glasses to Maggie and Billy.

"Speech! Speech!" came Jon's voice.

"Groom speech!" Chris called out. Billy smiled at Maggie and stood up.

"What can I say that you all haven't already said." He looked around at all of them with a huge smile. "Damn, it's good to see all your faces!" Everyone cheered. "Thank you all for sharing this special day with us, and everything you did to make it all come together." Then he looked down at Maggie and found himself choked up. He took a moment, smiling at her before he went on. "My beautiful wife... No words will ever be enough. You are my everything Babe." He stopped again and reached his hand out to hold her face. "It's always been you Maggie," he said, choking up again.

"Whoooo, kiss her Sweet Cheeks!" yelled Carla, and Maggie and Billy laughed. He bent down, grinning at her and with both hands, held her face and kissed her, softly, rubbing his nose with hers before standing up again.

"Well, I actually do have something planned, that I wanted to do instead of making a speech. Guess this would be a good time to do it." He got up and walked over to Del who handed him his guitar. Billy sat a chair down in the middle of the patio facing Maggie and started strumming. Then he started singing the most beautiful version of "The First Time Ever I Saw Your Face". With such soulful, whispered, loving expression in his voice Maggie was instantly crying. His eyes closing as he sang. His husky voice breathing the words so deeply as his voice grew stronger. It was as if everyone was holding their breath as they listened and watched the love dancing between the two lovers. As he started the last verse, Maggie placed her hands over her heart, staring at him with pure adoration. She had always loved listening to him, but the way he was singing the words to her now, made every cell in her body explode. She was filled with such abundant love she could hardly breathe. And the way he looked at her now, a higher love than he'd ever shown before. She stood up and walked over to him as he sang the last line, and he smiled at her. He stood up and sat his guitar on the chair, and she jumped into his arms, wrapping her arms around him, Billy holding her up as she kissed him so hard, holding his head in her hands. All their friends were yelling and clapping. They looked into each other's eyes.

"You are an amazing, beautiful, beautiful man Billy." He kissed her, then said,

"And you, my beautiful wife, you are such a gift. Damn, I love you, Mag." She flashed her big Maggie smile.

They heard music starting, and the steel drums playing, and Billy let her slide back down to stand on the floor. Everyone got up to dance, then they heard from Delroy,

"First dance!" he yelled. Billy walked over to him and said something in his ear. Del nodded with a grin and went over to the DJ, said something to him and he nodded. The music stopped and Maggie and Billy, followed by their friends, walked down to the dance floor. They stood in the center, everyone grouped around the edges, ready for their romantic first dance. Maggie saw a few cameras up and ready and grinned, hardly believing this dream she'd had, almost her whole life, was reality. Standing in front of each other, waiting, Billy holding her arms and grinning at her. She saw Del nod at him, and Billy winked at Maggie, ready to take his hand for their slow dance, just before "You Never Can Tell" started playing and Billy started dancing in front of Maggie, doing the twist. Maggie shook her head thinking, *she should have known,* then started laughing, their friends laughing and clapping too. Maggie joined in, twisting along happily. Having so much fun twisting together, both of them grinning, and being as goofily saucy and savvy as they could. They hugged and kissed at the end, then "At Last" started playing and Billy pulled her in, spinning her around the dance floor, kissing her and holding her close. Nose to nose, smiling at each other as they danced. Billy and Maggie sang softly to each other, and everyone joined in around them.

They all danced well into the night. Starting with the steel band, then the DJ was playing old 80s favourites with a reggae twist, all the cabiners enjoying their time together again. Maggie was so happy to see Cindy and Dave dancing to "Keep On Loving

You", holding each other close. A few people from the group running up to each other to watch and "ohhh" and "awwe" at them happily. They got lots of pictures, some down on the beach, a great one of Billy holding Maggie up, her feet up behind her and the sunset still glowing in the background, and they even managed to get a shot of everyone up on the patio together. Then later the steel drums started up again, and everyone was back up dancing. Alvita and Delroy, Maggie and Billy and Barkley and his girlfriend, teaching Maggie some moves, clapping and singing their hearts out. It was the best day of Maggie's life, and she couldn't have imagined sharing it with anyone else. Sometime near 1:00, everyone had the pleasure of noticing Cindy and Dave walking off together down the beach, and the whole group couldn't help but cheer at them.

"Woooo, dudes, just like old times!" Jon yelled out as they watched them walk off. Then, during a dance break, with a number of them back up on the patio, Billy came over to Maggie, reached out a hand and pulled her close.

"You know Mag, technically speaking, this marriage isn't legit until we consummate it." His cheeky eyed grin playing across his face, and he pulled her along, walking down the stairs onto the beach towards the dock. As everyone in the group of cabiners noticed, in turn, they followed, stopping and watching them walking away. As they reached the dock, Billy smiled at Maggie, then he bent down and scooped her up.

"Whoop Whoop! Billy! Maggie! Ya!!" they heard behind them, along with whistles and cheers. Maggie laughed and wrapped her arms around his neck as he carried her under the arbor and down the dock onto the boat. It had lanterns lit all along it, and inside were more fairy lights, another bottle of champagne and flower petals all over the floor leading to the bed. There were two red lanterns hanging on either side of the bed, casting a romantic glow. The sheets had been switched to red satin, and there were two thin, red house coats hanging by the bed with "Mr." and "Mrs." on the backs. As Billy sat her down on the bed, leaning over her, he grinned.

"I hope we still get this right now that we're a married couple Babe," he said, winking at her.

"Oh Billy, there's no doubt in my mind that we'll get it right." She grabbed his face, pulling him closer.

"Damn Mag, what if it gets better?" Billy asked, eyes twinkling, and a little chuckle escaping. Maggie's smile was enormous.

"Well I guess we might just spontaneously combust, Lover," she answered with fire in her eyes. They hugged and held one another tight, their hands sliding down to each other's butts and squeezing.

"Mmm," Maggie purred.

"Grr!" Billy gave a playful growl. Then, both grinning, looking deeply into each other's eyes, Maggie and Billy held each other's faces, fingers moving softly into one another's hair. They pulled tightly together, like magnets, kissing passionately and lovingly as they began the first chapter of their life as Mrs. Stanton and Mr. Ashberry.

THE END

About the Author

Katherine Waite-Gracie is a single, homeschooling mom of two great kids, two fur babies, and a fish named Mr. Malory. Growing up in a small town in Ontario, loving community and nature, she spent most of her time in the water or taking long walks with friends, daydreaming of a life full of wooded, secluded comforts and spending her days and nights with a partner as loving and as passionate about life as herself. Before writing romance novels, Katherine attained degrees and certificates in Intervention, Reiki, Children's Yoga Instruction, and Animal Specialist Programs. She spends her nights continuing to write and has recently finished the 5th and final book in The Maggie Ashberry Series, as well as working on four other novels.

Linkedin: www.linkedin.com/in/kat-waite-gracie-3681928a

Facebook: www.facebook.com/kat.waitegracie

Instagram: https://www.instagram.com/katsmyth/

Get ready to jump into The Maggie Ashberry Series by the International Bestselling Author, W K Waite-Gracie. This isn't just a collection of stories; it's an adventure you'll want to be a part of! With heartwarming moments and thrilling twists, this series mixes sweet and sexy romance that will keep you begging for more.

Join Maggie on her journey through love, challenges, and unforgettable surprises that will make you laugh, cry, and cheer. You won't just read her story; you'll live it! So go ahead—dive into this amazing series today and see for yourself why everyone is talking about Maggie Ashberry!

www.ingramcontent.com/pod-product-compliance
Lightning Source LLC
Chambersburg PA
CBHW060436310726
48977CB00001B/215